FORBID ME

IMMORTAL VICES AND VIRTUES: SHADOW SHIFTER BONDS

INES JOHNSON

PROLOGUE

Oz

I should've just let my mother kill me. Instead, it looks like Mother Nature will finish the job.

The forest breathed around me, heavy and alive, as I raced through its underbelly. Leaves the size of my head slapped my muzzle. My paws thudded against the soft, damp earth. I sank with each step, even though I barely weighed more than the branches I was careful to avoid. The line between predator and prey was so fine as to be non-existent. Safety was something I was not sure existed anymore. Maybe it never had in this world ruled by a mad god. The air was thick with the scent of moss, magic and murder, a potent, earthy smell that stuck to the back of my throat.

Tall weeds whipped at my face. Thorns snagged in my fur. I pushed on, driven by a heartbeat that drummed loudly in my ears, like the racing pulse of a hunted creature.

Which, I guess, was what I was now. The forest's magic tugged at me. Vines curled around my legs, trying to slow me, to hold me back. The night's breeze whispered of my guilt, of the terrible thing I'd done. The mistake that claimed me as predator. The decision that turned me prey. I tore through the foliage, but their thorny grip left stinging marks on my sleek black coat, little reminders of my betrayal.

I was just a cub. Would be considered an adolescent in my human form. The weight of my actions felt too heavy for my small shoulders. I couldn't shake the image of my brother, weak and fading, while I... I took everything. Even Mama's love, gone like the last light of day, leaving me alone in an endless night.

The trees closed in, their shadows like long, accusing fingers. Every snapped twig, every rustle of leaves sounded like a pursuer come to punish me for my selfishness. My heart raced faster, a desperate rhythm that synced with my paws pounding the ground.

I leapt over a fallen log. My starved body barely cleared it. My lungs burned with each breath. My sides heaved, threatening to let loose the little sustenance I had inside. This was my life now. Constantly running. If I stopped, I would die.

I wanted to howl, to release this ache in my chest. Fear clamped my throat shut. There were worse monsters in this forest than me.

The air was heavy, saturated with a sense of foreboding that clung to my fur like morning dew. The forest around me was a mix of shadows and whispers. Suddenly, a dark presence loomed over me, oppressive and ominous.

I froze. My instincts screamed at me to run. Lifting my head, I saw him—a lion, gaunt and ghostly, a skeletal figure in the twilight. His mane might once have been a majestic symbol of his might. It was now sparse and dull. The bones protruded sharply beneath his tawny skin, etching a map of his suffering that looked identical to mine.

Our eyes locked. In his gaze, there was hunger—a desperate, consuming need. There was triumph, too, as he saw in me his next meal. We could be reflections of each other. Except my coat was a dark void, absorbing the scant light, while his was a faded echo of glory lost.

A part of me accepted this as my fate. I had taken a life; it seemed only fitting that I should give mine in return. But as the lion charged, something primal awakened within me: survival. The need to hold on to what was left of my pathetic life clung to me, stubborn and defiant.

The fight began as a blur of motion and instinct. His claws swiped at me, sharp and merciless. But I was smaller and quicker. I dodged and wove. My own claws found his flesh.

It wasn't enough. I hadn't eaten in days. My strength was waning. My movements were sluggish.

The lion pinned me, his massive body a crushing weight. I gasped for breath, the earth cold and damp beneath me. His breath was hot and fetid on my face, the stench of decay and desperation. I saw the end in his eyes— a swift, brutal finish. I braced for the killing blow. But then he went slack.

Confusion mingled with my fear. What happened? I struggled out from under him. My body ached. My breath was ragged.

Lifting my head, I saw the cause of the lion's sudden stillness. Standing over us was another lion. His coat was a brilliant gold that I've never seen the likes of. However, he had no mane.

I looked again and realized he wasn't a lion. He was a jaguar. But without any spots. Not a single one. His coat was solid gold.

Recognition dawned. I rolled to my feet, struggling to all fours. I tried to shift back to the form of a human boy, but I couldn't. I haven't been a boy in days. Months? I couldn't remember the last time I'd shifted.

Because I couldn't kneel in front of the Prince of Panthera, I bowed my head and offered my neck as a show of submission.

The metallic scent of the lion's blood and the earthy fragrance of the forest floor were a potent reminder of the battle that had just unfolded. My heart still pounded in my chest, a relentless drumbeat echoing the fear and adrenaline that had coursed through me only moments ago.

As I crouched there, battered and bruised, the majestic golden jaguar before me began to shift. Its form shimmered and contorted in a play of magic and light. Within moments, where the jaguar had stood now was a boy. Dion, Prince of Panthera, stood before me in his human form, his aura radiating power and authority.

He was the same age as me, yet the difference between us couldn't have been more evident. His body, though smeared with the evidence of the fight, exuded health and vitality. A smile played on his lips with the blood that stained his mouth. It was a vivid contrast to the grim set of my own features.

"You almost had him."

I blinked, my gaze focused on the prince's bloody grin. There was something in his obsidian eyes. It was like the hunger I'd seen in the lion's dull eyes, but this prince was well fed. What I saw was clearly blood lust.

"If you had only dug your claws into his neck, he

would've gone down." Prince Dion demonstrated with sharp claws that glinted in the moonlight. "But it was good effort."

The prince was coaching me on my fighting skills?

His smile dropped as quickly as it appeared. He cocked his head and studied me. I wondered if I was wrong. Perhaps he was a lion and I was the meal he'd been playing with before he went for my throat.

"Shift."

My body heeded his command. Because it wasn't of my own free will, and because I was out of practice, the shift hurt. Four limbs collapsed as paws turned to fingers. My maw shortened into a broken nose, fur turned to soft flesh. I lay vulnerable on the forest floor, naked and shivering.

"I beg a quick death, your highness." My voice was barely a whisper, strained and filled with a short lifetime of doubt and hurt. Unused from years of neglect and solitude.

"I saw you. Inside my mind." The young prince pointed to his head. But those dark eyes looked through me.

Prince Dion was the son of the panther god. But the god of Arcadia, Pan, had lost his mind and trapped us all in his hell. Most on the realm was struggling with their sanity. Many in this world were caught in a partial shift. Stuck between human and animal, unable to transform fully into either. It was a disease known as the Call of the Wild.

I had heard that the prince was a seer, like his mother. But the Call must have finally caught hold of me to think the Panther Prince had a vision of a pitiful creature like me.

"Today isn't the day you die."

Prince Dion's words washed over me, stirring something deep within. My mother had turned her back on me, casting me out for a sin I couldn't undo. Now here was the prince, seeing worth in me where I saw none.

I felt a shift within, a flicker of hope igniting in the darkness of my despair.

I felt the damp earth beneath me, the coolness seeping through my skin, grounding me. The sounds of the forest hushed in reverence to his words. I felt an overwhelming urge to dedicate myself to this man, this prince who saw value in a life I had deemed worthless.

For the prince to come out and save my life, it must mean my life would be worth something. Perhaps I was meant to play some part in Panthera's future. Perhaps I was destined to be in service to the future king of my kind.

"What's your name?"

"Oz, sire."

"Oz, I had a vision about you."

Here it came; my true grand purpose in life. The reason I'd run instead of letting my mother claw my heart out and bury me next to my brother. Any second now, the prince would announce the reason for my redemption from the ugliness that had cast a shadow over me since the day I was born.

"I had a vision we'd be hunting squirrels today."

Managing to get my feet under me, I locked my knees and stood. "Squirrels, your highness?"

"If we hurry, we might be able to bust into their nut stash." The force of the young prince's laughter was so great that he bent over and slapped his knee. "Get it? Nut stash."

When I didn't laugh, he cocked his head and looked at me. His gaze narrowed, as though assessing me anew.

"Get it?"

I pushed past the lump in my throat. "I get it."

His grin rematerialized. "Then let's go."

And with that, the Prince of Panthers shifted and took

off running. I stared after him, bewildered. Before he could toss me another of those assessing gazes, I shifted and raced after him. It was a job I'd be doing for the next twenty years.

Not just chasing after the prince, but also protecting his nut stash. But hey, there were worse things. I knew that firsthand.

Stella

"It's not what it looks like."

What it looked like was my boyfriend's dick inside another woman's unshaven poonanny while her finger was lodged in his ass. I don't know what shocked me more, her lack of grooming or the back door entrance.

The door to Ken's apartment was ajar when I arrived. There'd been a sliver of light cutting through the dim hallway. I'd thought he'd anticipated my arrival. My heart had raced with anticipation, eager for the comfort of his embrace. I needed some cuddles after the day I'd had.

Lately, my visions had become clouded. My foresight had gone murky like a fogged mirror. Ken's touch, his affection always cleared the haze, sharpening my foresight. But the scene that greeted me was a gut punch, a brutal unraveling of my naïve hopes.

"You're in bed with another woman, Ken." My voice was

sharp, a blade forged in the fire of betrayal. The room spun, a whirlpool of emotions—anger, hurt, disbelief.

"What? Like she didn't see this coming?" drawled the naked Neanderthaless.

My foresight didn't work like that. I didn't see the people in my life. What I saw helped business decisions, trade, commerce. It was like being privy to a one-way mirror of economic fates, seeing how one move in the market could ripple out and affect a myriad of others.

When I concentrate, I can see the patterns of supply and demand shifting, like waves on a vast ocean. It was like watching the gears of a giant clock, seeing how one cog turning can affect the entire mechanism. I can sense market shifts, anticipate economic trends, and identify the best paths for financial and commercial success. Which made me a hot commodity in the Crossroads, but not so much in my boyfriend's heart. Or his bed.

Ken reached for me, his eyes wide with desperation. "Stella, please, let me explain."

I stepped back, repulsion and pain mingling in a bitter cocktail at the back of my throat. I tried to swallow and found it hard.

"Explain? What's there to explain? That you're a cheat? That I was a fool for trusting you?"

"It's not what it looks like."

"How stupid do you think I am? What? Did you slip and fall?"

"Yes, that's what happened. It was an accident."

"Your dick is dripping wet from being inside of me, babe," said the hairy skank, not even bothering to cover up.

We all looked down at Ken's dick, which was surprisingly still hard. Ken did like to be the center of attention.

His dick rose a bit higher and pointed at me, as though asking if it had next.

I did not. I had at least some self-respect. Even though all of my girlfriends had warned me away from Ken. But that was before the first time he'd cheated. By the third time that I'd complained of his wayward eyes or the lipstick I'd found on his collar or the phone number scribbled on the back of a business card in pink ink, they'd stopped voicing their opinions.

"Stella, you've got to believe me. I love you," Ken pleaded, his voice cracking under the strain. "This... this was a mistake. I don't even know what I was thinking."

"You call this a mistake? I call it a choice, Ken. You chose her over me."

People thought they had no choices in the Crossroads, where there were no Houses of protection. But that wasn't the truth. Every day was made up of little choices. Those choices could shape the direction of the world. It's what gave me a headache in my daily work. It's why I'd come here after watching waves crashing on the psychic plane.

Inside my belly, I heard the slightest snarl. The animal that slept inside me shifted in its slumber, as though it sensed my pain and wanted me to lash out. The magic within me swirled and churned like a tempest fueled by my chaotic emotions. My ability to see into the future, once a gift, now felt like a curse.

Had I seen this coming? Had I chosen to ignore the signs, the whispers of doubt that my friends had stopped trying to get me to see?

I stormed out of Ken's apartment. The door slammed shut behind me with a finality that echoed my shattered heart. The flickering lights of the dimly lit hallway cast long, dancing shadows that mocked my turmoil. The cool night air hit my face like a splash of icy water.

"Stella, wait! Please!" Ken's voice was desperate and pleading as he chased after me. I didn't have to look back to know he was following in nothing but his boxer shorts, his dignity as tattered as my trust in him.

Too bad the sun had set. I wondered if he would have run into the sunlight after me. He was still a relatively young vampire, thus allergic to the most visible star in the sky. Which was funny, since that's what my name meant.

I stood there, torn between the remnants of what we had and the bitter taste of betrayal that lingered in my mouth. My heart ached, a mix of anger and sorrow colliding within me.

"Stella, please, just hear me out. I promise, it was a one-time mistake. I love you." His words almost had me teetering on the edge of forgiveness.

He looked so sad, so forlorn. There was a wrinkle between his brows. My fingers itched to reach up and smooth it out. His boxers were rumpled, the fabric bunched up. Was he still hard?

My need to straighten things out almost had me reaching for the waistband and rearranging his clothing. A few people were well off enough in the Crossroads to have their clothing tailored. No one had their underwear fitted. Well, no one but me, my girlfriends, and my boyfriend. In addition to making predictions, my magic was good for one other thing. I had the ability to make people look good. I was excellent at giving makeovers. Externally, that is.

Maybe, just maybe, people could change their insides as easily as they changed their—

"Hey, Ken," a sultry voice cooed from down the way.

My eyes flickered to the source—an attractive fairy

with a knowing smile walked past us. She was familiar. She had been standing a little too close to Ken last month when I'd met him outside of where he worked. And then when he'd come home, I'd seen her cheap brand of lipstick on his collar. Now she tossed her hair over her shoulder, her gaze lingering on Ken for just a moment too long.

Ken's reaction was immediate and telling. His eyes trailed over her, a grin spreading across his face. All of a sudden, he was no longer the remorseful, pleading man, but someone unrecognizable. Or maybe he was recognizable.

This wasn't the first time I'd been cheated on. Not the second or third. Every boyfriend I'd ever had strayed at some point. Why would I think Ken would be different?

Because I was a hopeless romantic, that's why. Because I was a woman worthy of sometimes-love, that's why. Because I deserved more than someone who appraised another woman with a lewd gaze as he begged for my forgiveness.

The sight of it—the raw, undisguised lust in his eyes—was a slap to my own face. My hand moved before I could even think. My palm connected with his cheek with a resounding smack. The sound reverberated in the narrow hallway, a sharp punctuation to the chaos of my emotions.

"You'll never change, Ken. You're a cheat, and you always will be."

His hand flew to his cheek, his eyes wide in shock. But there was no remorse there, no understanding of the pain he had caused. Just the sting of my rejection.

I turned on my heel, leaving him standing there in his wrinkled boxer shorts, a symbol of the farce our relationship had been. Tears blurred my vision as I walked away.

They ran down my cheeks, bringing with them some of my mascara. That would not do.

With a wave of my hand, I conjured a spell to dry the teardrops away. With a wiggle of my fingers, I fixed my makeup, removing the puffiness of disappointment from beneath my eyes and adding a dab of gold sparkle at the corners to brighten the night.

It worked.

On the outside.

Because outside it was dark.

I halted for a moment, glancing at my reflection in a dimly lit store window. My golden hair, with its ombre of black at the roots, framed my face perfectly. It was an homage to the cat trapped inside of me, hidden beneath my flawless exterior. Every curve of my body was adorned with care. My outfit showcased my assets in the most appealing way. On the surface, I was stunning: a picture of confidence and allure.

The mirror reflected only the outer shell. Inside, I felt ugly, tainted by the betrayal of the man I had thought loved me. I saw the echo of the ones who'd come before him, promising me forever and stealing away moments of my life. The dissonance between my exterior and my inner turmoil was jarring.

A deep breath steadied my quivering emotions. The world would see the exterior, the image I projected. But I couldn't hide the pain entirely.

I pulled out my phone and scrolled to our group chat. *I'm in desperate need of a girls' night in. Ken is officially out of my life for good.*

The texts were hesitant, but my girls came through. Especially after I texted what I was bringing to the party.

CHAPTER

TWO

Oz

Having squirrel for breakfast was probably not the best decision.

Stepping through the portal, I felt that now-familiar lurch in my stomach. It was like being pulled under the water during a strong current or a vehicle swerving on an inch of water. Water in great amounts or small had the power to leave a man or beast helpless.

As a man, I was not good at being helpless. Inside my gut, my beast showed its disapproval by clawing at my intestines. The sensation of being pulled apart atom by atom and then stitched back together was something I would never get used to, no matter how many times I would do it.

No matter if it was by portal travel, or if I was being

physically sliced apart by the person I trusted most in the world—the person who had brought my life into existence.

Opening my eyes for my first look at this world left me less than impressed. I took a deep breath, allowing my senses to adjust, to take in the nuances of Earth. The air carried unfamiliar scents, a cocktail of odors that didn't fit the natural world I knew.

Exhaust from the vehicles, the sharp tang of technology, mingled with the natural scents of dirt and rain that underpinned this city's atmosphere. It was a far cry from the crisp, clean air of the forests and mountains I was accustomed to.

"You smell that, Oz?"

"What smell is that, my king?"

"It's the smell of success."

"You're feeling good about these negotiations with the House of Blood and Beryl?"

"Negotiations?" King Dion looked back at me over his shoulder. His canines glinted in the sunlight. "I smell brand new women eager to bounce on my cock."

"Your favorite smell," I deadpanned.

All the while, I remained stoic, not letting a hint of discomfort at the travel show on my face. This wasn't my first trip. I'd used witches' magic to travel short distances in my country of Panthera. In my role as King Dion's chief of security, I'd traveled the breadth of our home world, Arcadia. But I'd just traveled between worlds, from the realm of the gods to the mortal planet of Earth.

The light here had a different quality, too. The rays felt harsh on my skin, artificial even in daylight. It cast sharp shadows that fractured the world into a kaleidoscope of light and dark. It was disorienting, and I had to focus to keep my bearings.

As chief of security for the king, my instincts were always dialed to high alert. But here, in this teeming portal station, they were stretched to their limits. The place was a melting pot of beings. Shifters of all kinds mingled with vampires, fae, and witches, each with their own agendas, each radiating their unique energies and intentions. And my king, with his roaming eye, clearly wanted to touch more than he wanted to look.

The guards of the Portal Watch moved through the crowd with a brusqueness that bordered on aggression. Their eyes were hard, their movements sharp and deliberate as they herded the newcomers or managed those departing. Their demeanor spoke of the tension that simmered just beneath the surface, a reflection of the complex dynamics at play in this gateway between worlds.

I sensed the underlying currents of power, the silent battles for dominance and respect among the various beings. Shifters prowled with restrained grace, their eyes wary and watchful. Vampires moved with an eerie smoothness, their gaze piercing through the throng, assessing, calculating. The fae, with their ethereal beauty, seemed almost aloof to the chaos around them, yet their presence stirred the air with whispers of magic. Witches, cloaked in their arcane energies, navigated the space with inscrutable calm, their eyes gleaming with knowledge and secrets.

Everywhere I looked, there were negotiations, confrontations, silent exchanges laden with meaning. The air was charged with the potential for conflict or alliance, each interaction a display of power and diplomacy. But this was what we were here for.

Beside me, King Dion stood in his human form, his golden hair and cold black eyes taking in the world as well.

A charming smile played on his mouth. It was his poker face.

Dion smiled when he was happy. He smiled when he was angry. He smiled when he gave an order that would turn the hardest of generals' stomachs. The man never flinched. Why would he? He was the descendant of gods.

Our contrasting appearances were a visual representation of our roles within the envoy. Dion, the charismatic diplomat, was the face of our mission, his striking features and regal presence commanding attention. Meanwhile, I remained the vigilant protector, my dark form blending into the shadows, ready to act at a moment's notice.

The unfamiliar surroundings and the presence of powerful witches, ancient vampires, and unknown shifters kept me on edge. I knew that in this world, appearances could be deceiving, and I trusted only my instincts and my loyalty to the king.

Dion turned his piercing cobalt eyes toward me, a subtle nod of acknowledgment that signaled the start of our mission. We were here for diplomatic negotiations with the leaders of the House of Blood and Beryl. The potential alliance between our kingdom and the House was crucial for both our worlds, but I couldn't help but be wary. Trusting these other supernaturals, even in a diplomatic setting, was not in my nature.

I had always been fiercely loyal to Dion ever since the day he had saved me from the clutches of my living nightmare when we were both cubs. I would protect him with my life. Which often involved me cockblocking females trying to dig their claws into our charming king. While Dion liked having his cock stroked like a healthy big cat, I was the one often blocking my own family jewels from gold-clawing, wannabe queens trying to get past me to get to him.

"If you don't stop dogging my steps, the women here are going to get the wrong idea."

Dion was never without a woman at his back, at his feet, in his bed. I didn't slow my stroll or give the king more space. "This isn't Panthera. No one here is loyal to you."

"Except you."

I didn't bother to nod. He knew the answer to that.

"I'm not looking for loyalty, old friend. If these trade negotiations go the way that I want, with the portal reopened, there's more than wealth at stake. There's more power to be had. And you know what comes with power?"

I sighed deeply, knowing what was coming but not wanting to give voice to it.

"Say it," Dion said as he wrapped his biceps around my head.

I managed to get out of his hold, but he reached for me again. The prince had had a head over me when we were cubs. Over the years, I caught up to the king in height and muscles. In our human forms, we were evenly matched.

The headlock was his favorite move. His grip on me was strong. But it left his lower body relatively exposed. I could drive my elbow low, but I had honor now.

Besides, he was the son of a god, and my king. I owed him my life. He hated when I called him my savior. He preferred I call him my friend. And as his closest friend, I knew right now what he wanted from me, what he needed before the biggest parlay of his life, was a moment of play.

Before I could brace myself, he launched at me, a feint to the left followed by a swift jab to the right. Instinctively, I blocked, countering with a quick kick aimed at his side. Dion dodged with the grace and speed that only a jaguar shifter could possess. I knew better than to hold back; Dion wouldn't have respected me if I did. Our punches and kicks were real, packed with the strength of our animals. The sound of our combat, the thud of fists on flesh, and the scrape of shoes on pavement brought the first smile to my face since stepping out of the portal.

Then Dion got an arm around my neck. "Say it."

His hold was absolute. The only move I had to free myself was to say it. "Power comes with pussy."

"That's what I'm talking about!"

The king let me go with a hefty pat on my back. As quickly as it had begun, the fight was done. There was no victor, no vanquished—just two old friends who understood each other in a way few others could. We clapped each other on the back, the laughter still echoing between us as we climbed into the waiting vehicle.

Stella

The dimly lit room was filled with the sweet scent of vanilla candles. Soft music played in the background, casting a soothing ambiance over our little gathering. My girlfriends, Tori and Niamh, were sprawled out on my plush, lavender-colored rug. They wiped off the thick facials of strawberry-scented cream. Meanwhile, I carefully selected shades of nail polish, lining them up like a colorful palette of emotions, each bottle representing a different mood.

"How about this green for my mani?" said Tori.

"Hmmm, it doesn't exactly match." I ran my hand over the color in the bottle. Gradually, it changed until it was the exact shade of green I'd just dyed Tori's hair.

"I swear, Stella, every girl should have a best friend like you."

"Well, from now on, I'm only rolling with my ride or die

bitches. Only the women that I can trust. And that excludes those who slept with my boyfriend."

"Which is slim pickings," said Niamh.

I tossed a bottle of nail polish at her. She caught it deftly before holding it up to the light to see if it would match her skin tone. It did. Everything matched her skin tone.

"Too soon, Niamh," Tori admonished.

"No, actually it's not. I only promised to keep my mouth shut as long as she said she's happy. Now she's not. So I'm speaking the truth. Ken was a dickless dick. To say our girl deserves better is the most-duh statement of the year."

My eyes pricked at that impassioned speech. There was a small part of me that wasn't sure if the tears were from my shame at being used and abused or if they were from the unadulterated joy of being loved by my friends.

"I don't deserve you guys."

"Yes, you do." Tori reached back and grabbed my hand, squeezing it like I was sure she'd been wanting to squeeze life into me for the last year. "That idiot didn't know what he had. You deserve to be treated like a princess."

"Fuck princess." Niamh came to my other side and wiped the tear that threatened the corner of my eye. "We deserve to be treated like queens."

"Queens of the Crossroads," declared Tori.

I did love my girls. I wished I could live off their love alone. But contrary to Niamh's assertion, Ken wasn't dickless. And I had a dick addiction. I just didn't want a dirty community dick.

"Oh my God, Niamh, I need to touch up your roots. Your blond is showing."

They knew what I was doing. I'd changed the subject on them more than once when they started dissing my boyfriends. Like the best friends that they were, they let me get away with it yet again.

Tori scooted out of the way, and Niamh took her place on the floor in front of me.

"Having you as a friend is better than going to a beauty salon," said Niamh as she leaned her head back into my hands.

"Because you get me for free."

"We pay you in friendship," Tori chimed in.

I sighed, gazing at my friends' expressions. Tori, with her calculating eyes and cautious demeanor, was the voice of reason in our group. She was a realist and had always questioned my constant search for love. Niamh, on the other hand, didn't begrudge my need to be on the arm of a man. She only sniffed at my need to cling to them.

Both women had fae blood that made them stunning. I was part witch and part... other. The other part of me they didn't know about. No one knew about the sleeping animal that lived inside of me. The two halves added together made me a big, curvy girl.

Don't get me wrong; I loved my curves. Ever since I was young, I'd loved looking at paintings from the old world where the women were voluptuous and rosy. Growing up, that was all I knew. It's what I thought was the standard of beauty. Until I came in contact with the willowy fairies and the anemic vampires.

So while I might love my hourglass figure, it was a few centuries out of style, and the men of the Crossroads were looking at the present.

Niamh reclined gracefully on the floor, relaxed in the notion that I would enhance her beauty. Men and women alike adored her. My magical abilities seemed futile in adding to her already flawless features. She had the perfect figure, with a small waist and lean limbs that made heads turn wherever she went. Niamh often teased me about my quest for love, reminding me that I should treat men like side dishes, not the main course.

"You know, you guys could give me a little credit here," I said, trying to sound cheerful despite the sadness that lingered within me. "I just thought Ken was The One, that's all. He always paid for dinner. He bought me lavish gifts. He even said the L word first, just a few days after we started dating and—"

"Stop it," said Niamh.

"What?" I looked up.

"I don't need to be psychic to see you're doing it again. You're thinking about all his good qualities, which I still can't see a single one."

"He is pretty," volunteered Tori.

"Yeah, and he knows it, which is why he thinks he can get away with dipping his tool in every toolbox in the neighborhood," said Niamh.

"You get various tools dipped into your box," I shot back.

"That's true." Niamh grinned. "But unlike you, I don't let my feelings get involved."

"Then what's the point?" I flopped back on a cushion. "We're supposed to get fated mates."

"Not everyone gets them," said Tori.

"I know." I chewed my bottom lip. "Some people even reject them. I would never. I want him. Right now. In fact, I'm going to wait until he shows up. I'm not dating anyone else until I feel the mating bond."

"And you think he's here in the Crossroads?" asked Tori.

I had lived here my whole life. My mother had come here shortly after I was born. She'd come alone. I had no idea who my father was, but I assumed he was a shifter since my mother was a witch and there was a sleeping cat living inside me.

"Maybe if I was skinnier, he wouldn't have cheated."

"You're beautiful, Stella. And you know it."

I did know that I was beautiful. But every time I got cheated on, I had my moments of doubt.

"You don't need a man to define your worth."

Tori was right. My bank account proved how worthy I was. Didn't stop me from wanting to love someone and be loved in return. To have undying loyalty and know that someone always had my back.

I knew my girls had my back. But it was different with a fated mate. Couldn't I have both?

A knock at the door broke through the party. They looked at me and then away. We all knew who it was. I hesitated, wondering if I should answer it.

"He's going to keep knocking until I do. I'll just tell him to go away."

Neither woman said anything.

I moved foward into the dimly lit foyer, the soft glow of the chandelier casting an ethereal light that danced across the antique wallpaper. The scent of old wood and faded memories lingered in the air, a reminder of the building's history.

Ken stood there on the other side of the door. His handsome face was bathed in the golden aura of the hallway's light. He wore an expression of longing and regret. His eyes fixed on me with an intensity that sent a shiver down my spine.

"Stella," he began, his voice soft and pleading. "Can we talk for a moment? Just you and me."

I glanced back at Tori and Niamh, who sat enveloped in

the cushions of my couch, watching me with knowing eyes. It was as if they understood that I was drawn to Ken like a moth to a flame, no matter that I always got burned.

He took my hand gently, his touch sending a rush of memories flooding back. "I miss you, Stella," he confessed, his voice filled with sincerity. "I made a mistake, and I've regretted it every moment you've been gone. I want us to be together again, to make things right."

His words tugged at my heartstrings, and for a moment, I was tempted to believe him. Because I didn't want to sleep alone tonight. Nights were the hardest.

And then, as though the nightmares overshot their eagerness, the world went black. The last thing I remembered was Ken leaning in to kiss me. Before his lips touched mine, a vision flashed before my eyes, vivid and chaotic.

I saw a world in turmoil, flames and destruction consuming everything in their path. The sky was dark and foreboding, filled with swirling storms and a sense of impending doom. It was a vision unlike any I had ever experienced, and it left me breathless, dizzy.

Had I fainted? No, I was still on my feet. Ken's lips were a mere millimeter away from mine. I pulled away from him, my heart racing and my eyes wide with shock.

He stumbled toward me, entirely missing the target of my mouth and bumping his forehead into the doorframe.

"I... I need to go," I stammered, my voice trembling. "I need to lie down."

"I'll come with you. I'll take care of you."

I laughed at the notion of him taking care of me. It was always the other way around. I didn't feel like arguing, so I shut the door in his face. Niamh and Tori looked at me with their mouths open. They didn't say anything as they helped me to the bed.

I tried to recall the ominous vision that had come to my mind, but it slipped through my fingers. And then sleep claimed me. I dreamed of a man with dark hair and golden eyes. But then he shifted and had golden hair and dark eyes. And then, like clockwork, the nightmares came, and there was no one for me to hold on to.

CHAPTER

FOUR

Oz

My paws made soft thuds against the forest floor, a rhythmic sound that blended with the whisper of the wind through the towering trees. The wilderness before me was a vast expanse of untamed beauty that stretched far beyond where the eye could see. The forest underbelly was familiar terrain, yet the smells were different. There was no faint scent of sick here. No lingering whiff of madness.

Here, the leaves were smaller, the air crisp with the scent of pine and the distant roar of waterfalls. The towering trees of the Pacific Northwest cast long shadows that flickered in the failing light. Each snap of a twig, each rustle in the underbrush heightened my senses, a reminder that even in the role of the predator, one could easily become prey.

Though I was a panther in his prime, there were things

out there hungry enough to hunt me. Safety was an illusion in any world, a fleeting comfort that nature could snatch away at a moment's notice.

I cleared a fallen tree in a single, powerful leap, my muscles flexing with the effort. My body was a testament to survival, each scar a story, each mark a memory of battles fought, both within and without.

I pushed my limbs to their limits. The thrill of the chase coursed through my veins. The ground beneath my paws was a tapestry of fallen leaves and soft earth, each step propelling me forward with a burst of speed that only a fully grown panther could muster. The air was alive with the sounds of my pursuit, the rustle of foliage and the crack of branches breaking underfoot.

There was something exhilarating about being hunted, a primal excitement that awakened every sense, every instinct. I felt the presence of my pursuer. It was a creature that matched my pace with a persistence that was almost admirable. The scent of it filled my nostrils, a mix of musk and aggression, a clear signal that this was no ordinary predator.

My heart pounded in my chest. Not with fear, but with anticipation. I had long outgrown the vulnerability of my cubhood, the days when I was an easy target.

I darted through the underbrush, my sleek black coat blending seamlessly with the shadows cast by the towering trees. My ears twitched at every sound, my eyes scanning the environment for any sign of my adversary. The dense foliage offered cover, but it also obscured my view, adding an element of surprise to the chase.

As I raced across a clearing, the moonlight breaking through the canopy above, I caught a glimpse of my pursuer—a massive creature, its silhouette outlined against the night sky. Its size and shape suggested something wild, something not of this world.

I increased my speed, pushing myself to the edge of my abilities. The wind rushed past me, a cool caress against my fur. I heard the heavy footfalls of the creature behind me, its breathing a pulsing chorus of exertion and determination.

Then, without warning, the terrain shifted. The forest gave way to a rocky outcrop, the ground uneven and treacherous. I navigated the obstacles with ease, my agile body adapting to the sudden change. But it was here, amidst the stones and shadows, that I decided to confront my hunter.

I came to a sudden stop, my muscles coiled and ready. I turned to face the creature, my eyes glowing with an inner fire. The moment of truth had arrived, the culmination of this exhilarating chase.

The wolf stopped and howled. The howl was one of triumph. It thought I was cornered. It was wrong.

As it approached, I saw the intelligence in its eyes, a recognition of the challenge I presented. This was no mindless beast. It was a creature of power and purpose. The outcome of this confrontation would be determined by more than just strength and speed.

The wolf lunged. I met it head-on. Our forms collided with a force that shook the earth beneath us. The battle was on, a test of might and mettle under the watchful eyes of the moon and stars.

Our initial clash was a fierce clash of bodies. I swiped at the wolf with my powerful forepaws, my claws unsheathed and ready to strike. The wolf countered, its teeth bared as it aimed for my flank.

I twisted away, using my agility to my advantage. The forest around us became our arena. The sounds of our conflict echoed through the trees.

But as the fight wore on, a shift occurred. What started as a battle morphed into something else—something less deadly and more...playful. Our movements, still swift and powerful, carried a different energy. A swipe of my paw was met with a dodging leap, more akin to a dance than a duel. The wolf's growls took on a teasing tone, and I found myself responding in kind, my own growls mingling with what could only be described as laughter, if such a sound could come from a panther.

We were evenly matched, each of us giving as good as we got, neither willing to back down, yet neither truly seeking to harm the other. It was a game, a way to test our skills and enjoy the pure physicality of the moment. We darted between trees, leaped over fallen logs, our movements a blur of fur and muscle.

Then, suddenly, the wolf paused. Its ears pricked up in a way that spoke of attention being called elsewhere. I halted too, watching as its stance shifted from playful to attentive. There was no sound that my ears could catch, but I knew instinctively what had happened—Queen Dani, the wolf's other half, had called.

The wolf cocked its head back toward the House of Blood and Beryl. It was a very human move. Nova was more than the average wolf. A spell had separated the wolf from its human half, allowing the two to live as separate individuals but also intrinsically connected.

The twitch of Nova's ear, the lift of her nose, signaled that it was time to return to the House. Each of us to our masters.

Last night, after King Elias and his consort Dani had formally received us and dinner had been dined, Dion set about crowding the lavish bedroom he'd been appointed with more than one willing woman of the House. He'd invited me in like always. Dion liked to share his women. He was a good friend like that. But I'd grown tired of the orgies at some point in the last year.

What used to be fun and pleasurable now left me unsatisfied and feeling... lonely.

So last night I'd left Dion's quarters after assessing each woman to make sure she posed no serious threat. Then I went next door, falling into a lucid dream to a soundtrack of women climaxing on repeat. This morning, I'd left Dion to his diplomatic talks and taken the queen's familiar and gone on a run. I knew there wasn't much trouble my king could get into having discussions in a throne room. If he looked at Dani wrong, Elias would take his head. Or worse, the king would let his consort do the honors. And that would serve Dion right.

Together, Nova and I made our way out of the forest, skirting around what was termed as No Man's Land. The border was clear. Nature looked as though she had taken back the land unclaimed by a House.

Like Arcadia, this world had been torn apart as well. The planet had been divided into Houses where supernaturals gathered for protection. Pureblood humans were near extinct. Those that lived outside of the Houses in No Man's Land had little to no protection from the elements and the supernatural predators.

On our side of the border, where civilization held its grip, everything was meticulously arranged. Manicured pathways marked Blood and Beryl's territory. The scent of cultivated flowers mixed with the earthy aroma of the trails, creating an ordered environment. On the other side, nature had reclaimed this untamed realm with a vengeance. Towering pine trees, their branches heavy with lush foliage, stood like guardians, casting deep shadows upon the forest floor below. The ground was a rugged carpet of fallen leaves and moss-covered rocks.

In No Man's Land, where the raw forces of nature held dominion, the wilderness pulsed with untamed beauty. The air was thick with the scent of the forest—earthy, musky, and alive. It carried the symphony of the wild, with the calls of nocturnal creatures, the rustling of leaves, and the distant howls of coyotes.

I stepped a paw over the boundary, feeling the land call to me. The wild, untamed, lawless place was surely where I belonged. Not in the court of a king and his consort. But that's where my king was.

When Pan had been in his madness, many of the shifters in Arcadia who were stuck in their shifter forms succumbed to madness. Panthera had avoided most of the darkness, being settled in the far regions of Arcadia with a strong king who had godling blood. Pan's grip loosened when he found his queen. Now Arcadia was rebuilding and, with these negotiations, Panthera would grow in power.

Eventually, Nova and I made our way to the compound entrance of Blood and Beryl. With a silent understanding, we slowed our pace and made our way toward the grand entrance. Nova's amber eyes met mine for a moment before she turned and trotted away into the darkness.

I shifted back into my human form, the transition smooth and familiar. I grabbed my clothing from where I'd left the articles. I tried to shield my naked body, not out of modesty—I wasn't shy—but out of respect. Still, the women of Blood and Beryl were unapologetic as they craned their heads to get a good look.

I moved through the lavish gathering, my senses attuned to the opulent surroundings—the scent of perfumed air, the soft rustle of elegant garments, the flicker of candlelight casting shadows on the polished floors. Yet, amid the extravagance, I felt like an outsider.

Nova moved to stand by Dani's side. Seeing the two of them together, they were like two halves to a whole that forged to make a complete unit. There was an uncanny intelligence in the wolf's eyes, while there was a feral glint in the woman's.

Dion approached me, a teasing smile on his lips and two women on his arms. One of the women dislodged from him and approached me. I turned away. Eventually, she got the hint. Dion sent the other one off and looked at me with a huff.

"Do you not understand the term wing man?"

"We're here for diplomatic reasons."

"I can read a contract and fuck at the same time."

He could. More than one servant had made the mistake of going into his office without knocking first.

As I was deciding whether or not to open my mouth for a comeback, my king's expression shifted. The humor faded as a spark ignited in his cobalt eyes.

Immediately, I used my body to block him from the sight of others. I spoke to him in a low voice, making nonsensical statements. My words didn't matter. My position did. I needed to make our interaction look as normal as possible while a vision overtook him, leaving him momentarily vulnerable.

When Dion returned from the vision, his gaze locked on to mine. It was a silent acknowledgement that he was back in full control of his facilities and I could stand down. I didn't move a muscle.

Dion's gaze shifted from mine and found the vampire king's.

"You saw it too?"

Elias nodded. "There's a new portal about to open in No Man's Land, in a place called the Crossroads. We'll need to make an envoy there. But this won't disrupt our dealings, King Dion."

"Of course not." Dion smiled his charming smile, but it didn't reach his eyes. When the vampire turned his back, Dion turned back to me. "I need you to get there now."

I nodded, needing no reason, but the one he gave me had my brows raising.

"There's a woman there. She's in the midst of the chaos. She doesn't belong there. She belongs in Panthera, on the throne."

Dion's voice still had some of the awe of the vision, but one thing was clear to me: my king had sensed his mate.

"Bring her to me, Oz."

"I swear it will be done."

Stella

The morning sun peeked through my bedroom window, casting a warm glow over the disheveled sheets. I groaned as I stretched, feeling the aftermath of last night's indulgence in ice cream, facials, and my friends' unwavering support. A pang of sadness still lingered in my chest over the breakup, but I refused to let it consume me.

The vision from last night remained fuzzy in my head, like a half-remembered dream that slipped through my grasp. I blamed it on the hangover, the emotional turmoil of the breakup, and the pounding headache that throbbed behind my eyes. Today was shaping up to be a challenging one, and I needed to get my shit together.

Work had piled up, and I couldn't afford to fall behind. Usually, in times like these, I'd call Ken over for some cuddles, a bit of making out, and an orgasm—he was a master at finger-fucking—and cuddles again. It was our secret recipe to clear my mind and sharpen my predictive abilities. But today was different. Today, I refused to be weak, to seek relief or release in his arms.

I wanted to prove to myself that I was a strong, independent woman who didn't need a man to bolster her powers. Or maybe I was just too proud to admit that I missed him. Regardless, I was determined to face the day on my own terms.

Slipping out of bed, I padded out of my bedroom and into the kitchen. First things first, and that was coffee. While I waited for the brew to bubble me a cup of magic, I took in my domain.

My home, nestled in the heart of the Crossroads, was a luxurious haven amidst the gritty reality of our world. As a witch with the ability to foresee the future, my services were in high demand, and my employer, a powerful figure in the supernatural world, made sure I lived in comfort.

The place was a spacious sanctuary, adorned with opulent furnishings and lush fabrics. The walls were painted in warm, soothing colors that enveloped the space in a cozy embrace. Plush carpets covered the floors, their fibers sinking beneath my feet with every step. Soft, ethereal curtains framed the windows, allowing just the right amount of sunlight to filter through, casting a gentle glow on the room.

The living area was furnished with sumptuous sofas and armchairs, their cushions inviting and comfortable. A large, ornate mirror adorned one wall, reflecting the opulence that surrounded me. A grand chandelier hung from the ceiling, its crystals glistening in the soft light, adding an air of elegance to the room.

In the corner, a well-stocked bookshelf held volumes of

knowledge, from ancient spells to modern-day history. Nearby, a grand piano stood, a testament to my love for music, its rich tones filling the air when my fingers danced across the keys.

My bedroom was a haven of serenity, with a king-sized bed draped in silk sheets and plush pillows. The soft scent of lavender and vanilla filled the room, soothing my senses as I slept. A vanity table held an array of cosmetics and perfumes, a reminder that even in the Crossroads, I was expected to maintain a certain level of elegance.

The kitchen was a chef's dream, stocked with the finest ingredients and state-of-the-art appliances. I had everything at my disposal, from fresh produce to rare spices, ensuring that I could indulge in any culinary desire.

Despite the poverty that surrounded me in the Crossroads, my employer provided for my every need in exchange for the predictions I could offer. It was a life of luxury, but it came at a price—the burden of seeing the future and the weight of my employer's expectations.

Sipping at the magical dark roasted brew, I stood before my wardrobe, contemplating the day ahead. The Crossroads could be a harsh and unforgiving place, but today, I wanted to exude strength and confidence. That meant pink.

The pink power suit I pulled out of the wardrobe would serve as a symbol of my resilience. The jacket hugged my curves, and the tailored trousers elongated my legs. I cinched a belt around my waist, accentuating my hourglass figure. With a flick of my fingers, I used my magic to ensure the suit fit me perfectly, every seam and hem in place.

Next came the heels, sleek and sharp, adding inches to my height and an air of authority to my stride. My reflection in the mirror showed a woman who meant business, a woman who could hold her own in a world filled with uncertainty.

With the outfit complete, I turned my attention to my makeup. I reached for the cosmetics. Using my magical touch, I created a flawless look. My eyes were framed by perfectly winged eyeliner. My lips were painted a shade of deep red that demanded attention.

The woman staring back at me from the mirror was fierce, confident, and unapologetically herself. With every stroke of my brush and every adjustment of my outfit, I had transformed into a force to be reckoned with.

Feeling ready to face the day, I made my way to my favorite spot in my home — the pink recliner chair. Its soft, velvety upholstery enveloped me as I sank into its embrace. The chair was a sanctuary, a place where I could focus my thoughts and harness the power of my visions.

I pulled the lever, and the chair reclined, allowing me to find the perfect position for concentration. With my eyes closed, I let the visions flow, the sights and sounds of the future unfolding before me.

After that crazy vision of darkness and my rough sleep, I didn't expect much. Visions didn't come readily when I was unsettled. I took a deep breath, quieted my mind... and it was like a floodgate opened.

Stepping into the psychic plane was typically like walking into water. At first, it was a gentle lapping at my toes, a subtle whisper of the future brushing against my consciousness. It was the calm before the storm, the moment of anticipation that washed over me, both thrilling and unnerving.

As I delved deeper, the sensations intensified. The water pooled around my knees. Its cool embrace pulled me further into the depths of the psychic realm. It was as if I was wading through an ocean of possibilities, each wave carrying glimpses of what was to come. The visions swelled around me, a cacophony of sights and sounds pulling me in every direction.

Today was different, though. Today, as I stepped into the psychic plane, I was submerged, as if I'd been plunged into the depths of a vast and uncharted sea. The water engulfed me completely, surrounding me with its ethereal currents. I should be afraid, lost in the abyss of the unknown, but I wasn't. I'd learned to navigate these waters, to trust in my abilities.

The visions came rushing toward me like crashing waves, each one carrying a piece of the puzzle. I reached out, grasping at them with an urgency born from years of practice. It was a balancing act between staying afloat and diving deeper. In this vast sea of visions, I was both the sailor and the captain, charting a course through the turbulent waters of fate.

As I absorbed the visions, they became a part of me, merging with my consciousness. I saw the threads of destiny intertwining, the intricate tapestry of the future taking shape. It was a mesmerizing and overwhelming experience, like being swept away by the current of time itself.

As I focused, the visions began to materialize. Financial data, market trends, and economic forecasts unfolded before me like a map of numbers and charts. It was as if I was diving into a pool of knowledge, the water of foresight enveloping me.

I grasped the threads of the visions, pulling them closer, examining each one with a keen eye. The answers to Uziah's dilemmas slowly took shape, like pieces of a jigsaw puzzle coming together.

But just as I was about to emerge from the psychic plane, something unexpected happened. Another vision rushed toward me, unbidden and forceful. It was not a financial prediction; it was a glimpse of Uziah, my boss, confronting Ken.

My heart skipped a beat, and I was jerked upright in my recliner. My feet slammed down on the floor, but my eyes remained closed. Visions of people in my life were rare, and this one felt different, urgent. I saw Uziah's anger, his fist connecting with Ken's face. The realization hit me like a bolt of lightning. Uziah was taking action because of me.

Panic surged through me, and I knew I couldn't let Uziah hurt Ken. I had to explain, to make him understand what had happened. I scrambled to come out of the psychic trance and out the door. They were in the club in the vision. So I headed to Bite Me.

Oz

The world spun around me as I was unceremoniously spat out of a witch's portal. The sensation was even worse than the turbulent ride through the portal from Arcadia to Portland. My head felt like it was wrapped in a thick fog. My thoughts were sluggish and muddled. The disorientation was pure torture.

Gulping in a breath, I choked on the thick air. It was laden with the untamed essence of wilderness that clawed at the fringes of this ravaged civilization. I found myself standing in a dense forest, the canopy overhead a tangled mass of branches that barely let the waning sunlight through. The ground was littered with fallen leaves and branches and... were those bones?

In the distance, I made out the skeletal remains of what may have once been a thriving metropolitan city. Many of its once towering structures were now ravaged by time and neglect. The skyline was a jagged outline against the horizon. Buildings that once touched the sky were now reduced to crumbling monuments of a forgotten era.

I was literally at a crossroads. The irony—that was the name of this place in No Man's Land. A place where there were no rules, no protection offered by a House. It was in the center of the continent of what was once the most powerful union in this world. Now it was a place where survival of the fittest reigned supreme.

As the haze in my mind dissipated, I felt that a wild beast like me might just fit right in here. The instinctual part of me recognized the lawlessness of this land. I had been inside the palace for over two decades, but the feral creature in me was still very much alive.

I'd done my research to get the lay of the land before stepping into the portal. The Gateway Arch, once a symbol of hope and progress, stood as a corroded relic of a bygone era. Its stainless steel exterior had lost its luster, now tarnished and pitted with age. It loomed over the broken skyline like a sentinel of a forgotten time, its graceful curve in contrast to the surrounding decay.

The remnants of a sports stadium with a red bird were now reduced to crumbling concrete and overgrown vegetation. The roar of the crowd had been replaced by an eerie silence, broken only by the occasional rustling of leaves and the distant howl of a wild creature.

The streets were winding, chaotic alleys where makeshift markets had sprung up. Traders peddled magical wares instead of conventional goods, their stalls decorated with enchanted trinkets and elixirs. Neon signs that had once advertised businesses now flickered with mystical runes, casting an eerie glow on the worn façades of buildings.

Everywhere I looked, the city bore the scars of a world in upheaval. Magic flowed through its veins, powering the remnants of civilization in ways that were both awe-inspiring and unsettling. The Crossroads was a place where the past and the future collided, a city where the echoes of its former glory mingled with the enchantments of a new era.

I had arrived ahead of the House leaders, their voices still echoing in my ears as they debated the situation over comms. In my pocket, I carried a second portal potion, a lifeline, back to the House of Blood and Beryl to get there quickly before the portal opened. Portal magic had a tendency to make normal magic unpredictable. I had to find Dion's woman and get her back to Portland before the portal opened.

As I made my way through the bustling streets, a parade of supernatural beings marched around. Witches, their aura of power visible even to my keen panther senses, walked with purpose, their eyes often focused on the unseen currents of magic that flowed through the air. Shifters of various kinds prowled the streets as well, their animal forms occasionally peeking through in their eyes or in subtle movements of their limbs. Some moved with the fluid grace of big cats, like myself, while others displayed the strength and agility of wolves, bears, and even rarer creatures.

Fae beings with their unnatural symmetry added another dimension to the crowd. They shimmered with an otherworldly glow, their eyes filled with secrets as old as time itself. I admired their grace and elegance, even as I remained vigilant, watching for threats. It was often the beautiful ones that were the deadliest, their looks masking just how lethal they were.

It was still light out, which drove the vampires into the shadows of shops and doorways, where they sought refuge from the setting sun's harsh rays. Their pale skin and crimson eyes were unmistakable markers of their kind. They watched the world pass by with a mixture of resignation, forever creatures of the night.

And then I saw her. She was hard to miss. A vision of golden hair adorned with bold black spots, reminiscent of my king in his jaguar form. Even from a distance, her beauty was undeniable, her curves enticing and alluring. A primal desire stirred within me, a longing to protect and serve her, to become the fierce guardian this future queen deserved.

She was wrapped in pink, making me think she was more princess than queen. The outfit clung to her curves in a way that defied the laws of fabric. It was tailored precisely to accentuate her form—a form that was not that of a delicate princess but a comely goddess. A belt cinched at her waist, emphasizing her figure further.

Her heels, sharp and assertive, clicked against the ground with an authority that resonated in the air, marking her every step. It was as if she walked with an awareness of the power she wielded simply by being.

She turned to glance over her shoulder. Her gaze skated past me in her scan of her surroundings. For the fraction of an instant that her golden eyes touched mine, the entire world held its breath. Her face was utter perfection. Each feature was highlighted, from her full lips to her high cheekbones, to her eyes that sparkled with an intensity that did not belong on this godforsaken world. It made me wonder if there was fae blood running through her veins, lending her that ethereal glow that illuminated her from within.

And then, like a wisp of wind, she turned and was swallowed by the crowd, disappearing from my sight. But I'd already caught her scent. It lingered in the air, a delicate yet complex fragrance that wove itself around my senses like an imprint.

It was a blend of lavender and vanilla. The floral notes calmed the chaos around me, while the spice added a warmth and sweetness that felt like a comforting embrace. That wasn't all I smelled.

There was another layer to her scent, something deeper, more elusive—a hint of something I recognized from my years inside the palace. It was a scent I had always associated with Dion, a unique marker of his royal lineage, a scent that spoke of ancient forests and the noble blood that flowed through his veins. It was as if the very air around her was imbued with the promise of her destiny, intertwining her fate with that of our king and the future of our people.

My steps got more urgent. I watched her from a distance, my instincts sharp and focused. It was clear this golden-haired beauty was on a mission. There was a part of me that wanted to give her the space to handle her business. But I knew what was coming. So I picked up my pace.

Neon signs flashed all around, providing illumination as the sun dipped. The distant hum of conversations and laughter mixed with the thumping bass of music, creating a sensory symphony that threatened to disorient me. My heart raced as I trailed behind my quarry, a silent predator lurking in the shadows.

She was my target, the key to our mission, and she was headed toward a club guarded by formidable muscle. My orders were to take her quietly, not alerting the people of the Crossroads to what was about to happen to their world. I needed to be stealthy, but time was running out. The portal would open soon, and I couldn't afford to lose her in the chaos that would ensue if I went in fists blazing at the muscled men she approached.

When she disappeared into the club's entrance, I knew I had no choice but to act swiftly. I prepared to make some noise. The muscles guarding the club entrance were no match for my panther. But there were still a lot of witnesses on the streets.

The air shifted, along with the ground. It was happening. The portal was about to open. My time was just about up.

I crouched low, ready to pounce, my muscles coiled like a spring. My senses heightened. I smelled the sweat and tension in the air, felt the adrenaline coursing through my veins. I lunged forward, a predator on the hunt, ready to confront the obstacles in my path and ensure that my king's destiny unfolded as he commanded.

CHAPTER
SEVEN

Stella

I rushed through the streets of the Crossroads. The people around me gave me a wide berth, their eyes quickly averting as I passed. It was no surprise. They knew who I was and, more importantly, who I worked for.

Uziah was a name that commanded respect and obedience in No Man's Land. As one of his top earners, I was inextricably linked to his power and influence. No one in their right mind would dare cross him, and by extension, no one would even think of crossing in front of me when I clearly had somewhere I wanted to be.

There was another reason they might be averting their gazes. The legacy of my mother cast a shadow over me. My mother had been a seer, one who had glimpsed the shrouded veil of death itself. Her abilities were both revered and feared, as she had foreseen the assaults and deaths of countless individuals. My own skills were different. They didn't involve foreseeing death or the cause of harm. Yet the whispers and hushed conversations that followed me hinted at a lingering unease.

She'd seen my father's death. She'd seen hers, too. She'd known it would be in the Crossroads. I'd resented her for coming here. If she'd stayed away, maybe she would still be alive. But I knew better than anyone that you couldn't control the future.

What no one knew, not even me, was the secret I carried within me. I was part shifter, a fact hidden even from myself. The animal within me remained a mystery, dormant and concealed. It was a secret I guarded fiercely, knowing that it held the key to a part of my identity I had yet to discover. I doubted I ever would know more about the cat that chose to stay asleep inside of me.

Pushing those thoughts aside, I continued to navigate the streets toward Bite Me. The layers of secrecy and power that surrounded me were like a cloak, one I wore with a mixture of pride and trepidation. In the Crossroads, I was both a pawn and a player in a game I was only beginning to understand. Much like the vision that had propelled me out of my comfy recliner this morning.

I knew that Uziah was a violent man. He was a vampire, after all. I knew the organization that he ran was not tea and roses. People got bloody, and not just for meals. Ken had come home plenty of nights with bruised fists and split lips. But he had always been the one delivering the blows. In my vision, he'd been at the mercy of Uziah.

The problem was, Uziah was not known for his mercy.

The air around me crackled with an unsettling tension as I turned the last corner that would take me to the club. A sense of unease had settled over me. I couldn't shake the feeling that I was being followed. It was absurd, really. Who would dare to mess with me, knowing my connection to Uziah and my unique abilities?

I looked up at the sky. Today's forecast had called for sun. That had been predicted by a fae. Fairies were in tuned with the natural world. They didn't get their predictions wrong. However, those were definitely dark clouds forming in the skies. They reminded me of the vision I'd had before going to bed last night, the one where I saw darkness and destruction all around.

Part of me wondered if I was losing my mind. Or maybe if it was unlocking other powers. I was my mother's daughter, after all.

Even if the world was ending, I decided I wanted to save my ex-boyfriend. Not because I wanted to get back together with him. Probably.

The prickles at the back of my neck persisted, like a warning from some instinct buried deep within me. I couldn't ignore it. With a cautious glance over my shoulder, I scanned the shadows for any signs of an unwelcome presence. The street behind me appeared ordinary, with the same old rundown people trying to make it through another day, just like any other day in the Crossroads.

I quickened my pace. Just across the street was the club. *Bite Me* was illuminated in red letters. The exterior a vivid play of black and red that pulsed with an energy of its own. It was as if the very walls were alive. The red hues flowed like blood in a mesmerizing waterfall effect. Even in its dormant state of being closed, the building exuded a magnetic pull, an allure that was almost palpable, drawing people's eyes and making them swerve toward the club like moths wanting the burn of a vampire's bite.

Guarding the entrance were two imposing figures, bouncers with muscles that bulged against their tight shirts. They were the gatekeepers to Uziah's haven, a clear sign that not just anyone was welcome beyond the threshold. They recognized me, and without a word, they stepped aside to let me pass.

Stepping into the dimly lit interior, I was greeted not by the thumping bass of the music. Instead, it was a thud of fists. And then, as if confirming the vision I had seen in my head, there he was.

Uziah was the epitome of power and danger, cloaked in a suit as black as the night. Every piece of his attire, from the tie that hung around his neck to the shoes on his feet absorbed the light, making him a void in the vibrant chaos of the club.

It wasn't just his attire that commanded attention; it was those eyes, crimson orbs that burned with an intensity that was unnatural. They were framed by a mane of salt-and-pepper hair that cascaded down to his broad shoulders, giving him an air of distinguished menace. His bushy eyebrows and full mustache only added to the morally black image he presented.

There was blood on his knuckles. He was looking down on the floor as though there was a cockroach that had dared cross his marbled floors. But it wasn't a cockroach.

"What did I tell you about Stella?" Uziah growled.

"You told me to take care of her." Ken looked entirely cowed, his face drained of color as he shielded his head from his maker.

"Is this what you call taking care of her? Sticking your dick in another woman?"

"Sorry, boss."

As I watched, a wave of conflicting emotions washed over me. There was anger at Ken for betraying me, a sense of justice in seeing him held accountable, and a deep yearning for a love that had once been.

"I trusted you with her." Uziah grabbed Ken by the neck with one hand and hauled him up to his feet as though he weighed less than a teddy bear.

"You know how my girl gets when she feels neglected. Peaches gets antsy when I don't give it to her regularly."

Peaches? That was the name of the girl he'd been fucking the other day.

"You need to keep your girlfriend on a tighter leash, then. Stella is too important."

My head was spinning. I was Ken's girlfriend. Or I had been. He'd been cheating on me with Peaches. Not the other way around. Right?

"I know I screwed up." Ken licked at the blood on his split lip. It was already healing. "I'll win Stella back. I always do. She's so fucking desperate for dick."

"See that you do. I can't have my cash cow not giving up the milk. That woman's power is making us money."

"I won't screw up again. I know my job: keep Stella happy so the predictions keep coming."

"Either you do it or I'll get someone else. She's due for an upgrade, anyway."

"I'm the upgrade. Allan couldn't hack it."

Allan was my last boyfriend. He'd cheated on me, too. That breakup had been brutal. He'd also worked for Uziah. But Allan had been reassigned to another sector, and I hadn't had to see him again.

"I told you I can handle this. Keeping Stella happy comes with a promotion. I've earned a new rank. I'm ready for it, and I'll prove it. I'll eat her out every day until she's seeing stars."

"I don't need her to see stars," said Uziah. "I just want her to see the future so—"

He turned. I wasn't sure if it was because of my gasp. I had been holding my breath for so long that I was surprised I hadn't fainted.

"Fuck," sighed Uziah. "Stella, it's not what it looks like."

Really? Because what it looked like was I was being fucked over by every man I'd ever thought cared about me in this godforsaken place. And each time I'd caught them with their pants down, they'd blamed my eyesight. If someone said those words to me again, I was going to scream. Instead, I turned on my heel and ran.

"Grab her!"

EIGHT

Oz

Bite Me? What was throwing me off about the club was the façade that screamed insecure vampire having a centennial-life crisis. Standing at the doors were what smelled like two burly bears. Didn't matter what they were on the inside. After play-fighting with my king and Nova, my beast was ready for a real fight. Though I doubted I'd get much of one from these two.

The late afternoon air was cool on my skin in contrast to the heat building inside me as I crossed the street. There were only a handful of people out now. None were looking in my direction.

Without warning, I lunged at the first bouncer, my body a blur of motion. My claws partially shifted, elongating into lethal, razor-sharp extensions. With a lightning-fast strike, I slashed across his chest. The fabric of his shirt tore. Blood welled from the gash. He let out a guttural grunt of pain, stumbling backward.

The second bouncer reacted swiftly, attempting to grab hold of me. I danced out of his reach, my movements fluid and impossible to predict. I delivered a powerful round-house kick to his midsection, sending him into a stack of empty crates with a satisfying crash.

The bear let out a guttural growl. Instead of coming to his aid, the few people around disappeared into storefronts and alleyways. Only the sound of heavy breathing and the pit-pat of my victims' blood sounded on the street.

The first bouncer, clutching his bleeding chest, was far from defeated. He lunged at me with a wild swing. I dodged effortlessly, allowing his momentum to carry him past me. With a calculated strike to the back of his head, I sent him sprawling to the ground, unconscious.

My breath came out in ragged gasps. Adrenaline coursed through my veins. Bloodlust nearly consumed me. I wanted to tear their throats out, but they were no longer a threat. Their massive forms lay crumpled on the ground.

I was ready for more. My muscles coiled, my senses hyper-alert. That's when I heard it—a faint sound, a shift in the air that had me spinning around, claws at the ready, only to find the street eerily deserted.

The silence was unnerving. In Arcadia, if any other supernatural had dared an attack on one of us, it would have been met with a swift, collective response. Under King Dion, our kind rallied to each other's defense, bound by a pact of loyalty and brotherhood. But here in the Crossroads, it seemed such camaraderie was non-existent. Or perhaps the very name of this club and its owner cast a shadow too dark for anyone to cross.

I reached for the door to the club. On the other side was

my future queen. A woman who was destined to stand by the side of King Dion, my liege, my brother in all ways except blood.

The thought of her, so close yet guarded, ignited a fire within me. It mattered little whether the beings of this place chose to stand with me or against me. With a final glance at the shadowed alleyways and shuttered storefronts, I turned back to the club's entrance.

Just as I thought the battle was won, the door slammed open. A third man emerged from the club's interior. He was stockier than the previous two, with a determined look in his eyes. He had been alerted to the commotion. Likely by the second bear's cry of defeat.

I pushed him back into the interior of the club. The door crashed shut behind me, and then I slammed him into the frame. With my partially shifted claws, I swiped at another man's attack, striking his chest with enough force to send him stumbling backward. He hit his head on the post holding a velvet rope and was out. The room spun around us as I maintained my balance, my senses attuned to every nuance of the fight.

The man who'd had the bad luck to open the door lunged again, this time with a low, sweeping kick aimed at my legs. I leaped over his attack and cleared his reach. As I landed, I struck with precision, delivering a crushing blow to his abdomen.

With a gasp of pain, he crumpled to the ground, incapacitated. The entryway fell into silence once more, save for the labored breaths of the defeated men. My pulse raced and my chest heaved as I stood victorious.

When I looked around, I saw more men coming out of the woodwork and heading straight for me. I was outnumbered. But then the world shook.

It was the portal. It was opening.

The vibrations traveled through my body, disrupting the brawl. Confusion rippled through the men, their attention torn away from me. It was as though the very earth had rebelled against this violence.

I seized this moment of distraction to slip past them and make my way into Bite Me. I could taste her presence in the air—my future queen.

The lights assaulted my eyes. The base of beats that was a piss-poor form of music hurt my ears. Then, in a whirlwind of golden hair, she appeared before me. A vision in pink that seemed almost surreal against the backdrop of chaos.

Her hair was a cascade of gold, shimmering like the coat of a jaguar under the sun, with streaks of black at the roots that lent her an air of wildness, of untamed beauty. In those pastel colors, she looked like a flower blooming in a concrete jungle.

She stopped just short of me, her chest heaving, her eyes wide and filled with fear. Shame stopped me from reaching out for her. Was that terror in her gaze directed at me? Did she see past the royal treatment of cleaned fingernails and washed face to the feral creature that I truly was? Did she see me as a threat?

But as I followed her gaze over her shoulder, I saw the true source of her fear: two vampires, their faces twisted in anger, barreling toward us.

Conflict raged within me, a primal urge to protect her clashing with the violence that surged through my veins at the sight of her pursuers. I was torn between the desire to tear those vampires limb from limb and the duty I owed to the woman before me.

Her eyes met mine again, and in that moment, I knew

what I had to do. The duty to protect her overrode every-thing else. The decision was made in an instant.

I reached out my hand to her. "Come with me if you want to live."

I saw the indecision in her gaze. I was a stranger to her. The men at her back meant her harm. I saw the calculation in her golden eyes as she decided to take a gamble on me.

The moment her fingertips touched mine, the ground was ripped out from under my feet. My entire soul was squeezed in a vise-grip. My vision blinked out. My heart restarted.

It had all happened in a split second. I wasn't sure if I'd died. But I knew I had been reborn. I also knew that the impossible had taken place.

The two vampires behind us had fallen to the ground and were scrambling to their feet amidst the glassware and fixtures falling down around us. My focus was solely on the woman with her hand in mine.

I pulled her close, my arms encircling her protectively. Her eyes were closed, likely experiencing the same soul-stirring realization that I just had. When those golden eyes met mine, I knew that I would do anything for her, not because she would be my queen but because she was my fated mate.

Stella

They weren't even running after me; they were walking. I glanced back and saw Uziah and Ken casually strolling, their smirks telling me they didn't believe I could get far in my precarious situation. That situation being that I was an out of shape big girl who'd never moved faster than a quick stroll in a park.

I wasn't in a park today. I was in mortal danger. So I picked up my feet and ran. And promptly fell flat on my face.

I could hear their laughter looming in the distance. It got closer slowly, slowly. There was no urgency in their movements to collect me. I was trapped. Where could I go even if I could run?

Something inside of me demanded I get up. It had the grit in Tori's voice. It had the dare in Niamh's. But mostly, it sounded like my mom.

On your feet, kitten.

I'd always been an obedient child. I did what my mother told me. I got first one, then the other heeled foot under me and stood.

You can't let them catch you, baby girl.

I hated to disappoint my mother. They probably were going to get me. But they wouldn't get me without a fight.

I took off again, my heart pounding in my chest like a trapped bird. The staccato rhythm of my footsteps echoed across the dance floor, the sound of my heels clacking against the floor as I tried to flee.

I had never been a runner, especially not in the kinds of shoes I was wearing now. They were more suited for sitting on a bar stool waiting for a guy to buy me a drink than fleeing from danger. I'd never been in danger a single day in my life. Which I knew was all kinds of first world privilege while living in a third world territory.

But I had no choice. I couldn't stay with Uziah and Ken, not after what I had witnessed. They had been using me all along, manipulating my visions for their gain. Now that I knew the truth, I couldn't stay.

I felt cheap. Like a prostitute. Even though it had been my mind and not my body that had been used. But they'd used my body to get to my mind. Now they would keep using me without any of the perks.

Fear clawed at my chest, making each breath a struggle. They wouldn't play nice anymore. They wouldn't treat me with the same faux affection they had before. They would see me as a threat that they had to contain.

I stumbled on the steps. I knew they were gaining on me, their heavy footsteps and angry voices closing in. I needed a plan, a way to disappear, to hide my unique gift and stay one step ahead. But I couldn't even climb stairs properly. I was doomed.

My breaths came in ragged gasps. My legs were jelly. The ache in my side was unbearable. It hadn't even been five minutes of running. Barely a couple of yards of fast movement. I needed to keep moving, to find a place to hide, to disappear.

As I reached the top of the steps, I straightened myself, trying to regain my composure. There was someone blocking my way. Another of Uziah's many goons. Niamh called the men who worked for Uziah minions, but after seeing an old children's film about adorable yellow workers, I could never use that term to describe the imposing men that did Uziah's dirty work so he didn't have to get his dark clothes... Well, dark clothes didn't show off blood, did they?

The muscle blocking the door was also dressed in black. For some reason, he didn't scare me. In my messed-up mind, this guy screamed safety.

It's him.

I wanted to shout at my mother's disembodied voice. What did she mean this was him? Was this the man who would end my life and bring on our ghostly reunion?

He reached for me, his hand outstretching toward me. I knew I should recoil, but the closer his fingers got to me, the slower my heart rate became. I thought I was supposed to see my life flash before my eyes before death. Instead, all I saw was the gold of his eyes. They looked like a window to forever.

They also looked like the eyes of a man I'd never seen inside of Bite Me. This wasn't one of Uziah's minions or goons or muscle.

Tall, dark, and handsome did not do him justice. He was

over six feet tall and built, but his presence felt like it was touching the ceiling and both sides of the wall. He moved toward me with a fluid grace, like a sleek panther stalking its prey on two legs. And I was pretty sure I was his prey.

I was supposed to be running. But my legs slowed and began to walk toward him, in no hurry to arrive or get away.

His sharp teeth were bared, radiating danger and primal strength. However, as his piercing gaze landed on me, it softened into something gentle and reassuring. I knew deep down that I could trust this man. Even after the gross revelation of what every other lover in my life must have thought of me, I knew that this one was going to be different.

It's him!

I reached for him then. The moment my fingertips touched his palm, it all made sense. I was his fated mate. As he looked down at me, a sense of security washed over me. In his arms, I felt protected, wanted, and cherished. I knew that, no matter what, he would keep me safe.

"Come with me if you want to live."

Live? I could've died right there. This man was going to love me the way I deserved to be loved. He would never lie, cheat, or break my heart. Because he was my fated fucking mate.

I wanted to jump and cheer. But there was still danger behind us. And some kind of an earthquake going on outside.

I nodded my head, ready to be taken anywhere he was going. In the back of my mind, I heard Tori yelling at me to use my head and not my clit to make decisions. I heard Niamh saying to guard my heart and just have fun. But neither of them was here now. Neither of them was being held by the man that I was sure would never hurt me, never use me.

And so I let him clasp my hand, pull me close, and take me away. When we stepped out into the streets, it was pure chaos.

Oz

The bodies of the bear shifters and vampires who'd dared to stand in my way lay strewn beneath my feet, a macabre carpet that marked my passage. Each step I took was a declaration of the savage lengths I would go to fulfill my mission. Luckily for those on my tail, my mission was now in my arms.

As the heavy doors slammed shut behind us, a shift in the atmosphere greeted me. The sky, once a clear canvas of fading light, now roiled with ominous clouds, swirling into a vortex that appeared to devour light itself. The air, charged with anticipation and fear, crackled with the raw energy of magic unbound. People, mere shadows against the backdrop of impending doom, scattered in every direction, their screams piercing the growing tumult.

The ground beneath me vibrated, a sinister prelude to the catastrophe that was about to unfold. The portal, a gaping maw in the very fabric of reality, pulsated with a menacing glow, its edges blurred as if painted with the brushstrokes of madness. The magic that seeped through was tangible, a thick, intoxicating aroma that cloyed at my throat.

The weight of the woman in my arms was the only anchor I had to the physical world. Her rapid breathing was a counterpoint to the drumming of my heart. I felt the pulse of the portal's magic brushing against my skin. It was a siren's call that beckoned with the promise of power and the threat of oblivion.

The world tilted on its axis. The ground beneath my feet quaked, a violent quake of earth that threatened to upend everything I'd ever known. Having a portal open up in a new realm was legions worse than traveling between two portals. Portal travel was going to be my escape from the Crossroads, but with this crack in the world opening, all magic—including short-range portaling—would be too dangerous. I had to get us as far away as possible from this doorway.

The sky roared like a herd of wild beasts. Winds howled like the cries of a thousand lost souls, each one vying for attention in this apocalyptic nightmare. People scattered, their screams piercing the air as they fled the unseen terror of the portal. Their fear was a tangible thing, a thick, choking cloud that seeped into every pore, every crevice of this broken city.

The world around us might be descending into anarchy, but my focus remained laser-sharp. My gaze lowered to the woman in my arms. I didn't even know her name yet.

Liar, my panther called me. *She's mine.*

The feral creature inside me roared loud. Louder than

the people scrambling in the streets. Louder than the crack that rent the ground. She shuddered in my arms.

Had she heard the panther?

Was she about to run away from me?

Neither man nor beast would let that happen.

But she wasn't running. She clung to me. Her pink-tipped nails dug into my shirt. That lush body of hers pressed into mine. Her face tilted up, looking at me for answers.

I would give her the world. If it wasn't crumbling around us.

"I want to live," she said. "I can't die now, not when I just found you. That would be some serious bull—"

The ground quaked again. I brought her hard against my chest, enough so that her feet came up off the ground. She looked down at them dangling a few inches and then back up at me.

"Oh my gosh, you just swept me off my feet. No man's ever done that to me before."

Her voice was breathless. I could listen to her talk all day. I'd only barely heard her voice back inside the club. Now it rang just for me. And in that moment, everything else faded away.

The chaos, the noise, the fear—it all receded into a distant blur, leaving only her in a husky voice, the feel of her fingertips brushing the hairs at the nape of my neck, that golden gaze looking at me like I was ten feet tall.

The beast within me stirred again. It stopped pawing at my gut to get out, to have its own introduction to her. Instead, it sat down on its haunches, its tongue lolling out of its mouth.

Standing in a storm as the world fell apart around us, basking in the brilliance of her gaze was a calmness that

I've never known. The beast wanted to lie on its belly, to flatten its ears in submission and devotion. An itch tickled at the base of my spine, an odd sensation that I soon realized was the wagging of an ethereal tail—a manifestation of the beast's contentment.

It was ludicrous, absurd even, to think that this princess, this goddess, could be my mate. She was meant for the king, meant to be queen. The only thing a scarred warrior like me could do was lay down his life for her.

My loyalty to the king was unwavering, a bond forged in the fires of gratitude and indebtedness. Dion had saved me, given me purpose when I had none. To even entertain the thought of claiming his destined mate was madness, a betrayal of everything I stood for.

The ground continued to shudder, a relentless reminder of the world falling apart around us. The air was heavy with the scent of danger and desperation. Behind us, a familiar shout sliced through the chaos.

"You fucker. Like hell you'll get away with stealing my meal ticket."

The words hit me like a physical blow because of how they impacted her. Her response was visceral. Her body went slack in my hold. Her chest caved in. That proud forehead dropped. She reminded me of prey being cornered. Didn't she know she was being held by a vicious predator?

I could already taste that blond-haired excuse for a man's blood on my tongue. I was already spitting out the rancid taste of him. Every fiber of my being wanted to turn and confront the rat who dared threaten the goddess in my arms. My claws ached to show him the true wrath of a panther shifter defending what's his.

On my own, I would have done it. But the feel of fear in my future queen's body, the sight of her despair, reminded me of the stakes. I couldn't risk her safety, not for my pride or my anger.

And, as much as I hated to admit it, looking over my shoulder, I saw that I was out-manned. Only in numbers. That teething excuse of a baby vamp didn't know how lucky he was.

Putting my precious cargo on the ground, I pulled her along as I took off at a breakneck pace. I was acutely aware of her struggles to keep pace. She was no warrior. Her steps were hurried and clumsy. Frustration was a burning thing inside me, an anger at our helplessness, at her vulnerability, and at my inability to simply fight our way out of this.

When she stumbled again, I felt the weight of the witch's potion in my pocket. It was a dangerous gamble, but it seemed like our only chance. My fingers closed around the vial, its surface slick with the sweat of my apprehension.

I pulled it out, the potion that would open a portal back to Portland. A flicker of doubt crossed my mind—portals were unpredictable, risky in the best of times. The sound of footsteps growing closer banished any hesitation. I hurled the glass to the ground. It shattered with a sound that was quickly swallowed by the night.

A cloud of purple smoke erupted from the broken vial, swirling and coalescing into a shimmering gateway. It was now or never. I pulled her toward the portal, and it was just in time.

The blond vamp's hand reached out, grasping just inches from her back. A sense of impending doom clenched my gut, but we were already stepping into the cloud. The world around us blurred, reality bending and twisting in ways that defied comprehension.

There was a sensation of being stretched and

compressed all at once, a disorienting tug that made my head spin. Sounds and smells warped around us, the stench of the city's decay giving way to something fresher, cleaner. The chaotic noise of our pursuers faded into a distant echo, replaced by the quieter, more mundane sounds of Portland.

And then, just like that, we were through. The portal closed behind us with a soft whoosh, cutting off the baby vamp's enraged howl mid-crescendo. It was a howl of rage loud enough to follow us through the portal.

When I looked up, it wasn't the House of Blood and Beryl I saw. I could still see the jagged skyline of the Cross-roads. I could still see the clouds of the opening portal. We'd gotten away, but we hadn't gotten far. Maybe a few miles out of the city at best.

It wasn't far enough. They could be on us in no time, and I was all out of quick travel magic. We were going to have to run.

"Shift!"

CHAPTER
ELEVEN

Stella

A wave of nausea hit me like a bear shifter after a pot of honey. I doubled over, dry-heaving the buttered avocado toast I'd had for breakfast. I've always hated portal travel. It was like being churned inside a cosmic blender. The world spun and tilted in impossible ways, leaving my stomach lurching in protest.

This time it wasn't so bad, though. Likely because of the strong arms that were circled around me, holding the world together as I almost fell apart. I'd thought the portal opening was going to snatch my dreams from me. That had almost been my miscreant of an ex. Neither had managed to snatch me from my man's arms.

And oh boy, did my man have a set of arms on him. They were strong and reassuring, steadying me as the world slowly righted itself. Thank God I didn't heave on his boots. That would not have been a good look.

I leaned into his warmth, grateful for the solidity of his presence. His scent, a mix of forest and something distinctly him, enveloped me. It was a grounding force in the middle of my disorientation.

Finally, the world stopped spinning. We were somewhere new, safe from the immediate threats that had chased us. I gasped for air, my heart pounding not just from the portal's disorienting effects but from the sheer exertion of running.

I was never one for physical activity. A laughable thought, considering I'd once used magic to cheat on a fitness challenge, making a treadmill seem like I was running on it while I wasn't. My running shoes were probably still collecting dust somewhere in the back of my closet. My body, built for comfort and not for speed, had somehow carried me through life-or-death sprints.

Looking up at my unexpected protector in this whirlwind of madness, I saw concern and a depth of emotion in his gaze that took my breath away. There was an intensity there. A fierce protectiveness mingled with a gentleness that appeared at odds with his formidable presence. And man, was he in top form. He was breathtaking, his features striking in a way that transcended the conventional handsome. There was a raw, untamed beauty about him, as if he'd been carved from the very essence of the wild.

His eyes, dark and penetrating, saw right through to my soul, offering a sense of security I had been craving since my mother's passing. The connection between us was palpable, a tether that pulled with a magnetic force. It was a strange, inexplicable trust, one that defied logic or reason. I didn't even know his name. However, the bond I felt with him was as solid as the ground beneath my feet.

His lips parted, and he said something, but my brain

was still ringing from the intradimensional opening and the portal travel. The world was still trying to right itself. Thankfully, he held on to me.

"It was real," I whispered, more to myself than to him. "Everything I saw in my vision." The vision of the portal's opening in the Crossroads was not just a figment of my imagination.

"You have visions?" He let out a huff and looked away from me. "Just like him."

"Just like who?"

If he answered, I didn't hear him.

Another vision hit me—a car hidden among the trees, a secret refuge for two teenagers caught in their own world. I saw the keys left in the ignition, a lifeline thrown to us as our pursuers closed in. The car was fueled by magic. I saw us taking it, leaving behind a story the teenagers would struggle to explain.

"Shift," came the deep, growling voice of my savior, my fated mate.

I realized this wasn't the first time he'd said that. Earlier, I'd been too caught up in the sight of him. There was an elegance in his stance, a predatory grace that spoke of his strength and agility. Yet it was the softness in his eyes when he looked at me, the slight curve of his lips that hinted at a smile that truly mesmerized me. It was in that moment I understood the true power of a fated mate—not just a partner chosen by destiny, but a soul so perfectly aligned with one's own that their mere presence brought a sense of peace to the plaguing chaos.

Yeah, my entire worldview had certainly shifted.

"We're not out of danger. They're still after us. We need to shift and run."

"Shift?" I echoed, puzzled. I was on the verge of

mentioning the car I'd just envisioned when he dropped that bombshell that left me reeling.

Me? He wanted me to shift and run? But how did he know I was—

"Into your panther," he said, discarding his leather jacket.

"How do you know I'm a panther?"

His gaze on me sharpened, as if he found my ignorance baffling. "We don't have time for this, princess. We have to get back to King Dion."

"King?" The word felt foreign on my tongue. "Princess?"

Was this a term of endearment or an actual title? Was I, by some twist of fate, a princess from another realm? The timing of his arrival, coinciding with the portal's opening, hinted at a reality far beyond my imagination.

It all made sense. I hadn't come from the Crossroads. I'd never believed I belonged there, having never quite fit in. And my father and my animal had both been kept secret from me my whole life.

A crown and a mate in one day, and it wasn't even my birthday.

"They're coming. You need to shift now. Shift into your panther."

Shame enveloped me, the realization of my inability to shift into my animal form exposed in the most vulnerable manner. I'd never managed to shift, a failure that haunted me, now laid bare before him. He was tugging at the back of his shirt, about to do one of those one-handed tugs to pull it over his head. It was one of those things I loved watching a man do, so I was surprised I found my tongue instead of watching the free show.

"I don't even know your name," I managed to say, an attempt to deflect from my inner turmoil.

"It's Oz," he revealed, his identity adding another layer to himself as well as a new layer of skin. "I'm the panther king's second."

"Nice to meet you, Oz. I'm Stella, your fated mate."

His reaction was not what I expected. He visibly clenched his jaw. The lines of tension etched across his features felt like the prelude to my greatest fear being realized.

A wave of icy dread washed over me. My heart thudded painfully, the sensation echoing against my ribs. I wanted to take a step back, to head back through that portal right back to the Crossroads, and back under Ken's thumb, than face this possibility.

Was I about to be rejected?

Oz's rigid stance, the set of his shoulders, every minute signal from his body screamed a warning. He was going to do it.

He was going to reject me as his fated mate.

I was about to be cast aside, deemed unworthy by the one person who had awakened a sliver of hope in my battered heart. All because I was defective. Because I couldn't shift.

Then it crashed over me, a vision so sudden and forceful it took my breath away. I was about to get whiplash from all of these visions. I had never had so many in the same day.

This time the vision was of me and Oz. We were standing in a grand palace, surrounded by statues of panthers, jaguars, leopards, and cheetahs watching us with their stone eyes. I was draped in an exquisite gown, the fabric flowing around me like water. Oz stood beside me in military regalia, every inch the warrior prince. But he wasn't smiling. He looked so sad, so dejected.

That look twisted into a grimace of rejection as he turned away from me. The pain that shot through me was so sharp, so bitter, it sent me tumbling to my knees back in reality.

I didn't hit the ground. Oz caught me. Somehow, I knew he would.

I fought for breath, each gasp a battle against the despair clawing at my insides. The vision clung to me, a cruel reminder of my deepest fear. Rejection. It had always been my companion, a constant in a life filled with fleeting shadows.

Oz's arms encircled me, his embrace a fortress in the midst of the storm inside me. Within the safety of his hold, the world's chaos dimmed, even as the earth trembled with the opening of the portal.

"Please?"

"Tell me, princess. Anything you need, I'll make it happen. Just say the word."

"Please," I repeated, my voice a fragile whisper. "Don't reject me."

My hands shook as they clutched at him. Even as I sought to anchor myself to him, the vision's shadow loomed, a relentless reminder of a possible future filled with pain.

"My job is to keep you safe. I will not fail you."

"You'll keep me?"

He bit at his lower lip, like he was holding in a lie. I'd seen Ken do that. All of my other boyfriends, too. Oz was struggling to hold on to the truth.

"Just give me a chance," I begged. "Please."

"Know this, Stella; I would give my life for you."

It was a vow, a vow I believed. Still, I wasn't sure he was promising me what I wanted.

"If it were up to me, I would tear out the throat of that blond bastard that dared to hurt you."

More truths. Nothing but the truth. And the violence of those facts was turning me on.

"I will always protect you. But right now, I need you to shift so that we can run."

"I can't." The truth spilled from me, a confession I'd never dared voice. Because no one ever knew to ask about the animal hidden inside of me. "I can't shift. I've never been able to."

The words hung between us, bright light of revelation shone on my darkest inadequacy.

TWELVE

Oz

"**P**lease don't reject me."

My brain stopped working. When it restarted, all I saw was red. Suddenly, I was no longer the chief of security and second to the king. I was on all fours, a cub again, vulnerable and pleading. The scene from my past unfolded with painful clarity: the cold, distant look in my mother's eyes as I stood before her, small and desperate.

"Please don't reject me," I had begged, my voice quivering with fear. It was a plea for compassion, for a sign of her love, for any indication that I mattered. But the response was a harsh lesson, a backhand across the chest with claws out, a wound so deep it felt as though it had carved into my very soul.

"Just give me a chance," Stella begged. "Please."

The damp earth of the forest underfoot snapped me back to the present, but the sting of that memory clung to me, as present as the scent of pine and moss that filled the air. My mother's rejection was a scar that would never heal. My mind was still reeling from the flashback that had sent me alone and into danger when I came to a full understanding of the dire straits I now stood in.

This goddess among mortals thought any man would reject her. The blond suckface didn't count. He was not mortal, and much less than a man. A woman as beautiful as Stella, with curves that had my canines aching, my molars throbbing, and my tongue damn near lolling out of my mouth? Rejection?

If she were mine, I would have stripped her naked upon sight and given my tongue worship duties on that lush body of hers. Starting with removing those ridiculous spiked shoes which had to be murder on her legs. But she wasn't mine.

Liar, roared my panther, making me wince with the force of his certainty.

I shut out the sound of the beast and focused on the most important thing she just said.

"I can't shift."

The forest around us was a blur of green and brown, a wild tapestry that was both familiar and alien to me. Like the wilderness of Portland, the land looked as though it was trying to reclaim the space from the supernaturals that stubbornly clung to them when they were at the top of the food chain. They mistakenly thought they had a leg up on nature. But as the skyline was reminding them, there were far greater powers out there than them.

"You can't shift?"

Stella stood before me. Her eyes shimmered with vulnerability and fear. Fear of rejection. Fear of shame.

I couldn't fathom a life devoid of the freedom to shift, to

feel the power and grace of my panther form. There was a time when I feared I might be trapped forever in that primal state, the wildness of the panther nearly consuming the boy I used to be whole. But to have never known the exhilaration of the run was unimaginable to me.

Without conscious thought, my hand reached out to her, intending only to coax her gaze upward, to remind her of her divine nobility. A goddess should never bow to any man, not even her king. But at the slightest contact, at the first brush of my fingertip on her soft flesh, she surged toward me, her body pressing against mine with a desperation that took my breath away.

My initial instinct was to retreat, to maintain the respectful distance her impending queenship demanded. Yet, as her warmth enveloped me, I found myself unable to resist the pull of her need. My arms wrapped around her as though she commanded it. It was of my own volition that I sniffed at her hair, gulping down the sweet vanilla scent of her and feeding it to my hungry beast.

"It's all right, princess."

She was not mine. She was destined to be my king's, to be my queen. But as of now, she was not. That's probably why I'd been calling her princess; she hadn't assumed the throne yet.

Despite everything I knew—that she wasn't my fated mate, that my ultimate loyalty was to my king—I found myself unable to push her away.

She calmed in my hold, and so did I. Even though I knew danger was gaining ground on us, I was loath to let go of this moment. It was like a dream. I hadn't dreamed since... I don't think I'd ever had a single dream in my life. Only waking nightmares.

The weight of my past, the guilt and regret, still shadowed me. It was a constant throb in my heart, a relentless reminder of the cub I had once been and the errors I'd committed. The loneliness that ensued had shaped me, transformed me into the leashed weapon I'd become. It also etched scars, deep and unforgiving, that ached sharply as Stella gazed up at me.

I gazed down at her and saw more than just the woman standing before me. I saw a kindred spirit, someone else touched by the stiff hand of rejection. My instincts as a protector roared to life. I couldn't let her experience that pain, that desolation. Never again.

A part of me wanted to wait for that suck hard vampire who hurt her. I could almost taste his blood on my tongue. But duty overruled that.

"I need to get us out of here."

"There's a car about a mile away," she said.

"How do you know that?"

She tapped her temple. She possessed the sight, just like Dion. Yet another sign they were destined for each other.

It took us twenty painstaking minutes to reach the car. Her shoes were the culprit, slowing us down. Countless times I wanted to yank them off her feet, but then she'd be barefoot and entirely at the mercy of the wilderness. I also fought the urge to hoist her over my shoulder and carry her. That right wasn't mine.

The car roared to life, its rumble resonating with the panther within me. I scented the two teens a distance off. Heard a male grunt of pleasure. Heard a feminine gasp that was fake pleasure. Then a fruitless scramble of clothes and shoes as I steered through the dark, tree-lined path.

The night wrapped around us, a cool shroud of secrecy. The dashboard lights cast a soft glow on Stella's face, high-lighting her features in a serene light. I held the steering wheel tightly, a battlefield within me where man and panther collided.

The beast within was agitated. Drawn to Stella, to her scent that filled the car — a blend of wildflowers and that sweet essence of vanilla. Vanilla was said to be calming. Instead, it called to my primal side, demanding I claim her as mine.

But my duty to Dion, my king and savior, acted as a shackle. The internal struggle was relentless, a war between what I desired and what I owed. The panther inside clawed at my confines, its longing clear. I had to quell its desires. I could not—would not—betray the one who gave my life meaning, who'd rescued me from a fate of isolation and sorrow.

The silence in the car was a third passenger between us. A quick glance at Stella showed tears shimmering in her eyes, a sight that sliced through me sharply. She was still under the impression I'd reject her, resigning herself to a fate devoid of a true mate.

I yearned to unveil the truth, to confess that Dion, the best man I knew, was her destined mate. Well, he would be the best man. Now that he had a mate. He would give up all the women and whoring.

I was certain.

My hands fidgeted on the steering wheel as I recalled my last sight of Dion as I left the House of Blood and Beryl. He'd helped me procure the portal potion from a witch. It was clear that payment for her services would be handled in his bedroom. He'd waved me off with a salute as the witch had tugged him down the hall.

But that was likely his last time with another woman. When he caught the scent of his mate, saw her for real and not just in a vision, he would be devoted to her. I was sure.

And when he did, Stella would see that he was the best man for her. He was dedicated to his kingdom, to his people, and to his duties. He would dedicate himself to her. And so would I as chief of security. It would be my duty to ensure my queen was protected.

"I'm not worthy of a beautiful princess like you. But I vow to protect you with my life until my last breath."

It was a promise I intended to keep, no matter the cost. It was the only vow I could make her.

"Do you really think I'm beautiful?" She turned to me with eyes seeking affirmation, seeking something honest and real.

I met her gaze, letting her see the truth in my eyes. "I will always tell you the truth. I might not be able to tell you everything, but a lie will never leave my lips. You have my complete loyalty."

The words were a balm to the turmoil within me, a bridge between the man and the beast. From the smile that spread across her face, I knew they pleased her. Inside my chest, I felt something unlock. Which was odd because that space had been hollow for more than half my life.

The road stretched out before us, a ribbon of possibilities and uncertainties. I drove on, the sound of the engine a steady heartbeat in the quiet of the night. Stella sat beside me, a presence that both soothed and tormented me.

"I know I'm weak," Stella said into the quiet of the night. "But I'll try to be better. I'll be what you need."

Her words were a slash at my chest. The thing that had unlocked moments ago made a groaning sound. I scratched at my chest instead of reaching for her. I wanted to growl. Not at her, but at the circumstances that had made her doubt her own worth. I glanced at her, taking in her downcast eyes and the determined set of her jaw.

"You're not weak, Stella. You don't need to be anything other than who you are."

She didn't look at me. Her gaze was on the moon. Her teeth worried her bottom lip, begging for me to steal it from her and kiss it into believing me.

"What I need," I continued, "is for you to let me protect you."

It was the truth, but not the whole truth. I'd omitted the part that screamed inside me—that she was my future queen, that she was the one my beast yearned for. It was a truth too dangerous, too volatile to acknowledge right now.

THIRTEEN

Stella

I hadn't seen this part. The moment the car sputtered to a final, jarring stop. When it did, a sense of foreboding washed over me. We were stranded. In the middle of the night. Outside of civilization.

The Mississippi River was just a stone's throw away. I could smell the swampy funk of the waters. Somehow, the moonlight shimmered on the surface of the murky depths. In the air was the unmistakable smell of death and decay.

As I stepped out of the car, my foot immediately sank into the soft, mucky ground. Panic fluttered in my chest as the rank water seeped into my shoes. Aside from my expensive pumps, the cold, unpleasant sensation on the ball of my foot made me shiver. The riverbed was a treacherous place. Its beauty was deceptive, hiding dangers beneath its serene surface.

Oz was beside me in an instant, his expression as

unreadable as it had been on the drive here. The only time I had a hint of what he might be feeling was when I was in his arms and my cheek was pressed against his chest.

His heartbeat had accelerated. His breathing went shallow. I felt the pinpricks of claws dig past the fabric of my outfit and meet my skin.

Had it been anyone else, I would've been pissed off. But this was my fated mate. He could've ripped my clothes off and I would've been all in.

Why hadn't he ripped my clothes off yet? We'd been together for a few hours now, and I was still fully clothed and unmolested. That's when he reached for me.

But his aim was off because he reached southward. A grin spread across my face, thinking my man was going for the honey pot. Instead, he reached for my shoe.

Okay. Okay, I could get with a foot fetish if—

"Hey!"

He snatched off one shoe and then snapped the heel. Then he reached down to do the same with the other. Outrage filled me at the destruction of my beloved heels.

"How could you?"

"It's your heels or your life."

I opened my mouth—to say what? I wasn't sure? When he reached south again, his big hand went around my calf muscle. I couldn't have pulled away even if I wanted to.

I did not want to.

Oz's hold was gentle as he balanced me against his body while lifting my bare foot. Carefully, he put first one and then the other shoe back on my feet. Then his hands were on my waist as he made sure I was steady before letting me go.

Honestly, I was not sure what pissed me off most, the

fact that he ruined my shoes or that he grabbed my feet instead of—

"Now we'll move faster."

With a huff, I snatched the broken heels from the ground and jammed them into my bag. Losing my heels was a small price to pay for safety, but it still stung. I took a tentative step. To my surprise, I found that it was easier to walk on the uneven, soggy terrain without them.

We made our way through the swamp, the sound of our footsteps squelching in the mud. The air was heavy with humidity. It clung to my skin like a damp cloak. Every so often, the eerie call of a night bird pierced the silence, a haunting melody that had me pressing my shoulders up to my ears.

The moon cast a pale light over the swamp, creating a landscape of shadows and silvery reflections. The water around us was a dark, opaque mirror, its surface occasionally disturbed by the ripple of some unseen creature. The thought of what might lurk just beneath the surface made tingles of apprehension crawl over my arms.

Oz moved with a grace and ease that was almost enviable, his steps sure and confident. I followed him, trying to match his pace, but the swamp was an unfamiliar terrain, challenging and unforgiving. My blouse clung to me, heavy with moisture. My hair had long since come loose and now hung limp around my shoulders.

I wanted to take a minute and fix myself up. Oz was a panther. He could see me in the dark. But it wasn't my outfit he was concerned about right now. It was my life. Ken was still after me. I would be damned if I let him catch me.

I knew without a doubt that Oz wouldn't let that

happen. I believed him when he said he would give his life to protect mine. It's what a fated mate was supposed to do.

Oz's silhouette was a steady presence against the shifting backdrop of the swamp. There was a determination in his posture. He would snap Ken's neck if he came near me. I found my steps slowing in anticipation of that event.

"We need to find shelter for the night." Oz's voice cut through the natural symphony of creepy crawlers and a night owl.

There were boats and barges that went up and down these waters. I'd been on a riverboat cruise with Niamh and Tori once years ago. It was a Samhain party hosted by Uriah. But it looked like they'd all hung up their anchors for the night.

"Yeah, rest sounds like a dream right now." The thought of stopping, even just for a few hours, to lay my head down and close my eyes was more inviting than I could express.

Oz was busy scanning the dark landscape, assessing the safety of every shadow. "Once it's light, we can try to find a riverboat or a ship captain. Get us out of this swamp and on our way to Chicago."

"Why Chicago?"

"There's a train there. It'll get us to Portland, where the king is in residence at the House of Blood and Beryl. From there, we can get you back to Arcadia, the panther home-world. There, you'll be able to shift. Arcadia doesn't have latent panthers. You'll be in your true form."

The promise in his words sent a thrill through me. The idea of transformation, of finally becoming who I was meant to be, was both exhilarating and terrifying. But for now, the promise of rest in a safe shelter kept me moving forward, following Oz through the moonlit night.

The swamp gave way to firmer ground. The landscape

subtly changed as we moved away from the riverbed. The sounds of the water grew louder, a soothing rush that promised a path to escape, to safety. The air here was fresher, the heavy scent of the swamp replaced by the crisp, clean smell of flowing water.

Despite the exhaustion that pulled at my limbs, the idea of shifting was what kept me moving forward. Inside my belly, my cat perked up. I could almost feel the power of her form simmering just beneath the surface, a force waiting to be unleashed.

A simple structure came into view, a quaint cabin nestled by the river's edge. Its timeworn walls whispered tales of bygone eras. The structure, modest in its make, seemed to have been a silent witness to the clandestine dealings of river traders or smugglers seeking sanctuary. Its rustic charm was evident in the faded wood and the slightly crooked shutters that hung loosely at the windows. The roof, though aged, appeared sturdy, offering a semblance of shelter against the elements.

Oz moved with a quiet efficiency, his tall frame silhouetted against the backdrop of the dark, flowing river. He gathered some wood, and soon, a small fire crackled to life in the crumbling fireplace inside the cabin. It cast a warm, flickering glow over the hideout's interior. The sound of the fire, the gentle popping and crackling, was a soothing counterpoint to the constant, soft rush of the river outside.

He handed me his jacket, and as I snuggled into it, the scent of him enveloped me. It was a complex aroma of forest, a hint of leather, and something wild, untamed, and reassuringly solid. The jacket was large on me, the fabric worn but comfortable. It felt like a protective cocoon, shielding me from the chill of the night.

Lifting my gaze, I caught Oz watching me. His eyes were

intense, dark pools filled with a raw desire. The firelight danced inside the gold, lending a warmth that belied the restraint in his posture.

"Want to lie down with me?" My voice was barely above a whisper, an invitation hanging between us.

He gave a stiff shake of his head, his expression torn between longing and duty. "I'm going to keep watch over you while you sleep."

The statement hit me with the force of a revelation. It wasn't just the words but the conviction behind them—a promise of protection, of unwavering vigilance. It was the hottest thing any guy had ever said to me.

Lying down, I let the sound of the river and the warmth of the fire lull me toward sleep. The hideout was a humble shelter, but wrapped up in Oz's jacket with his sentry's gaze on me, it felt like a sanctuary. Outside, the world was a wild, harsh place, but here, with Oz standing guard, I felt a sense of security I'd never known. Sex could wait when the safety he brought was practically orgasmic.

As sleep claimed me, my last thought was of Oz. In my heart, I felt a growing certainty that he was going to be different from anyone I'd ever known. He wouldn't betray me, wouldn't lie to me. In him, I sensed the possibility of a perfect fated mate—a partner who was loyal, true, and utterly devoted.

FOURTEEN

Oz

The night was a dark canvas stretched over the world. The river's gentle murmurs were a constant backdrop to my restless thoughts. Stella had drifted into sleep cocooned in my jacket. My scent surrounded her, and the panther approved.

She fell asleep almost instantly, as though she didn't have a care in the world. Even though a portal had just opened miles away, spilling gods knew what onto this planet. There were men after her, itching to imprison her—or something worse. I didn't even ask. Didn't really care. They'd never get their hands on her so long as I lived and breathed. And even after that, I'd turn hell upside down so that my spirit could haunt them.

Stella's breathing was deep and even. She rested like someone who felt safe and secure. Like she trusted that I would do all that for her and more.

Just like my king.

Dion had no fear walking into negotiations in Blood and Beryl. Not when I did the security sweep. If I said it was safe, he did not doubt it. Though at the same time, Dion could take down half a dozen adversaries with his bare claws without breaking much of a sweat.

I remembered the first time I'd walked back into the palace after years in the wild. The way people stared got to me. Not because I minded, but because they were right. I was more beast than boy then. More comfortable in the shadows of trees than under the chandeliers of the palace. That fact was still true today.

Back then, I jerked at each sound of laughter, certain it was a predator closing in to snap my bones. That first day after catching squirrels with Dion, I followed him into the courtyard. I saw a bunch of cubs playing, tumbling around like they owned the place. A couple were messing with yarn, another group was all over a laser light, failing miserably at catching it but having a blast all the same. I just watched from the sidelines, feeling like I was on another planet. I couldn't help but think about my own brother, how we'd never get to play like that. That was on me.

Out of nowhere, something smacked me right in the face. I looked up, claws extended, teeth bared, ready for the attack. All I saw was Dion.

The prince grinned like we were in on some private joke. He'd tossed a ball my way. That's what had hit me. It rolled to a stop at my bare feet.

Looking back up, Dion was making a motion with his hand. It wasn't a challenge. It was an invitation. To play.

The realization took me a minute to understand. He wasn't looking to put me in my place. He was just... playing.

But by then, one of the females had caught his eye. Even

at a young age, Dion was a flirt. He abandoned the game before I had my turn to go and chase tail.

He came back moments later. Did the hand motion again for the ball. This time I kicked it to him. He kicked it back. It went on like that, back and forth between us. Soon, others joined in, which annoyed me. But we formed teams, and Dion put me by his side. I'd liked that. From that day on, I was always by his side.

Looking down, I saw that my claws were out. Taking a deep breath, I retracted them. Then I reached into my back pocket and pulled out the phone.

Dion had handed it to me at the same time as he'd given me the witch's portal potions. I'd scoffed, believing this mission to only take a couple of hours. There would be no need for communication. He'd smirked and winked. Of course, he'd known it wouldn't be so simple. Had he also known that my panther would lose its mind and hunger to claim his mate?

Looking down at the blank screen, I guessed the device wouldn't work with the portal magic still spewing across the land. The moment my thumb brushed across the surface, the screen illuminated, casting a pale glow in the shadowed interior of the cabin. I scratched my nail over the protective screen. There was only one number programmed in the device. All I had to do was press the call button.

Stella shifted in her sleep. Her lips parted, and she let out a soft moan. A crease formed in her brow.

I moved closer to her, crouching over her form protectively. I could scent fear on her. My ears perked, searching for signs of any foe coming near.

I heard nothing. Her fear must be from dreams.

For a few moments, I warred with whether or not to wake her. I couldn't protect her from the visions in her head. Dion probably could. He saw visions just like she did. The two of them could probably meet each other on the psychic plane.

I crab-walked backwards until my back hit the wall. The rusty end of a nail pierced my shirt and broke skin. It would serve me right to catch some form of bacteria. What the nail did do was clarify the lines between duty and desire.

Even if there was no Dion, a woman like Stella was not meant for a man like me. I had a future queen sleeping on the floor, for fuck's sake, her soft skin wrapped in my rough jacket. She was covered in dirt and grime. It was no wonder she was having a nightmare. I needed to get her to my king, and fast.

I pressed the call button. The phone rang. And then rang again.

It was night. I knew what my king liked to do at night. The thought of him wrapped around a woman or two while his mate was in danger had me growling into the receiver.

There was a click from the other end. But as I pressed the phone to my ear, all I was greeted with was a hiss of static. The portal's turmoil had woven a web of chaos through the magic currents, rendering this lifeline useless. The silence on the other end was a reminder of our isolation, of the distance that lay between me and my king, between me and clarity.

The phone's glow dimmed. I set it aside, my gaze lingering on Stella's sleeping form. I barely blinked through the night as I watched her. The sight and scent of her comforted me. So much so that I must have drifted off to sleep.

The sudden shake on my arm snapped me awake. Every

inch of me was ready for a fight—claws unsheathed, teeth bared, every muscle coiled tight.

But then my eyes focused, and there was Stella. She was so close I felt her breath on my bottom lip. A surge of panic hit me—I'd almost hurt her. I did hurt her.

My hand was around her throat. A tiny stream of blood trickled from where the tip of one claw punctured her swan's neck. My hand wasn't even tight around her, but I'd still caused the damage.

I released her instantly. My eyes struggled to meet hers. There was fear there in her gaze. Her golden eyes were wide open and scared, reflecting the dying firelight like she'd caught every spark inside them.

But it wasn't me she was scared of. I could tell. It was something else, something beyond us both.

I pulled her close. Iron was at the edge of my senses as my nose rested above the place where I'd broken her skin. I smelled something else in the air. Something wild.

A branch broke. Leaves rustled. There was a small change in the wind that let me know something was out there, and it was coming for us.

CHAPTER

FIFTEEN

Stella

In my sleep, a dream took hold, so real it could be mistaken for another life. It was Oz and me, wrapped in a future that promised joy and companionship. Our home, bathed in warmth and light, rang with the laughter of our children. Twin cubs, a gift common to panther shifters, darted around us with youthful yips. Oz's presence beside me was solid, reassuring. Our laughter intertwined, building a sanctuary of happiness. The vision of us, surrounded by our cubs, was the life I'd longed for.

Even as I dreamed, I realized this picture never had Ken in it. Not a single man I'd dated before ever fit in this vision. Oz wasn't a cardboard cutout. He was the man who molded perfectly to me. This was going to be our life.

I sighed happily, lucid in the dream. All of my dreams were lucid. Sometimes I could change things in the dream, if they were solely my dreams. But when it was a vision, a prediction of the future, I was only a silent witness. So when the dream warped and the light in my mind dimmed, I knew something beyond my control was happening, and I would only be allowed to watch, like so many of my nightmares.

In the midst of the dream, the atmosphere shifted. From the shadows of our imagined sanctuary, four beasts emerged, their forms large and menacing. Their growls were a guttural chorus of hunger and aggression. The sound filled the air, sending a wave of terror through me. Their teeth gleamed, sharp and ready, promising pain and destruction.

Oz's arms encircled me, his embrace a fortress of safety and assurance. He leaned in, his lips meeting mine in a kiss that was both a promise and an assurance. He was going to protect me. Just me, because our cubs weren't born yet. This vision was about to happen. Right now.

I should make myself wake up. But I could see that there was more about to play out. I decided to spend a few more seconds watching the outcome so that I could give all of this information to Oz when I opened my eyes.

Back in the vision, Oz released me and stepped forward. The transformation was swift; his human form melded into the shadows, and in its place stood a panther. His animal took my breath. His coat was a deep, absorbing black that swallowed the light. With a roar that echoed the fury of the storm outside, he launched himself at the intruders.

The cabin became a battleground. Oz was a whirlwind of dark fury. One by one, he confronted the beasts. Each encounter ended with a beast subdued, their threats silenced by my man's overwhelming strength.

I jolted awake, my heart thundering against my ribs as if trying to escape what was about to happen. But my head was in the game. My mind was clear. I knew what was coming, and I was ready for it. I only just stopped myself from reaching for my lip gloss for a fresh coat before I had my first kiss with my fated mate.

With a hesitant touch, I reached out, stirring Oz from his rest. He was sitting up as he slept. The only thing that let me know he was resting was his closed eyes and even breathing.

The moment my fingers brushed his, his eyes flickered open, immediately alert. His hand went around my neck. I felt the puncture of claws. This should not be a turn-on. But it was. My blood wasn't the only thing dripping.

His gaze lingered on my lips. I leaned into his touch, ready to be claimed even though I heard the scratching at the door. Oz looked from the mark on my neck into my eyes and then at the door.

Understanding flashed in his eyes, and like a switch had been flipped, he was all action. He positioned himself protectively between me and the ominous sounds outside. The air hung heavy with a sense of impending doom. The scratching grew louder, a sinister promise of the nightmare lurking just beyond our makeshift sanctuary.

Behind him, I blew out a puff of air between my neglected lips. A surge of longing washed over me, a desperate wish for him to have taken just a second to close that distance between his lips and mine with the same fervor from my vision. Sometimes I didn't get it all right. But damn if I wished I'd gotten that one detail right.

The door burst open with a violent crash. The sound of splintering wood echoed through the small space. Three feral coyotes stood on the threshold, their eyes wild and hungry, gleaming in the faint light. So I'd gotten the math wrong too.

They were not shifters but wild animals. Their gazes fixed on Oz and me with a predatory hunger that chilled me to the bone.

In a fluid motion that was completely awe-inspiring, in the sense that my lips parted and I said *awe,* Oz shifted. His clothes couldn't contain the transformation. They tore away as his human form gave way to that of a dark, majestic panther. The sight was breathtaking.

Just as I finished saying *awe,* I had to inhale deep and slowly. Oz was a creature of raw power and grace. His fur was darker than midnight.

The ensuing fight was brutal, merciless. Beautiful. In his panther form, Oz became poetry in motion. His every movement was lethal grace. His body was a weapon sharpened by instinct. His paws struck with precision, his bites fatal. The coyotes, wild and uncontrolled, stood no chance against the might of a lethal panther shifter.

The sounds of the conflict were primal—growls, snarls, the sickening crunch of bone. The air filled with the metallic scent of blood, turning my stomach as Oz dismantled the coyotes.

One coyote, gaunt and driven by desperation, dodged Oz's defense. It lunged toward me, its gaze wild with the desperate urge to survive. Defenseless, with only a lipstick and the heels of my shoes as weapons, I acted on impulse. I hurled the tube of gloss at the coyote. It might as well have laughed at my feeble attempt. Panic surged, threatening to root me to the spot.

But then Oz acted. With startling speed, he spun. His movement morphed from pure animal instinct to something disturbingly human. His paw, now eerily hand-like, shot out, snagging the coyote by the neck in a grip so precise, it seemed the man within had momentarily taken control.

The coyote's choked yelp was abruptly silenced as Oz ended it with deft finality. The sound, a harsh, guttural snap, reverberated through the hideout, a grim reminder of the thin line between life and death in the wild. Oz's eyes met mine. Within them, I saw a tumult of emotions—rage, regret, and an unspoken apology for the violence I'd had to witness.

As quickly as it emerged, the human-like quality in Oz's actions disappeared, and he was once again purely a panther, completing the grim task of neutralizing the remaining threats. Witnessing Oz, so controlled, sent shivers down my spine. It served as a reminder of his dual nature, the man and the beast, existing together in a sometimes unbalanced equilibrium.

The coyotes were defeated. All three lay still on the ground. The danger had passed. Wearied from the fight, the panther made its way to me. His steps were slower now, the aftermath of the battle showing in the slight slump of his form. He settled at my feet, resting his massive head on his paws. With each breath, his sides expanded and contracted, signaling the exertion from the confrontation.

I knelt beside him, my hand shaking as I reached out to touch his coat. It was soft yet bristled with the remnants of the fight. Our eyes locked, and in his golden gaze, I found an array of emotions that no words could ever fully capture. Relief, weariness, and an undiminished sense of protectiveness.

Even though I'd missed a few details in my vision, I knew my dream would come true. I was going to spend the rest of my life with this man. I would have his cubs. We would live in a big, sprawling house. And we would be happy.

Oz

The hideout was thick with the scent of blood and death. My panther had the reins of my body. I didn't try and snatch them back. There was too much adrenaline still coursing through my blood.

My sides heaved with exertion. The taste of the fight lingered in my mouth. One of those fat rats had nearly touched her. It was lying in four—maybe five—pieces now in the corner of the room. My incisors sharpened, wanting more of its blood for penance at daring to come near my mate.

I gave a shake of my head. Stella was not my mate. But the panther was still in control. That shake of the head only served to land its head in her lap.

Instead of crying in fear or turning away in disgust, Stella scratched the fur behind my ear. She cooed nonsensical words that soothed the savage beast at her feet, in her lap, wrapping us both around her manicured fingers.

I wrestled with a different kind of battle then—one within myself. My panther was asserting its claim over Stella, insisting that she was ours. It was a possessive urge, strong and unyielding. With every gentle touch from Stella, every tender stroke, it sent waves of comfort through my panther form and straight into a chest that was becoming less and less hollow. I felt the bond between us stretching, while the one I shared with Dion thinned like a thread pulled too tight.

I needed to shift back, to put an end to this dangerous game. Both the man and the beast in me craved to claim her, to mark her as ours in a way that would leave no room for doubt. But that was a path fraught with betrayal and heartache.

Mine, not hers.

Once she saw her choices laid out in front of her, there was no way I would stand the victor. My best friend and I were a physical match. But the scales tipped in his favor when it came to worth. King Dion, with his strength, his nobility, his seat on the throne, was far more deserving of Stella than I could ever be. It was a bitter pill to swallow. But even my panther, with its fierce possessiveness, couldn't deny the truth of it.

It lifted its head from Stella's lap, taking its last look at her in this form. She gifted me with a smile. It was a look so full of warmth, so brimming with affection, it cut through me.

I'd seen many women look my way before. Their eyes were calculating, seeing me as nothing more than a means to an end or, more often, a path to Dion. Stella's gaze was different. It was devoid of any ulterior motives, filled with a devotion that was all... for me.

My panther and I were utterly undone by her. The fierce, protective emotion that surged within me was overwhelming, a tidal wave that threatened to wash away all reason and resolve. I wasn't good with emotions, having experienced so few early in my life that I had trouble identifying feelings inside me or radiating from others. But I knew with a clarity that pierced through the foreign sensations in my chest that I would be hopelessly, irrevocably loyal to this woman until my dying breath.

I focused inward, calling on the magic that bridged the gap between man and beast. The shift was always a struggle, a battle of wills between my two halves. But this time it felt even more daunting. Every fiber of my being was at odds, torn between the duty that anchored me and the desire that threatened to sweep me away.

The shift ended. I was back in my human form. The vibrant sensations of my panther self dimmed to the more familiar, muted human senses. I found myself on my knees, the cool air of the cabin brushing against my bare skin. The brief disorientation that always followed the shift ebbed away as the full weight of my human thoughts and responsibilities returned.

Without thinking, I turned my back to Stella. It wasn't about modesty—I'd long ago lost any sense of embarrassment about my body. It was the scars that crisscrossed my chest I was hesitant to show. Each scar was an open wound, a connection to my past, a time of turmoil and survival I never spoke of. They were more than just marks; they were stories of pain and endurance etched into my skin. I wasn't sure I was ready to share them with her.

I caught sight of my clothes, now nothing more than

shredded fabric on the floor. A sigh escaped me as I acknowledged my current state, stripped of defenses both physical and metaphorical.

"You don't need to hide from me, Oz," Stella said, her voice soft but carrying an undeniable force that made me pause.

I stayed still, my back turned to her. I closed my eyes and took a deep breath. Even her voice soothed me. I wondered if I'd gotten it wrong. If she was a siren and not a panther.

The sound of rustling fabric reached my ears. I opened my eyes to see that Stella had reached for the remains of my clothes. Before I could voice any objection, her hand moved in a graceful arc. The torn pieces of my pants began to weave back together, threads moving as if guided by an unseen hand. But I saw her hand, her magic. In no time, the garment was restored, looking as good as new, without a single sign of the battle they'd been through.

Turning to face her, I let her see, scars and all. Her gaze met mine. There was no disgust there. Only a profound acceptance that pierced right through me. She handed me the repaired pants, keeping her gaze trained on mine and not dipping lower.

"It's kind of hot that you're shy. Luckily for us, I'm not. But I also believe in consent, so I'll wait a little while before I claim you."

Her boldness took me by surprise, almost drawing a laugh from me. My mouth curved up in half a smile. Her gaze dipped to my lips. Her smile stretched wide and lit up her face.

Damn, the woman was beautiful.

I slid into the mended pants, which felt almost new. Though they did fit a little snugger in the derriere department. I caught Stella looking back there now, an appreciative grin on her face.

Then she focused her attention on my ruined shirt. Her fingers whirled through the air with a grace that reminded me of a music conductor. The threads of the fabric, torn and scattered, began to move as if alive. The sleeves, once hanging by mere threads, reattached themselves with precision. The seams pulled tight, each stitch perfect, as if the shirt had never been torn. The dirt that had clung to the fabric lifted away as if carried by a gentle breeze. Stains of blood, reminders of the fight, dissolved without a trace, leaving the material pristine and unblemished. It was as if time itself was being reversed, the damage undone by Stella's will alone.

As she handed the garment back to me, our fingers brushed. The contact was brief, but it was enough to send a jolt through me. I wondered if her weaving magic would pull me to her, tie me up in knots that only she could unravel.

"Fashion I can magic," she quipped, her focus now on her clothing. She lifted the dirt and mended the tears. "That's about all I'm good for, really. Tailoring clothes, doing makeovers, and having visions. My ex-boyfriend Ken... he used me. He pretended to love me, to care for me, to have sex with me. All so I'd keep giving his gang visions."

The fury that rose in me was instant and visceral. Rage, red-hot and furious, coursed through my veins. My head was a kettle, the steam screaming to be let loose.

"I'm going to kill him," I promised, my voice as casual as if I'd announced the date and time.

She might not be my mate, but she was mine to protect. As soon as I delivered her to Dion, I would come back and hunt that vampire down.

"No one uses you and lives, Stella. No one."

Her shock dissolved into a pleased grin. My golden princess was a little bloodthirsty. "That's really sweet. Thank you, Oz."

Then her grin turned sultry. She took a step toward me, those full hips swaying as she did so. Both man and beast went on high alert as we realized we were being stalked.

"You know, the full moon is just two nights away."

I did know that. Even though the moon cycles on this planet were different than on Arcadia, the shifter part of me could still sense its incoming pull.

"I'll go into heat with the full moon. It's what happens when shifters find their fated mates. Maybe we should... take care of the mating now."

She took another step, those hips now brushing up against mine. The word *no* was on the tip of my tongue. But the tip of my dick had other plans.

In my mind, I heard the ominous ticking of a clock. I was on more than one deadline now. The edict from my king to return her to him. The danger of the men chasing us to steal her away. And the moon's call that would rob me of all rational thought, save the one to claim her body and soul. I have no idea where I found the strength to speak the words that I said next.

"Stella, you're a princess. You deserve more than this." I motioned around the dirty shack I'd procured for her, resplendent with dead carcasses. "You deserve to be claimed and marked with honor and ceremony in the palace, not here, not like this."

Her eyes met mine, searching, seeking the truth behind my words. I gave her the truth like I'd promised. But also like I promised, I didn't tell her everything. Like the fact that it would be a king giving her that claiming mark.

"Well, then"—quick as a cat, she nipped at the corner of my mouth—"you better make it worth the wait, mate."

I wanted to tell her that I'd wait an eternity for her if I could. Instead, I dug my claws into my palms to keep from reaching for her. I got the feeling I'd have blood on my hands for the rest of my days.

SEVENTEEN

Stella

I found it difficult to keep up with his long strides as we walked along the riverbank. The mud had a vendetta against my shoes, sucking them in with each step I took. The once fashionable footwear was now a victim of the relentless muck. I could use my magic to fix them, but it would be a perpetual battle, and I doubted I'd win the war.

I kept my complaints to myself, not wanting to burden Oz with more than we were already facing. A portal opening in the Crossroads, Ken coming after me, and finding my fated mate. I'd had all three of those visions. Though the one with Ken had been grossly misinterpreted. Still, this was the best batting average I'd ever experienced in my career as a foreseer. What I couldn't see clearly was Oz falling for me.

He should be all over me. Instead, he kept me at arm's

length. He should be kissing me senseless. Instead, he clamped his mouth shut, saying as little as possible.

Since I was all in my head and not watching where I was going, I stumbled over an exposed root. Oz caught me just as my knee buckled. When he began to let me go, I clamped down on his arm, feigning that whole damsel routine.

Technically, I'm far more damsel than badass warrior like Tori. Niamh would tell me to use what I got, and so I did. But as I held tight to my fated mate's arm, I hoped my girls were doing okay in the chaos back in the Crossroads. They were far more capable than me, so I was sure they were fine.

Oz set me to rights. Instead of offering his arm or copping a feel, he turned and trudged on.

The steady silence between me and Oz was about to drive me crazy, so I decided to fill it with the dream I'd had, which felt more like a vision of our future. "We were in this incredible palace, surrounded by twin cubs. They were so full of life, laughing and running around..."

I trailed off, looking up at Oz, hoping to see a spark of interest or perhaps a smile. His face was set in a grim line, his eyes clouded with what looked like anger or perhaps deep frustration. It was hard to tell with him still being so much of a mystery to me.

"My visions aren't always one hundred percent accurate. In fact, I've never seen myself in a vision until yesterday. When the portal opened."

"Portal energy is known to enhance magical powers."

"Are children something you want?"

"What I want is to get you to safety, to get you to the palace. Then we can talk of futures."

There was another moment of silence between us. The

only sounds were the gentle lapping of the river against the bank and the distant calls of night birds. The humid air was thick with the scent of wet earth and growing things. But now it was tainted with the bitterness of unspoken words and unfulfilled desires. Either he didn't want kids, or he didn't want me. Possibly both.

What was so wrong with me that every man in my life used me? That when I said 'I love you,' what they really said in return was, *I love what you're going to do for me*. That when I found my fated me, he had buyer's remorse.

I was a good person. I had a good heart. Sure, it constantly picked wrong, but after every time it got stomped on or discarded or broken, it picked itself back up and tried again. That had to count for something. Didn't it?

"I know I can be a bit much sometimes." I looked down at my mud-stained shoes. "I can tone it down if that's what you need. Be less... high maintenance."

Oz's reaction was immediate. He rounded on me, his hand shooting out to lift my chin so that our eyes met. "Promise me something, Stella."

"Anything," I agreed without knowing what this man would say. But if he would just try to love me, I'd give him anything. Which, yes, I knew, was the root of my problem. But all I'd ever wanted in this world was to be loved.

"Promise me you will never dim your light for anyone." His voice was low and fervent. "Not for me, not for the king, not for anyone. Your spirit, your strength, it's part of what makes you who you are."

He didn't know me, but I wanted to be the girl he thought I was. His words resonated deep within me, a warm glow that countered the chill of my desperation. I was drawn to him, the space between us charged with an unspoken connection. Our faces were inches apart, the pull between us undeniable.

"I know that." Truly I did know my value in my head. That wasn't the problem. "But sometimes I have trouble believing, which makes it hard to act on the knowledge."

His eyes softened as they regarded me. His thumb caressed my cheek back and forth, soothing the hurt that was so deep within. Somehow, this man managed to touch it. I wondered if he had the same trouble with inner light as I did.

I cupped my hand over his, trying to warm the light inside me so that I could share it with him. "I don't need a palace if I'm with the man I love. I could live the rest of my life in that shack back there if I'm there with the person who loves me back."

Oz's gaze softened as he looked down at me. The eye contact was steady, not invasive. Not probing to see how to manipulate me. Yes, I knew each time Ken or my past lovers were manipulating me. I just pretended not to because I wanted to—needed to—believe that this time it might be real.

This time, with Oz, it might be real. I could believe he loved me.

One by one, his fingers lifted to lace with mine. I think he'd meant to take his hand away, but I had his hand cornered. He could've slipped my grip. Instead, he spread his fingers to make way for each of mine to join him at the knuckles.

His proximity was intoxicating, sending my senses into overdrive. The sound of the river faded into the background. All my focus was on the man in front of me.

He leaned in, his breath mingling with mine. The moment stretched out into an eternity. I thought I would've been impatient for our first kiss. But this felt like the moment right before an orgasm, that slow climb up a mountain before jumping off into oblivion. I could've stayed here forever.

I was literally on the precipice. Our lips were just a second away from meeting. But just as our lips were about to touch, someone cleared their throat and shattered the moment.

An old witch appeared on the riverbank. It was crystal clear she was a witch. The magic oozed from her pores. Including the illusion spell. She was not as old as she looked. Just as I wasn't as clean as my dirt-less clothes made me appear.

Oz pulled me behind him, but his claws didn't come out. He couldn't scent the illusion on her. But her hands were in clear view, palms up on her dark cloak. She broadcasted that she meant no harm. But something about her still sent a shiver down my spine.

"You seek passage." It wasn't a question. She knew. She likely had foresight, too. "I can get you on the next riverboat going north."

"What's the cost?" Oz asked, posture still defensive as he stood in front of me.

"Blood," croaked the witch.

Oz held out his forearm. "Take mine. It's panther blood."

The witch's eyes flicked to Oz's arm, then back to me. "No, hers is more valuable, a powerful witch and panther royalty."

CHAPTER 18

Oz

The vessel was sturdy. Its wooden structure bore the marks of countless journeys down the Mississippi. The deck stretched out invitingly, leading to a modest cabin at the back. The steamboat, with its broad, flat bottom, was designed to handle the river's moods, its shallow draft perfect for the varying depths we'd encounter.

We waited for an age as the crew refueled with a new spell. The opening of the portal stretched its unpredictability even this far as magic behaved contrary to how it was meant to. That gave time for others to board.

I assessed the potential for danger with each body that came onboard the boat. The majority were women, their faces etched with lines of worry and fear. They held their children close, whispering words of comfort and reassurance or hushing their youths into quiet so as to not have others take notice of any weakness. Among them were the elderly, their steps slow and measured, supported by younger relatives or walking sticks. By all appearances, I was the strongest and most dangerous on board.

What struck me as odd was the scarcity of young men. In any other setting, they would have been the majority, the protectors and providers. But here, their absence was a gaping hole. One I should consider. But the lack of threat as the boat pushed off the bank promised me a moment of respite.

Stella had stayed close, her arm entwined with mine, sending jolt after jolt of awareness through me, straight to the hungry panther inside. I knew I should discourage her dependence, maintaining a distance to remind me of her impending role in Panthera. But every instinct in me rebelled at the thought. Her proximity felt right, necessary even. I justified it to myself as a protective measure. She was, after all, safest by my side.

Our greatest threat was a boy who didn't come up to my chest and was actively trying to hide his tears. There hadn't been a single sign of Ken or the other vampires, mostly thanks to the sun high up in the sky. It would set in a few hours by the time we reached the shores of the Quad cities, which was just under two hundred miles from Chicago where we could take a train direct to Portland. The journey up the river would take the rest of the day. I needed that time to rest and recharge.

I reached for Stella's hand, which was resting on my biceps. My intention had been to loosen her hold on me. But when my fingers touched hers, her golden gaze swung to me. I was wrong about there being no dangers on this vessel. With just one glance, this woman had me ready to fall to my knees to do her bidding.

"Stella, I need a moment."

"Me, too. I've been needing a bathroom break since we came on board. I think they're over there."

She gave my arm a tug. I nearly followed. Planting my feet on the creaking boards of the boat, I halted her forward momentum like my body was a dropped anchor.

"I'm going to need some space."

"Space?" Stella's brow furrowed, confusion and hurt flashing across her face. "Did I do something wrong, Oz?"

She reached up to her hair, pushing at the perfectly styled strands. Then her fingers glanced down her outfit, which was as pink and bright as when I'd first seen her crossing the street. I caught the subtle hints of the fabric tightening here, loosening there. Contouring to her figure to highlight some assets, like pressing her breasts upward.

I ground my molars, wishing it was Ken's jugular between my teeth. "No, it's not you," I said, the words feeling like ash in my mouth. "I need to rest."

"Right. Yes. Rest. I'll come with you."

"No. Go freshen up." As soon as the words were out of my mouth, I knew they were the wrong thing to say. "I mean, take in the sights. Relax for a bit. You're safe. No one on this boat will harm you. I need a minute to regain my strength. Do you understand?"

"Mmmh-hmm," she hummed.

I knew she didn't. She wouldn't meet my gaze. The sparkles from her fingertips that had been tailoring the bust of her top dulled and then fizzled.

I felt like an ass. But it was for the best. She wasn't mine.

As Stella walked away, her shoulders hunched. Her head hung low. I felt a chill settle over me, a premonition of the loneliness that awaited me once she was truly gone from my side. I had pushed her away to save her from heartbreak. But also to set her up for the life she deserved, as queen.

I found a place on the opposite side of the boat. It gave me a vantage point that I would be able to see her no matter where she was. Even though I planned to rest, I doubted I'd close my eyes for long.

The air of the river should've been fresh. Instead, it was a mix of dead fish, stagnant mud, and whatever else was in the process of dying in the waters. The sound was a contrast, though. Even though it stank, the water lapped gently against the boat's hull. Death could be a quiet business.

As the boat sliced through the calm waters of the Mississippi, I took a moment to observe the surroundings. The riverbanks were adorned with trees, their leaves shimmering with the morning dew under the gentle dawn light. The world was waking up, shedding the remnants of night to reveal the day's splendor. Yet, the scenic beauty did little to calm the storm raging within me.

The further we journeyed, the more acute the reality of our predicament became. Stella was right there, within arm's reach, but it felt as though a vast chasm lay between us. I found myself caught in a relentless tug-of-war between my allegiance to my king and the magnetic pull Stella had on me. Every fleeting touch, every shared look, was a torturous pleasure.

I snuck a peek at her now. It was a mistake, of course. Both man and beast were captivated by the way the early sunlight bathed her in a soft, otherworldly light. She appeared contemplative, her gaze fixed on the river, seemingly adrift in her thoughts. I wondered what she saw in those reflective waters, what future visions were dancing before her eyes.

The engine of the riverboat rumbled beneath me, its steady hum blending with the soft splash of the waters as we sliced through the river. I couldn't get comfortable. Stillness was not my thing.

I made my way to the deck, my eyes assessed every passenger aboard. My gaze swept over the women's attire, searching for any bulges that I might have missed. Even in this second scan, I didn't find any hint of concealed weapons. My eyes scrutinized their hands for signs that spoke of familiarity with combat. My every sense was on alert, parsing each sound, each movement for hints of danger.

Among them, a woman stood out, her scent unmistakably human. Humans had become a rarity, even in their native realm, and her presence in this group was notable. There was no trace of magic about her, just the simple, unadorned essence of humanity. She kept to the shadows, never giving anyone her back.

Scattered through the crowd were a few shifters, their postures relaxed. None bore the distinctive smell of predatory beasts like myself. They were of the milder kind, perhaps birds or small mammals, their magic subtle and unobtrusive.

My gaze lingered on another woman, her demeanor hinting at something delicate. It was the delicate features that had me suspicious. I suspected she might be a fairy. Fae kind had bonds with nature. However, the air around her was free of any toxic whispers, the kind that sometimes clung to the fair folk like an unseen shroud of menace for those with power over poisons.

Once again, I concluded that there was no immediate

danger to Stella. My shoulders relaxed slightly. The constant vigilance ebbed but never fully dissipated. I regained the seat on the opposite side of the boat, positioning myself where I could keep a watchful eye on her.

I sat there, my muscles coiled tight, ready to leap at the first sign of trouble. As the journey continued, the sun rose higher, bathing us in its warm light. I kept my gaze on Stella, her very presence a balm and a curse all at once. I thought I was born to protect the king. I saw now that my true calling was to protect my queen. I contented myself with that thought for now.

I might never feel the brush of her lips against mine or feel her body move beneath me. But I'd never needed that. I'd only ever wanted to have a purpose in this life. She was that. I would lay down my life for her without a second thought. It was that thought that soothed me.

CHAPTER 19

Stella

From my spot on the riverboat, I watched Oz as he surveyed the other passengers. His gaze lingered on each person with a careful, calculated assessment. The thing about all of the other passengers was that they were all women.

It was happening again. My man was looking at other women to step out on me with.

I'd gone to the bathroom to check my appearance. Despite everything we'd just been through—the running, the coyotes, the mud—I looked damned good. Hell, even if I had been getting ready to go to the club with my girls and I'd walked in looking like how I looked in the bathroom mirror, it was clear; I was looking fierce.

Why couldn't he see that? What did I have to do to keep a man's gaze fixed on me? What good was my magic—my foresight, my tailoring, my touch-up abilities—if I couldn't keep a man's attention?

The Mississippi River flowed steadily beneath us. Its waters glinted in the late afternoon sunlight. The breeze carried the stench of water mixed with the faint odor of whatever magic was used in the motor. It smelled surprisingly like diesel, but there wasn't much of that ancient energy source left in this world. There certainly was little need for it when magic was an infinite source of power.

Even with the unpleasant smells, the setting was serene. The Mississippi River, vast and mighty, stretched out before us. The banks were lush with life. Trees lined the edges, their leaves whispering secrets to the breeze. Grass, foliage, and bushes crept toward the bank. It was as if nature itself was trying to get away from the land where all the people were.

Despite the serenity of the setting, a part of me remained on edge, watching Oz as his gaze ran up and down, over and around each and every woman on the boat. I tried to tell myself that he was just being vigilant, protecting us from potential threats. The small, insecure voice in my head had whispered nonsense in each of my past relationships. It was high time I tuned her out and listened to my own voice.

Problem was my voice sounded just as insecure.

I wished I could transform my body as effortlessly as I could mend a tear in fabric or style my hair with a simple magical gesture. What if I could just wave my hand and morph into a slimmer version of myself, more like all of these women Oz appeared so interested in? Would that make me more appealing? Would it prevent him from looking elsewhere?

Truth was, I'd walked this path before, molding myself

to fit someone else's ideal, only to end up in pain, feeling a loss of my true self. This was my body, the one that had endured every trial, every moment of joy and sorrow. There was a hidden strength in these curves, a resilience that went beyond the physical. It was woven into my identity.

I knew the fault never lay with me or my body. It was always the men who chose to wander. It was never a flaw in my being.

I knew that. Every woman who had been cheated on knew that. Didn't change that gnawing feeling, that nagging voice in our heads.

As Oz's eyes moved from one woman to the next, that insecurity gripped me tighter. Tighter than the belt cinched around my waist to show off my bust line. Big girls like me looked best when we highlighted the skinniest portion of our waist, which was usually right under the boobs. Bringing attention to that spot formed the shape of an A from the top of the head on down to the feet. An added benefit of drawing the eye to the A-line was focusing on the boobs, which were my best asset.

Oz had barely glanced at my boobs earlier when he told me to go fix myself up. Men always looked at my boobs. Always.

The woman he was looking at now barely had an A-cup.

Maybe Oz was an ass man? But my ass was fabulous. That other woman's was flat as a fairy's.

Not that all fairies had flat asses. Niamh had a killer backside. But she wasn't pure fairy, so she had more curves than those leafy leeches.

"Hi there."

I blinked to see that the fairy was standing in front of me, a tentative smile on her face. Glancing over, I saw that Oz had closed his eyes as he leaned back against his perch.

Either the fairy was no threat, or she was coming to ask me about him. Everyone had seen me come on board with him. Then they'd seen me on his arm.

Did this fairy think we weren't together? Or maybe she didn't think I could hold on to him? Well, she was in for a rude awakening.

"I just wanted to tell you that I love your outfit."

My gaze narrowed at her. Was it going to be kindness killing? Well, two could play at that game. "Oh, thank you. I love your..."

And there she won this game. The woman was pretty much in rags. Her clothing was tattered and dirty. But she smelled like a bed of flowers. Of course she did, frigging fairy.

"I'm sure I look a mess. As soon as I saw that portal open, I ran for it. I've been through one before -a portal opening, I mean. I didn't want to wait and see what came out. So I ran, and here I am, trying to put as much distance between me and it as possible."

The fairy shivered under the late afternoon sun. It was an involuntary body reaction. She was telling the truth. I knew when someone was lying to me. I just preferred to pretend I didn't know.

"It's magic."

"What magic?" She cocked her head in that way that fairies did. Suddenly I was missing Niamh. If she was with Tori, she would be fine. Even if she wasn't with Tori, she was smart enough to stay safe.

"Here, I can fix your top for you," I said, feeling a bit of transferred loyalty since my friend might be this fairy's kin.

"Really?"

Extending a hand toward her, I let my magic flow. A soft, warm glow emanated from my fingertips. The threads wove together, mending the tears and holes with delicate precision. I decided not to make the mending too perfect. I didn't need any unnecessary competition, especially not from a fairy who already possessed that rose-blush beauty.

The fabric mended, looking much better than before but still carrying a hint of its previous war. "There," I said, pulling back and admiring my handiwork. "Not perfect, but it should hold up for a while."

"You're with the brooding shifter, aren't you? He can't seem to take his eyes off you."

I looked up at Oz again. But he wasn't looking at me. His eyes were opened but focused on another woman. "Yeah, we're... together."

"That's an understatement. He's been clocking everyone on board. I almost didn't come over to you."

"He... what?"

"I can't wait to meet my fated mate. I just hope mine is as protective of me as yours is of you."

The fairy gave me a playful punch on the arm. When she did, her bare fingers brushed against my skin. It must have been the contact that triggered the vision.

A chill coursed through me. It was the same chilling shiver that shimmied over her shoulders when she'd spoken of the portal opening. Like her response, this vision wasn't a lie. It was about to happen.

From the murky depths of the river, a dark horse emerged. It was the darkest black, like looking into a void. Its form was massive and menacing. It rose, water cascading from its shadowy form. Its eyes blazed with a malevolent light.

Its neigh shattered the silence, a sound so piercing it clawed at the very fabric of the air. The calm of the boat flipped like a switch. Everything, everyone descended into chaos. The scent of fear and the shrill echoes of screams came from everywhere and nowhere. I wanted to cover my ears, but the sounds were coming from inside my head.

In the vision, I searched for Oz. He wasn't far. He stood with his back to me. He was an immovable statue, frozen and unresponsive to the pandemonium around us. That didn't seem right. He should be the first into action. But he wasn't even trying to protect me. The sense of abandonment, of utter isolation, gnawed at my heart, a cold dread settling in my stomach.

Turning, desperate for any sign of safety, my inner gaze fell upon the fairy. The vibrant life that had animated her moments before was extinguished. Her body lay eerily still on the wooden deck, a crimson stain spreading beneath her. A silent scream caught in my throat.

Back on the other side of reality, the scream found its voice—my voice. The last thing I saw before everything came true was Oz moving toward me, coming to my rescue. The problem was, he was already too late.

CHAPTER 20

Oz

My mouth was dry even though we were surrounded by nothing but water. It wasn't drinkable water, but it was wet. It didn't soothe the rawness in my throat or the tightness in my chest. Something was off.

It was why I couldn't relax. I had been covertly keeping an eye on Stella as we made our way down the lazy river. My gaze had flickered across the deck, taking in the other passengers. There was no beware vibe coming off of any of them.

Then it happened. My worst nightmare come true. The reason I hadn't fully closed my eyes. Stella's body stiffened.

My claws extended immediately. I bared my teeth. A non-predatory boy that had been playing near me scurried away. Ignoring the kid, I held my ground. Stella wasn't in danger. Not from anything external, anyway.

I knew the signs. The tension in her body. The glaze over her eyes. The part of her lips. She could've been Dion at that moment. The two had so much in common.

I always blocked Dion from others' view when he was having a vision. My instinct was to run to Stella. To gather her in my arms. To have her confide in me. But that would only get me three steps back to where we had been. Back to her falsely believing I was her fated mate. This woman would have a crown on her head. She would have jewels to drown in. She would have the very best, and that wasn't me.

Stella wasn't in danger on the other side of the boat. There was no immediate threat at present. So I held my position. That was until the vision loosened its hold on her.

The color drained from her face. Her eyes widened in unmistakable terror. She exhaled a shaky breath, and I tasted the bitter tang of fear.

The panther took over. It cut through the distance with swift, predatory efficiency. The deck beneath my feet might as well have been the underbrush of a dense jungle for how quickly I moved, every muscle coiled and ready to strike at whatever threat had managed to instill that kind of fear in her.

My hand shot out, gripping the fairy's slender wrist with a force that was probably more than necessary. The fairy's cry of pain barely registered in my consciousness. My focus narrowed to Stella, to the pallor of her face and the tremble in her limbs.

"Stella, I'm here. I've got you."

I did have her. My hand went to her cheek, cupping her chin and brushing a thumb over her trembling lip. My other arm wrapped tightly around her, pulling her body against mine. I heard a click like the cock of a gun or sluicing sound a blade made coming out of its sheath. But it was neither of those weapons. It was the sound of Stella's body fitting perfectly against mine.

"Stella, look at me."

My voice was a low rumble, barely concealing the turmoil of emotions that raged within me. Her eyes, wide and haunted, slowly focused on mine. I saw the terror that gripped her soul.

"Oz?"

"Yes, it's me. You're safe. You're safe with me."

Breathing in deeply, I inhaled her scent, a soothing balm to the adrenaline coursing through my veins. Stella placed her hands over my heart. It beat fiercely beneath her touch. Man and panther belonged to her, heart and soul. She owned every part of me, and I was willingly hers to command. She need only unleash me to dispatch whoever, whatever had upset her.

A gasp escaped her lips. Her gaze shifted from me to something over my shoulder. Instinctively, my body tensed, ready to confront whatever threat had caused that reaction in her. Turning swiftly, my eyes landed on the crumpled form of the fairy, lying in a heap on the deck. Her gaze was fixed on me, wide eyes filled with a fear that mirrored Stella's.

"Did she hurt you?" It came out as a growl.

"No, she..." Stella pressed her lips together, not letting the rest of the words out.

The fairy crab walked away from us. I corralled Stella into a corner of the boat. Everyone gave us a wide berth. Only the occasional spray of the water dared break into our privacy.

"What did you see?"

"She's going to die."

"Who? The fairy?" Relief flooded through me. I didn't care about the fairy. Call me callous, but that skinny frond wasn't my responsibility. She wasn't my world.

"And you..."

"Me?"

Had Stella seen my death? It wouldn't bother me as long as she was safe when I died.

"You turned your back on me."

"Never."

"I saw it," she insisted.

"Not possible."

"No? Is that why you've been avoiding me? Keeping your distance from me?"

I choked on my words and swallowed hard. I had the woman of the dreams I'd never dared to dream of in my arms—and I choked. I didn't tell her that I'd never taken my eyes off her the whole time we've been on this putrid river. I didn't tell her that I saw the changes she made to her eyeliner and how it brightened her eyes. I didn't tell her that her lip gloss had worn off and it made me want to kiss the rest away.

Avoiding? Distance? It was the furthest thing from the truth.

"I know how men are. They cheat. It's just a fact of life." Stella's voice wavered, but her eyes were resolute. "I'm not like that. I'm loyal. I'm a one-man woman."

Even though her eyes were resolute, I saw the slight wince before she continued. I heard the hitch in her breath as she pushed the words out. I felt the curl of her fingertips as they tried not to clutch at the fabric covering my chest.

"I can share you with others as long as I have your heart. Deal?"

The words struck me like a physical blow. The idea of

her settling for anything less than she deserved, of her sharing me with others because of some misplaced belief about men and loyalty, it was unbearable. And then I thought of Dion.

Dion and his voracious appetite. Dion and the women piled in his bed each night. Dion who sent me to fetch his fated mate while he went off to bed another.

"Deal?" Stella pressed.

"No!"

She closed her eyes. I felt the tears pricking at the corners like they were my own. I felt my throat constrict as she swallowed down the lump that had formed in hers. I placed my hands over hers, pressing them into my chest as my heart stopped beating for one, two beats.

"No," I said softly. "No," I said, pulling her closer. "You should never have to share your heart with anyone."

"I won't."

She looked up at me. That golden gaze was dull at the edges as she made her request. My heart raced as I pressed her hands firmly against my chest. I knew the moment I lost her touch, I'd be lost.

"I won't say this again," I said. "You do not dim that light inside of you for anyone. Do you hear me?"

She nodded, but her head wobbled.

"You are worth more than anyone on this godsforsaken world. You're worth more than all the gold in the palace. It pales next to you. Nothing is worth a single one of your tears."

The intensity of the moment hung between us, a tangible force that pushed the sounds and smells of the river to the background. I saw the conflict in Stella's eyes, the fear of being hurt again warring with her desire to believe in what could be. I swore I would gut Ken if ever I caught him in my sights again. Dion was now on my hit list if he didn't treat this goddess right.

"You have my heart, Stella. Sole possession of it for as long as it beats. And my loyalty. I would die for you."

"I don't want you to die. I want you to live. I want us to be together. Just the two of us." Stella glanced at my lips, her desires clear as the setting sun's rays on the murky waters.

I stood there, wrestling with a desire so strong it threatened to consume me whole. Kissing Stella was not only in direct contrast to my protection duties, it was a betrayal to my king, my best friend. I had said I was willing to die for her. As our faces drew dangerously close, I knew this would be the end of me.

The air crackled with a tension that was thick with unvoiced yearnings. There was an electric current that pulsed between us, urging us closer. We were inches apart, the space dwindling to nothing, our breaths mingling in the nearly nonexistent distance that remained. Anticipation wound tight within me, a coiled spring ready to snap, propelling us into the inevitability of our lips meeting.

I felt the warmth of her breath against my skin. Her fingers snaked around my neck, beckoning me closer. Her very presence was a siren call, enveloping me, drawing me in with an invisible thread that tugged at the core of my being. But if she was a siren, I was the snake offering the apple.

Every rational thought, every duty and obligation, faded into the background. The only truth that mattered, the only force that held any sway over me, was the pull I felt toward Stella. It was a pull I was powerless to resist, even if it meant facing the wrath of my king and the ruin of my own honor. I knew with a bone-deep certainty that no matter the consequences, this was my choice. Stella was my choice.

Her lips met mine, and I felt... nothing.

No, not nothing. A jolt ran through me. The electric shock seized my body. I couldn't move. Not a muscle, not an eyelash. Man and wolf alike had seized up. All because I'd chosen my will over my king's.

But as dark figures swarmed onto the boat, I realized this wasn't my conscious playing guilt tricks on me. This was an invasion.

CHAPTER 21

If the boat is a-rocking, don't come a-knocking. No, that's too corny.

Raise the sails cause we have liftoff. Hmm, too obscure.

When his lips met mine, the world fell away. Ugh, too purple prose Harlequin.

Yes, this was every thought that went through my brain in the split second before Oz's lips met mine for the first time. I was crafting a text message in my head to send to my girls. But I had no idea how to begin it. And then my brain short-circuited when my fated mate finally did kiss me. Because it was nothing like I'd ever experienced before.

Yeah, that would make a good email subject line: Nothing like I'd ever experienced before. It would definitely get Niamh and Tori clicking to read the rest of the story. But first I had to finish experiencing the kiss for myself.

It was gentle at first, a tentative exploration that quickly ignited into something more intense—and the color purple exploded all around me in flowery prose.

The moment our lips met, it was as if a dormant volcano within me erupted into life, its lava coursing through my veins, igniting every nerve in my body. His bottom lip was a soft, gentle brush that painted me in vivid colors, while his upper lip was a raging storm that had been gathering force ever since I'd laid eyes on him.

In truth, it was the kind of kiss a girl dreamed about. It was the kind of kiss grown women read about in paperback books from a bygone era. It was the kiss I knew I deserved after swapping spit with frogs for all of my teenage and adult life.

Oz's kiss consumed me as it left me starved for him. My heart raced as it skipped a beat. His hands, strong and tender, found their way to my back, pulling me closer, erasing any space that remained between us. And then he stopped and let me have control.

My tongue darted out. I tasted the dark spice of him. It spoke of wild, untamed places and whispered promises of protection and devotion. My hands traced the lines of his shoulders, feeling the power that lay beneath his skin. My body pressed against his, feeling the heat of him blanket me with a comforting warmth that enveloped me, making me feel cherished and safe.

It was the best kiss of my life. And it was only our first. There would be tens of thousands from this moment on.

I wanted to tell him that I took back everything I'd just said. I was not going to share him. He was my man. Mine.

Inside my belly, where my heart was climbing back up into my chest, I felt the panther inside me stir. She uncovered her eyes and blinked out at the man who was the other half to her soul.

Was that all she'd needed to wake up? To find our mate?

I leaned back to tell Oz my exciting news. When I did, I felt something wasn't quite right. Oz was stiff in my arms.

He stared down at me, unblinking. There was struggle in his golden gaze.

Had I done something wrong? Was it my breath? My kissing technique? Had I done something he didn't like when he'd let me take the reins? Maybe he didn't like my take-charge attitude?

Maybe he wanted a submissive woman? I'd tried that once in a relationship. It hadn't worked out for me. The guy could never make a decision. I'd had to top from the bottom the whole time, and it was exhausting.

It wasn't just Oz who was stiff. The fairy who had crawled away from us was frozen in place. The shifter kid who'd been bouncing a ball had his arms extended in a throw, but the ball had rolled away from him. Every adult on the boat had stopped moving, like they were playing the game Red Light Green Light. But no one had asked me to play.

The world around me tilted on its axis as a sudden eerie stillness fell over the riverboat. No, actually, that was the boat tilting to the side as a dozen men boarded. Not just men—predators.

Pirates had boarded the boat. Shifters with their canines out. Dark elves with malice in their eyes. And vampires. Though none of these vamps were from the Crimson Roses. They were dressed in dark pants that smelled of the river. Uziah would have never let them anywhere near him and his tailored suits.

I felt a moment of relief that they were not after me. Then I realized they didn't have a clue who I'd once belonged to. And then there was the fact that everyone around me was frozen, their bodies rigid and unresponsive. I stood alone in a sea of motionless figures, a surreal and terrifying tableau.

"Your blood is more potent than I thought, little godling."

I knew that voice. I'd heard it earlier this morning. I looked over to find the witch moving slowly toward me from behind, the men fanning out across the deck.

"Your blood is priceless. It will get me off this swamp. So you'll understand why I'm going to bleed you dry."

I pressed my body to Oz's, seeking protection. But he had none to give in his frozen state.

His golden gaze was dull now. But there were sparks at the center. Those sparks urged me to do something. But what? I could barely make it walking through swamp land earlier. What was I supposed to do against a dozen supernatural pirates and a blood-hungry witch? Launder and tailor their clothes with a flick of my wrist?

Actually...

Drawing a deep breath, I extended my hands, palms outward, and concentrated. With another flick of my wrist, the dirt lifted from their garments, coalescing into a tornado of refuse. The dust cloud grew denser and darker, swirling with all the filth I had pulled from their clothes. With a final push of will, I released the cloud, directing it toward their faces in a blinding, choking mass.

The effect was immediate. The pirates stumbled, coughing and swatting at the air as the dirt cloud enveloped them. Their rugged faces twisted in irritation, providing me with a momentary advantage. But it was just that—momentary. As the cloud settled and their vision cleared, they laughed it off and advanced forward.

They were undeterred, their eyes alight with the thrill of the hunt and the promise of plunder. But I wasn't out of tricks yet. I had just found my fated mate. The hell if I was going to go down before I'd at least tapped that booty.

My gaze darted around, desperate for another solution, and that's when it hit me. With a flick of my wrist and a focused intention, I called upon my magic once more. This time, I targeted their clothes—those ill-fitting garments that had momentarily been cleansed. I envisioned the fabric tightening, constricting, becoming a second skin that would hinder their movement and buy us more time. And it worked.

Their clothes began to shrink, seams pulling tight against muscles and joints. Especially in the crotch areas. It was a little exhausting because there was a lot of fabric to pull together. But once I hit the spot, it was like watching a scene from a comedic play.

They stumbled, tripping over their own feet as they tried to adjust to their suddenly restrictive attire. But once again, my victory was fleeting. People might call fashion cutthroat. Too bad there wasn't much I could do to actually cut someone's throat.

"Cute," said the witch. "But that's enough play time. No, leave her to me."

A couple of the men had nearly reached me. But under the direction of the witch, they about-faced with a snarl. The first one went to the fairy. I only just managed to look away when he sank his fangs into her neck without any of the finesse that said he wanted to preserve his meal's life.

That bite was one that a living being didn't come back from. Just like I'd seen in my vision.

The other two men went behind me, headed straight for Oz.

CHAPTER 22

Oz

Frozen in place, I was a prisoner within my own body, silently witnessing the chaos unfolding on the riverboat. The scene before me was my nightmare come to life. Stella was in danger, and I was impotent to do anything about it. The pirates had moved away from her at the witch's direction, but the witch was now cornering Stella outside of my peripheral view.

A brutal assault played out across the boat's deck. A bloodthirsty vampire snacked on the neck of the fairy Stella had been talking to. A dark elf prowled up to a non-predatory shifter and used their claws to rip open the blouse of the woman. The small child who'd been playing with a ball bore witness to the whole scene. There was the barest flinch in the kid's left eye. I'd made a mistake about the notion he might be non-predatory. If the kid was strong enough to move even one muscle under this spell, he likely harbored a dangerous beast. Unfortunately, by the looks of its current predicament, that beast would never grow into lethal maturity.

The heat of my anger caused sweat to drip down my forehead and burn my eyes. Frustration came out of my nose like a steam engine. I did not do helplessness well, not since that day I'd faced a lion as a cub. Dion had saved me that day. And today I'd kissed his fated mate.

It had been less than five minutes, but it was enough time for the pirates to do serious damage. The vampire had drained the fairy, and she lay motionless on the deck, her blood staining her top. The other assailants went about filling their pockets with magical currency instead of their hunger. Yanking teeth out of some shifters, taking blood samples from others, cutting off the hair of fairies. It was a robbery, but the kind where no one would get off this boat alive.

The urge to shift, to tear through the constraints holding me back, grew with every snip of hair, every pull of teeth. My panther snarled inside of me. It raged, its fury threatening to consume me. I felt the spell's hold on me beginning to weaken, the edges fraying as my beast pushed against it.

The hairs on the back of my neck rose. I was now in the sight of one of the predators. Through the paralysis, I couldn't move, but I could scent him—a lion shifter. The smell transported me back to my youth, to that emaciated lion that had almost ended me. He had been in his natural form, but this one in front of me walked on two legs with a glossy mane of vanity.

Still, I saw the beast in his eyes. It was no match for me as a man or a beast. If circumstances were different, if this was a fair fight, I could take him down with one hand tied behind my back.

My muscles twitched involuntarily, a sign of the fierce battle raging within me as both the man and the panther struggled against the magical constraints. The lion shifter noticed the slight movements. His confidence faltered for a moment as he hesitated.

The memory of the lion from my past, its hunger-filled eyes as it looked at me, not as an adversary but as food, fueled my determination. That and the knowledge that Stella was unprotected somewhere near was enough to get the fingers of my other hand twitching.

The lion shifter's hesitation was brief, showing he wasn't stupid. Spells could be broken, and I was close to figuring out how to break out of this one. And then a few things happened in succession.

A heard a gasp from behind me. It was just a slight intake of breath. As tuned into her as I was, I knew that it was Stella.

The lion shifter reached for my arm. With another burst of will, I shoved at the spell and managed to turn my hand. My claw caught the fleshy part of his wrist right at a nice juicy vein.

The last thing that happened went over my head. Literally.

A loud crash echoed from the water, drawing everyone's attention. A dark horse emerged from the river. The horse's black coat glistened in the moonlight. Water droplets cascaded off its powerful body.

"Kelpie," cried the witch. She appeared from behind me with Stella close on her heels.

The kelpie was like something out of a myth or a fever dream. The floorboards creaked and cracked as the horse landed on the starboard area of the ship. The pirates, so menacing just moments before, halted in their tracks. Their expressions shifted from aggression to confusion and then fear. As if under a spell, one by one, they dropped their victims. Then they turned and started walking toward, and then off the plank.

The splashing into the Mississippi River was a steady drumbeat, like a bell tolling the hour of death. It struck twelve times: once for each pirate.

The horse reared up. Its hoofs were high enough in the air to smash down on my head. But when it landed, it was not on my head, and it was not as a horse.

The moment the kelpie transformed, it was like witnessing a force of nature take on human form. Her shift from the majestic beast to a woman was seamless. Her eyes crackled with the energy of a storm, alive and commanding. And she was completely naked.

Moving with an otherworldly grace and power, the woman pulled metal chopsticks from her hair with a flourish like a swordsman unsheathing his weapons.

"Let them go." The kelpie's voice was like lightning in a bottle.

Instead of doing as she was told, the witch smirked. I felt the binds of the spell tightening on the places I'd gotten loose.

"You came out of the portal," said the witch.

The kelpie said nothing.

"You have a lot to learn about how things are run here, Tartarian."

"Not interested in any lessons from people who treat water like it's a garbage can."

"This whole planet is a garbage can."

"For the last time, let them go, bitch."

"I'm a witch."

"I said what I said."

"Give me the girl." The bitch pointed at Stella. "And I'll be out of your horse hair."

"Doesn't look like she wants to go."

The two were at a standoff. The witch's finger twitched as she grabbed for Stella. But the kelpie was too quick for her.

The metal chopsticks, once benign accessories nestled in her hair, became extensions of her will, gleaming like twin swords in the faint light. The air around her crackled with anticipation, charged with the imminent release of energy. Then, with a flourish that seemed both rehearsed and instinctive, she thrust the chopsticks forward, directing her focus onto the witch.

The lightning bolts she conjured were focused beams of energy, each one a spear of pure power. They sliced through the air with a sound that was part thunder, part tearing fabric, illuminating the deck with blinding brilliance. The bolts zigzagged toward their target, an unstoppable force seeking to neutralize the threat the witch posed.

The witch couldn't hold the spell, grab for Stella, and ward off the kelpie all at the same time. Self-preservation won out, and the spell broke.

Man and panther lunged for Stella, bringing her into my arms.

As the bolts struck, the air exploded with light and sound, the aftermath of the clash sending ripples across the deck. The witch, caught in the onslaught, had no time for countermeasures. Yet, when the light dimmed and our eyes adjusted, the bitch was gone. But the tang of portal potion lingered in the air.

CHAPTER 23

Stella

As the witch vanished in a puff of smoke, relief made me sag. The tension that had gripped my body released, leaving me unsteady on my feet. Before I could wobble, Oz's arms were around me, pulling me close.

The world righted itself. I was inside the safety of his embrace. The sight of the shifter advancing on him had filled me with a fear so guttural that the panther inside of me had come fully awake. She had clawed to get out. I just didn't know how to let her out. The helplessness of watching, unable to protect the one person who had come to mean more to me than anyone else was a torment I wouldn't wish on my worst enemy.

No, scratch that. I would take joy in watching Ken and his hairy Neanderthal take our places.

As Oz's hold tightened around me, I burrowed into him,

seeking the warmth and protection that only he could offer. His scent enveloped me, a reassuring blend of the wild outdoors and something uniquely Oz. It calmed the storm of emotions swirling inside me. I nudged against him, a silent plea for him to hold me closer, tighter, to never let me go. He responded, his arms constricting around me in a protective cocoon that made me feel as if nothing could ever harm me again.

A sharp pain lanced through my forearm. It broke through the haze of comfort and security. I couldn't stifle the yelp that escaped me.

Instantly, Oz's embrace loosened. He pulled back to look at me, his eyes scanning my face and then my body for the source of pain. The sight that greeted him was the blood welling from the deep gash on my forearm, a cruel souvenir from the witch's greed.

She thought my blood would get her out of here? Why, when it hadn't gotten me anywhere?

Oz's reaction was immediate, his hands gently cradling my arm, examining the wound with a focus that belied his worry. His hands went to the hem of his shirt. A ripping sound filled the air.

I should've stopped him. I was going to stop him. But I wanted a peek at what my man was packing first.

His abs did not disappoint. Hello, eight-pack.

"I'm fine," I said, staying his hand before he shredded his entire shirt to form a bandage. "I can fix it."

I extended my arm, watching as my magic emanated from my fingertips. It was like weaving a complex fabric, each thread of the spell meticulously pulling the edges of the wound together, knitting the flesh back into wholeness. The sensation was a tickling tingle. The process was like the detailed work I put into my clothing. I imagined the threads of my magic as fine silk, weaving a pattern of healing over my skin. The edges of the wound closed, the magic mending the torn flesh as easily as it altered a garment's fit.

I hadn't known I was capable of that. Not until the moment before I knew my body needed it. And then, I realized I had the ability to do it.

The pain subsided, replaced by a cool, soothing sensation that spread through my arm. It was working. The wound, which had looked so angry and raw moments before, was now nothing but a thin, red line. I flexed my arm, testing the strength of my work. It was as if the injury had never happened.

"See? Good as new."

Oz ran his fingers over my skin. I tingled in a very different way. Especially with the way he was looking at me. Whatever wall he'd had up between us was gone now. Funny how a near-death experience could do that to a person.

Breathing in deeply, I smelled the stench of death coming off the boat and not just the waters where the pirates had all jumped. As my gaze wandered over the deck of the riverboat, I saw I was far from the only one bearing injuries.

People were huddled together, many of them bleeding from their mouths where teeth had been brutally extracted, a horrific currency in the Crossroads. Others sported bald patches where clumps of hair had been torn out, and still others bore cuts similar to mine.

The air was thick with the scent of blood and fear, a pungent, metallic aroma that mingled with the earthy smell of the riverbank. It was a smell I knew would haunt me, a reminder of how close we had come to losing everything. The sounds of soft sobs and whispered comforts filled the boat, a low murmur of despair that was almost worse than the screams that had preceded it.

And there, lying on the floorboards as I'd predicted, was the fairy. Unlike in my vision, someone had closed her eyes and covered her with a dirty blanket. I took a step toward her but was halted.

"No." Oz's hold on me tightened.

His heart beat steadily against my ear. It was a reassuring rhythm in the midst of the calming madness. But even as I sought solace in his arms, I couldn't ignore the pain of the others.

"I can help." I'd never been able to help in a time of crisis. Unless there was a wardrobe malfunction or makeup mishap.

"No one is near death." His hold on me was absolute. "They'll live."

I wanted to protest, but I didn't have the energy to. The adrenaline had left my body. Mending my arm had left me exhausted. Being brave and strong had been hard. I decided to let Oz manhandle me into being coddled and protected instead.

"I'm so sorry," he murmured, his breath warm against my skin. "I've got you now. I'll never let you go, never let anything happen to you."

His words were a balm to my frayed nerves, soothing the storm of fear and uncertainty that had been raging inside me since he'd frozen as I kissed him. I'd thought he was rejecting me. But it had been a bitch of a witch flipping my Oz to off.

Now it was on. He was on. His words were practically a declaration of love. Just without the L-word. Other than that, it was everything I had ever wanted to hear, a promise of safety and belonging I had longed for all my life.

I tilted my head up to meet his gaze, seeing the sincerity and resolve shining in his eyes. I leaned in and kissed him, a soft, heartfelt expression of all the emotions churning within me. This time, Oz responded instantly. His lips moved against mine in a kiss that spoke of protection, commitment, and a budding love. The kiss wasn't the only thing budding. My nipples became tight buds of desire as he pulled me close and deepened the kiss.

"You two look like you'd be good in charge."

Oz and I broke apart to find the kelpie standing before us. The woman was completely naked, her boobs up high and perky. Her waist was snatched like an actual hourglass which flared down into smooth hips and long legs. Even though she'd just saved my life, I hated her instantly.

"I'm turning this over to you." She dropped the keys to the riverboat into Oz's hands.

"Who are you?" I asked. I'd never seen a kelpie before.

"Name's Styx. I came through the portal from Tartarus."

All I knew of Tartarus was that it was a prison planet. But she didn't have the desperation of an inmate. She looked like someone who was in charge and used to dealing with miscreants.

"I'll be back to clean this mess up later."

She waved her hand, not at the bruised and bleeding people on board the boat, but at the murky river water.

Before we could react, she leaped gracefully back into the water, disappearing beneath the surface with barely a ripple. I wondered who else had come through the portal and if they weren't all bad. Styx was definitely one of the good guys.

The passengers, who had been watching in stunned silence, let out a silent sigh of relief. The tension that had been holding us all in its grip dissipated, replaced by a sense of safety.

I knew it was all because Oz was now in charge. That sensation everyone was feeling was all I was willing to share of my man. I laced my fingers with his as we made our way to the wheelhouse. Unfortunately, there were windows where onlookers could look inside. So I'd have to wait until we reached dry land to finally bang my new man. But I still had every plan to stake my claim. Publicly.

A low hum filled the space as the engine came back to life. Oz navigated the controls with ease. The man clearly possessed many skills that I was still discovering.

Finding my place in his lap, I wrapped my arms around his neck, drawing him closer for a kiss. Once again, he came willingly.

The riverboat's steady thrum beneath us was just like his heartbeat, rhythmic and reassuring. Oz's hands found their way to my back, pulling me closer, as if he couldn't bear even a sliver of space between us. His touch ignited a fire within me, a desire that had been simmering since the moment I'd laid eyes on him. The ugliness of the world outside dimmed in the evening light, leaving only the warmth of his embrace, the taste of his lips, and the promise of a future together.

CHAPTER 24

Oz

I had one hand steady on the wheel as I steered the riverboat. The other hand was wrapped around Stella. My fingers dug into the curve of her hip. Gone was the shame. Guilt was a faint memory. I had nearly lost her. She would not slip through my hands again.

The rhythmic churning of the boat's engine and the soft lap of the Mississippi River against its sides formed a soothing soundtrack to our moment of calm. Stella nuzzled into my neck like the cat that she was. Her warmth pressed against me as the night lifted its curtain and a new dawn greeted us.

Stella's scent, that calming blend of lavender and vanilla, wafted up to my nostrils, mingling with the crisp, salty breeze that swept over the river. I breathed her in, taking a moment to do some of my own nuzzling in her hair. The color fascinated both man and panther. Her hair, a crown of ebony strands with golden highlights cascading down her back, was reminiscent of a leopard's coat. Her locks tickled my chin as she nestled closer, her breath soft against my neck as she dozed.

Her eyes, closed in peaceful slumber, revealed nothing of the danger that had just passed, the near death experience we'd narrowly escaped from. And we weren't out of danger yet.

Now, in addition to the vampires from the Crossroads chasing after her for her visions, I had to also guard against a pirate witch intent on draining her royal blood. I would've thought each supernatural would've wanted the other: the vamps her blood and the witch her foresight.

Didn't matter. Neither would get so much as a fingernail from her so long as I breathed.

As the first light of dawn painted the sky in hues of pink and gold, a surge of protectiveness washed over me. I vowed to keep her safe, to shield her from the dangers of this world, until my last breath.

"Mmmh." The rumble was low in her throat, like a lover awaiting pleasure.

She moved to tilt back her head. The movement brought her bottom lip against the pulse in my throat. That spot I'd only ever shown to two people: my mother, who had clamped down on it, causing pain, and Dion, who'd told me to rise and then extended his hand in friendship.

My shoulders slumped, but as they did, they curled around Stella. She inhaled, her lips parting in a quiet gasp. The intake of air cooled the vulnerable spot on my neck. I ached for her to bite down there.

Her scent was all over me. I wanted her mark on me, too. I had been claimed body, mind, and soul by her. There wasn't an inch of me that this woman—this goddess—

didn't own. Instead of biting me, she planted a lingering kiss at my pulse point.

The claws came out then. There was the sound of fabric being ripped. Looking down, I saw that the bottom of her blouse was in shreds. There was a tint of red on the pink—her blood.

I let go, holding my hands up in surrender. My fingertips were tinged with the evidence of my desire. "I'm sorry, Stella."

She shrugged, waving a hand over the ruined fabric. "I can fix it."

But she couldn't. The shredded, unmendable thing wasn't her clothing. It was me. "I don't deserve you."

Stella leaned into me. Her arms wrapped around my neck, the fingers of one hand finding my nape. She kneaded the skin she found there. I'd seen this kind of behavior between parents and cubs, pack mates, and mated pairs alike. It was a sign of affection, of ownership. The feeling of it almost robbed me of my words. And then her words robbed me of all sense.

"I deserve you. I deserve a man who fights for me. A man who is honest with me even if the truth might hurt me."

"When did I hurt you?"

"You hurt me every time you try to put distance between us. Every time you try to push me away."

My claws came out again. I cursed as another rip of fabric rent the air. I couldn't take care of this woman's clothes. How could I be expected to take care of her heart?

"Fate has brought us together for a reason," she went on, waving her hand once again over the torn fabric, making it look like new. "I can mend my clothes. I can't mend a broken heart if you reject me."

"Fate wouldn't be so cruel a to pair a goddess like you with a man like me."

"I've dated criminals, liars, cheats, and users. You can't be any worse than—"

"How about a murderer?"

Her gulp was audible. Her right eye twitched as she studied me. That twitch was only for a second before her gaze steadied again. "You said you worked for the king as head of his security. You killed as part of your job?"

"My first kill was before the king took pity on me."

Now her claws dug into my shirt. It was her human nails. The pricks felt like her panther refusing to let go.

I took a deep breath, the weight of my past heavy on my shoulders. I opened my mouth and said the words as fast as I could before I lost my nerve. "When I was a cub, I killed my brother."

Her claws released my shirt. The loss of that tiny pinprick of pain felt like the exact opposite of relief. Her hands hovered in front of my heart. The organ thumped hard against my chest to reach its mistress.

"He was the runt, and I... I was stronger."

"The two of you fought?"

"No, never. He was my brother, my twin. I never lifted a hand to him."

"Then... how?"

"I was greedy and growing so fast. I suckled all of my mother's milk, leaving nothing behind for him."

The confession felt like a wound reopening, raw and painful. I remembered the sight of my brother's frail form. I'd only seen the color of his eyes a few times when they'd been open. They were a dull rust to my vibrant gold.

"You're a shifter. Your mother could have given him other sustenance."

Stella was still trying to rationalize my actions, still trying to make me out to be a hero. She refused to see the villain that I was.

"We were born in our panther form. He couldn't shift into a human. He was too weak. He wouldn't take any other form of sustenance. And he died. It was all my fault."

"You were a baby, barely cognizant. It was not your fault. He had two grown, adult parents."

I shook my head. Dion had said the same thing to me when I'd told him my shame. I'd shut him down, gone mute as he continued to protest. He'd never brought it up again.

My father had succumbed to madness before we were born. The Call of the Wild had claimed not only his body but shifted his mind to madness.

"My mother... she rejected me after that. I was alone, a lone panther, until King Dion found me. He saved me, gave me purpose. I owe him my life."

"Then I owe him, too, for saving your life so that you could find me."

"I just told you I was a murderer."

Stella made a dismissive sound in the back of her throat. She waved her hands in the air as though she was tailoring my words. "I've dated murderers. I grew up in the Crossroads. Don't judge me, and I won't judge you."

She pointed a pink-tipped nail at me when I opened my mouth. I shut it mutely. Mainly because I wanted to hear her words. I wanted her words to absolve me.

"My point is you don't feel like a murderer to me. You don't have that dead look in your eyes. Your nostrils don't flare when you see an easy target." Stella's hand found mine, her touch gentle and reassuring. "Your mother should've taken better care of both of you. That's a mother's responsibility. When I meet her, I'm going to have words with her."

"She's dead."

"Oh. I'm sorry." She bit her lip like she was trying to hold in the next words. She quickly lost that battle. "But also good riddance if she made her baby think her neglect made him a murderer."

Her words struck a chord deep within me, a longing I didn't realize I had.

"I've changed my mind, Oz."

Stella had been holding my hands. She let go now. Her arms crossed over her chest. That regal nose went into the air in a show of defiance.

"I'm not going to share you. I want to be the only woman who gets access to your body and the sole caretaker of your heart."

CHAPTER 25

Stella

As the words spilled from my lips, a pang of doubt clawed at my heart. Maybe it wasn't a pang. Maybe it was my panther.

I felt her clawing at me to get out. Would she bow her head and accept less from her mate? Would she lower her eyes when confronted with another woman's carnal gaze as she looked at Oz? Would she try and conform and contort her shape to appear more desirable to him in the face of all the sleek pantheresses in Arcadia?

"I deserve more."

But even as I spoke those words, a torrent of worry flooded my mind. Would he think I was too bossy, too needy? Would he see my request for exclusivity as a burden?

Beneath my tailored clothes, behind the contoured blush on my face and under the surface of my confident façade, I harbored doubts about my own desirability. What if I wasn't enough for him? What if he longed for someone more alluring, more captivating than me? The thought gnawed at me, threatening to unravel the fragile threads of hope I had woven around my heart.

But then, as I looked into Oz's eyes, I saw something that washed away my fears. There was a tenderness, a depth of emotion that mirrored my own. An animal peered out at me from behind those golden irises. It rose to the surface, a raw and untamed presence that sent a shiver down my spine. It was the panther in his gaze.

The beast within wanted me, all of me, just as I was—flaws and all.

It was the man who kissed me.

The kiss was consuming. I was engulfed in the taste of him, like a wild forest after rain, earthy and alive. His essence filled my senses, overpowering me in the most intoxicating way possible. My heart raced in my chest, matching the rhythm of his own.

Oz kissed me like he was a skilled tailor weaving delicate threads. Each brush of his lower lip against mine stitched our souls closer together. The brush of his upper lip felt as though the fabric of our beings was being expertly mended. The fractures in my heart from past relationships faded away with each of his tender nips.

The feel of his fingers against my chin was like gentle embellishments. He swiped a thumb over the corners of my mouth as his tongue tasted mine. His index finger caressed the soft skin of my eyelids, adding intricate details to the masterpiece we were creating together. With every caress, I felt myself becoming more and more like precious fabric, delicate yet resilient, as if his touch had the power to transform me into something even more beautiful.

In his arms, I felt the magic of our connection, the stitches of the bond weaving us together in a way that felt both inevitable and absolute. This man would never hurt me. He would never lie to me. He would never leave me. Because it would hurt his very soul.

That was all before he deepened the kiss.

The once tender connection we shared cracked under the weight of his intensity. I wasn't sure if it was the panther or the man who growled. The sound had me pulling him closer at the same time as it had me pressing my thighs together.

But why the hell was I pressing my thighs together when I wanted this man right in my thigh gap? I bet he was strong enough to catch me if I hopped up and clamped my legs around his waist. I'd always wanted to do that. But none of my exes had been man enough.

Before I could even go up on my toes to get a running leap, Oz's touch grew more demanding and wholly possessive. His hands slid down my face, my shoulders, coming to rest at the curve of my ass. I wondered, was he going to lift me up himself? He stood, and I came with him. My feet came flat onto the earth. He pulled away without lifting me up.

As our lips parted, I was met with the fierce intensity of Oz's gaze. It was raw emotion. I'd said I'd seen the dead look of murderers. Oz looked at me like he was going to smother me with more than kisses. Oh, man, this was going to be a good death.

However, he didn't come for my mouth. Gently, he pushed aside a lock of my hair, exposing my shoulder to him. I knew his intentions before I saw his canines. I'd had the same urge when I woke up with my nose in his neck.

Never had I felt my panther more at the surface than

when I'd tasted the salt at his pulse point. I'd wanted to bite, to mark, to claim. But with my human teeth, I'd have done more damage than anything. Somehow I doubt he would've minded.

I cried out at the pierce of his teeth. The sensation was sharp, sudden, sending another shiver down my spine. As quickly as the pain came, it melted away into a warm, pulsing pleasure. It was as if a part of him was being sealed into me, marking me as his own, binding us together in a way that transcended the physical realm.

I gasped at the unexpectedness of it all, a mixture of surprise and overwhelming happiness coursing through me. This was it. This was my dream coming true—being marked by my fated mate, claimed in the most primal and intimate way imaginable. I felt a sense of completeness, of belonging, of happiness so pure that I nearly passed out.

As the sensation of the bite subsided into a dull throb, I was overcome with a sense of affection and belonging. I was marked. I belonged to Oz, and he belonged to me. And with that realization came an indescribable joy, a sense of fulfillment that I never knew was possible. In his arms, I had found my home, my sanctuary, my everything. I looked into his eyes, and I knew without a doubt—I was his, in every way that mattered, and he was mine.

I was floating. I was levitating. No, actually I was being lifted off the floor.

Oz had made two of my dreams come true. He'd claimed me as his fated mate, and he'd swept me off my feet. But he wasn't done.

Oz tugged the tucked tails of my shirt out of my pants. When his knuckles rubbed against my belly rolls, I wanted to stop him. Then his fingers delved into my panties, and I surrendered.

I moaned as his fingers traced along my most intimate places. His touch was both gentle and demanding, careful and coaxing as he began his sweet assault. I'd been fingered before. One by one, each memory dropped from my brain. It was like the light switch being flicked to off in a house that was going up for sale. That girl named Stella didn't live in the house of past lovers any more. She'd moved in with the wizard named Oz.

The man was really a magician. Each stroke, each caress, sent waves of ecstasy crashing through me, building and building until I teetered on the edge of oblivion.

I gasped as Oz's index and middle fingers entered me, crooking to stroke against a spot that only I had managed to find with the help of a curved dildo. My mate's thumb continued to rub tight circles around my clit as his other fingers tugged at the spongy patch of nerves inside of me. I did not stand a chance.

The twin flames of his touch were like fire and gas, igniting an explosive desire within me that I couldn't deny. As his fingers moved with practiced skill, exploring every inch of my most intimate places, I felt myself unraveling in ways I never thought possible.

I wasn't orgasming yet, which was a little frightening. This was already more pleasure than I'd ever experienced in the throes of passion with any other man. At least that's what I believed. I couldn't remember. The lights were all out in that house that was buried deep in my memory.

Each stroke of Oz's fingers brought murmurs of ecstasy out of me. I was a shivering, whimpering mess, and I still hadn't come. He kept me dancing on the edge of bliss as he built my body up to an inevitable release that I knew would shatter me to my core. My breaths came in short, ragged gasps as he expertly manipulated me, bringing me closer and closer to the—

"Ahhhhh, Oz!"

I arched my back and cried out his name, my body trembling with the force of my orgasm. It hit me harder than the ground had shaken when the portal opened. It swallowed me whole. The orgasm at the hand of my fated mate was overwhelming, earth-shattering, world-ending.

His lips found mine once more. But I had nothing left to give. Still, I let him take from me, and he did so.

Oz continued to pet my core as the aftershocks zinged and zipped across my ragged nerve endings. He sipped at my mouth as I alternately sighed and took in deep breaths. He whispered in my ear, but I couldn't make out anything he was saying. Didn't matter because my panther got every word. I felt her presence growing stronger in my belly. I knew she had every intention of getting out to claim our mate. She could have at him because for now, I was done.

A knock at the door made both our animals growl.

CHAPTER 26

Oz

As the boat docked in the port of the Quad Cities, exhaustion settled over me like a heavy cloak. The journey had been long and bloody, like most missions I'd been assigned back on Arcadia. But this one was far from over. There were nearly two hundred miles of ungoverned, gang-managed, lawless terrain ahead of us through No Man's Land to reach the trains in Chicago.

I was tired just thinking about it. I hadn't slept in two days now. I was running on fumes. Forget my muscles. My bones were tired. But as I stepped off the riverboat, a surge of unfamiliar warmth flooded through me. My first thought was that it was magic, and I was being put under a spell. Then I looked down to see that Stella's hand was in mine, our fingers interlaced.

I'd never held anyone's hand before, never felt the weight of someone else's trust resting in my palm. It was her touch igniting a fire within me, her fingertips reaching to the depths of my soul. The heat of her affection radiated from her palm and seeped into my skin to soothe the ache in my weary bones.

"You're tired." She brushed her fingers across my brow and through my hair with her free hand. "We've gotta get you to bed."

The woman already had my soul. I'd been erect since I first spotted her walking down the street. Now my heart was a goner. It pounded right at my sternum, trying to get closer to her.

Looking around the docks, I saw that the other travelers had dispersed. Few had thanked us for our intervention. That didn't bother me. Out in the wilds of No Man's Land, friends turned into foe and then back again quick enough to give anyone whiplash. Everyone was scurrying away and watching their own backs. I never had any intention of watching out for any of them aside from steering the boat to safety.

The clang of metal against metal, the shouts of sailors, and the creaking of ships created an assault against my senses. I was tired of the salty tang of the river on my tongue. I wanted to get us away from all of it.

I pulled Stella into my side as I made my way through the crowd. A ball rolled up to my foot, halting our steps. I looked down to see the shifter cub from the boat. Once again, he looked expectantly from me to the ball and back again.

I almost moved around the ball. Almost. Maybe it was Stella's hand in mine. Maybe it was the sleep deprivation. Maybe it was the fact that we'd just survived a near death experience.

I stopped the ball with the tip of my boot before it rolled

off the side of the pier and into the water. Turning my foot, I gave it a kick that sent it back to the cub. He caught it with a gleeful grin.

The kid rejoined his group. A woman put a hand on his small shoulders and pulled him close. She bent and bussed a kiss to the top of his head. I swallowed hard before turning sharply to the right, giving the mother and cub my back.

I fisted my hand but didn't get very far. Stella's fingers were still wrapped around mine, making it hard to ball my feelings up. I avoided her gaze, not wanting to invite any discussion.

She said nothing, only pressed her palm more tightly to mine. Sending me more of that bone-melting warmth.

"You're a good man, Oz."

She was wrong. I knew she was wrong. But her words didn't feel wrong.

Everything she said to me sounded like the truth. I was under this witch's spell. I wanted to be her hero. I wanted to worship her for the rest of her days. I wanted to be a good man.

The scent of her on my fingers called me a liar. I'd just finger-fucked my best friend's fated mate.

Mine, said the panther.

The mark on her neck spoke louder. It was something I couldn't hide, like my feelings. Something my king would kill me for.

He could do that once Stella was safe in Arcadia. She would choose the king over me, and that would be the end of it. With that thought, something in me shifted. My life would be over soon. Might as well enjoy it.

Stella didn't balk at the story of my past. She didn't blame me for my brother's death, just like Dion didn't. The only one who did was my mother, and she wasn't a glowing beacon of maternal warmth. So maybe I wasn't as bad as I thought.

The settlement, teeming with activity, carried an unmistakable air of danger. I sensed it in the wary glances and hushed conversations of the passersby. My instincts, honed by years of survival, remained on high alert.

Stella walked beside me, absorbed in the task of mending her designer clothes with her magic. The threads twisted and turned under her deft control. I couldn't shake the feeling that her actions were drawing unwanted attention. Her elegance and the evident quality of her attire marked us as outsiders, making us targets in this rough settlement.

I reached for her hand, halting her movements. Even the slightest touch sparked a possessive impulse within me. She stopped what she was doing. A grin spread across her beautiful face, and she tilted her head up for a kiss.

I could not deny her. Allowing her lips to brush against mine, I seized her mouth. I was the pirate now, and I'd plundered the most precious treasure in this realm and any other.

"Stella." I reached out to trace the mark on her collarbone. "You need to be cautious. We have to blend in."

I tugged at the hem of her blouse, which shifted the top of the garment. Her gaze followed my movement, a salacious grin turning to a frown as my fingers didn't go lower than that hem.

"You're suggesting I don't blend in?" Her tone was laced with amusement.

I regarded her, this woman destined for royalty, in the middle of the gritty streets. These alleys were unworthy of her grace. The people should lower their gazes in her presence. "No, princess. You do not."

I reclaimed her hand in mine. Now that I'd experienced this hand-holding business, I had no intention of stopping it. As we forged ahead, a sense of belonging and rightness enveloped me whenever I glanced at her, even as my mind cautioned me about the complexities our bond entailed.

There were more shadows and whispers in the streets than people. The remnants of a bygone era stood as silent witnesses to the chaos that reigned in this city that had once been. There were remnants of what once were notable architectural and tourist attractions. A dilapidated shell of what looked like an art museum was now marred by graffiti and shattered windows. A pavilion lay in ruins, its exhibits plundered and its machinery rusting in the harsh elements. A botanical center had been reclaimed by nature. The gardens were overgrown and untamed, the pathways cracked and broken.

Stella, adorned in her tailored garments enhanced by her magic, stood out like a beacon announcing a big pay day. Her pristine appearance called many eyes to her in the grimy surroundings, drawing unwelcome attention from those who sought to exploit her magic. The only thing that made most stop in their steps toward her was me at her side.

A hungry person might act mindlessly. Hungry people didn't need to think straight if they had numbers on their side. The farther we got into the city, the more people I saw walking in pairs, in threes, and in groups.

The need to get us off the streets as quickly as possible gnawed at me. In this unforgiving landscape, safety was a luxury we couldn't afford to take for granted. The panther within me emitted a warning growl. The crowds backed up a step, but that trick wouldn't work again.

Surveying our surroundings, I assessed our limited options. Most buildings that could pass for shelter appeared as black holes that fed off violence. Stella gestured toward a hotel across the street. It exuded a seedy aura, the type likely offering rooms by the hour, a far cry from the safety and comfort I yearned to provide her.

I hesitated, torn between fulfilling her request and my instincts clamoring that it wasn't the safest choice. It wasn't like we had many others. So we crossed the street.

CHAPTER 27

Stella

I'd like to say I've stayed in worse places... but I would be lying. It might have been nice a hundred years ago. Though I was also pretty sure it hadn't been properly cleaned in all that time.

The exterior of the hotel loomed before me. And when I say loomed, I was a bit worried it might topple down on top of me like an old man leaning hard on his cane. The hotel's once-grand façade was now weathered and worn. It bore the scars of neglect and decay. The neon sign flickered intermittently, casting an eerie glow over the cracked pavement below. The broken windows and peeling paint were more evidence of years of neglect than disrepair.

Stepping into the lobby, we were greeted by a wave of musty air that assaulted my senses. The dim lighting did little to dispel the gloom that permeated every corner of the space. There were plenty of wall sconces and chandeliers. It looked like the lights were on actual electricity and not magic. Human-made electricity was an old-fashioned oddity in short supply.

The carpet had seen better days -likely one hundred years ago when it had been installed. It was worn and frayed in places, the once-vibrant colors faded to a dull, mottled gray. It had a musty, lingering scent that seemed to have seeped into every fiber of the worn carpet beneath my feet. The unpleasant aroma clung to the back of my throat.

It was clear that this was not a place accustomed to luxury or comfort. But as long as we had a roof over our heads and a bed to sleep in, I was willing to give it a try. Turning to Oz, I offered him a small smile.

"Well, it's not exactly the Ritz, but I suppose it'll have to do for now."

Famous last words. There was a part of me that would rather go back outside and search for a Ritz, or even a Holiday Inn Express. Bugs skittered under our feet as we walked down the hall. A heavy realization settled over me like a suffocating blanket. Gone were the days of luxury and comfort I'd once taken for granted. Instead, we found ourselves in a small, dismal space, barely deserving of the title *room*.

The faint sound of a dripping faucet echoed through the room, accompanied by the muffled voices of other guests drifting through the thin walls. I refused to let any of this dampen my spirits. If anything, it only strengthened my resolve.

I was alive. I was away from the men who had used me for years. I was with my fated mate. And he'd claimed me.

In the dim light of our modest accommodations, I saw an opportunity, a chance to deepen our connection even further. Despite the room's shortcomings, it had everything we needed—most importantly, a bed. That wasn't all it had.

"We can't stay here," Oz said, backing up into the hall as he tried to shut the door to the room.

Oz had gone ahead of me, so he was blocking most of my view inside the room. All I could see was the bed.

"Oz, I'm tired. Do you really want to go back out there? At night. In the dark."

I was starting to learn my man's expressions. He wore a combination of a frown and furrowed brow. There were degrees to the downset turn of his lips and the depth of the lines in his brow. Right now, they were at the highest setting on each.

"I trust that you'll keep me safe," I said, putting my hand on his chest.

His heart was racing. That didn't make sense, since we were inside and out of harm's way. Unless there was someone in the room.

I was tall, but Oz had a few inches on me. I came up to his chin, which meant I could peer past his shoulder. And that's when I saw it.

"Oh," I managed.

Oz's shoulders didn't so much as relax as they heaved out a sigh of weariness. Or was that wariness? I always got the two confused. With his guard down, I slipped past him.

There was a musty smell in this room, too. Instead of carpet, there were rugs on the floor. Made sense so that management could change those out more frequently. The walls were painted a faded shade of off-white, with patches of peeling paint revealing the years of neglect. But there wasn't much of the wall visible. Framed artwork dominated most of the area.

Boobs were on display in all of the artwork. Lots and

lots of boobs. And sliced peaches that were de-seeded. In the place of the seeds were dripping wet purple eggplants. And then more boobs. I was surprised there were no penises. At least not in the paintings.

There were penises on a shelf beside the bed. Pink penises. Black penises. A purple one that had a glowing attachment. Because of the subtle hum of the vibrations, I knew these were not battery operated with ancient electrical technology.

"So that's where the magic happens."

Oz did not laugh at my joke. Tori and Niamh would have. I made a mental note to repeat it to them once we got to Portland and I could send them a message. It was going to be a long text.

I was no longer so disappointed in our accommodations. I saw that it had everything I needed to allow my mate to claim my body. Including the sex swing hanging from the closet door.

Oh, and I'd missed the BDSM paraphernalia inside the closet. Masks and handcuffs. Whips and chains. And... a lot of things I could not identify. I rubbed my hands together, thinking of all the fun that we were about to have.

Unfortunately, my intended boy toy looked like he was going to be sick. His brows were still furrowed. His nostrils flared like he smelled something bad. But instead of a frown, his lips were pursed. He was not a man aroused.

He did not want to be in this room. With sex toys. And me.

"This place is not befitting a goddess," he managed to say in a hoarse whisper.

I took a deep breath, pushed back my shoulders, and lifted my head. "I need a bath."

His lips unpursed and turned upside down into a frown. Good; a frown I could deal with.

"I'm dirty from running through the swamp and fighting pirates."

Those words deepened his frown even more. I made a mental note: his thinking back to me being in danger drew him closer to me.

"I think I'm bruised, too."

"Bruised? Where? Let me see."

I crossed the threshold of the bathroom. Inside the space, I was met with the scent of dampness and mildew. The fixtures were worn and aged. Opposite the sink, tucked into a recessed alcove, sat the sunken bathtub. It was a surprising haven of cleanliness amidst the room's decay. Made of faded porcelain, the tub offered a spacious sanctuary. Its surface was smooth and inviting despite its age. It was the cleanest piece of furniture in the entire room, likely because of its constant access to water.

I heard Oz's footsteps approaching rapidly, the concern evident in the quickness of his stride. He came up behind me, his presence making the space feel smaller, more intimate.

"The bruise? Where?"

I turned to face him, seeing the worry etched in his features. "It's probably nothing serious," I reassured him.

The concern in his eyes didn't wane. "Show me, Stella."

His proximity, the intensity of his gaze, and the protective care in his touch filled me with a mixture of reassurance and longing. I let him check for any bruises. I hadn't lied. There were plenty. He would have to get my clothes off in order to find all of them.

As I popped the first button of my shirt open, I could see the panther in his eyes. He blinked, and the man was back.

I popped the next button and watched his Adam's apple bob. It was the panther that flashed his teeth at me. It was the panther that growled low, making me press my thighs together. And then he blinked again, and the man was back in control.

"You *are* bruised."

"I am?" I'd forgotten my whole ruse. Looking down, I saw the trail of red and slight purple on my bare arms.

Oz ran a finger over my skin. "I want to dive into the water, find each of those pirates, and kill them again."

"I'd rather you soak with me in the tub."

He shook his head and started to retreat.

"You're bruised, too."

"I'm fine. I'll keep watch while you bathe."

"You're not fine. You're more bruised than I am. It's my job to look after you, too, as your mate."

That Adam's apple bobbed up and down like it was caught in a barrel at a kid's birthday party. He did that every time I referred to myself as his fated mate.

I knew he wanted me. I didn't understand why he kept holding himself back. When I put my hand to the hem of his shirt and gave a tug, he didn't stop me. So I pulled the tails up and out. When I got to his torso, I stopped. And gasped.

CHAPTER 28

Oz

The fluorescent light flickered above, casting a harsh glow on the peeling wallpaper and the old, chipped tiles. I breathed in, filling my nostrils with the warm, sweet scent of Stella. Her fingers trailed fire as the soft pads met the hard ridges of my abs.

I was a man unused to softness, unacquainted with gentleness. I'd had a hard-on for this woman since the first time I saw her back in the Crossroads. The erection was easy to ignore. What was happening in my chest with my heart beating erratically; what was going on at the back of my throat, where the rhythmic pounding of my pulse took over my voice; what was happening in my head, where I no longer remembered or cared about the reasons why this woman should not be touching me so intimately, why I should not reach for her in turn. All of that took a back seat.

All I could think of was how to be gentle in return. How

to hold myself from tossing her up against the bathroom wall and sinking into that lush heat. How to keep my claws from piercing the honey-golden flesh peeking through her lacy bra. How to keep my incisors from nipping at the clit I knew had to still be plump after I'd played with it on the riverboat.

And that's when she gasped and pulled away.

No shit, she'd pulled away. Because she'd probably heard me. She'd heard each of those dirty things I'd wanted to do to her and she was balking now. She finally realized that I wasn't the man for a goddess like her.

"How did this happen?" she demanded.

Back in the shack, there hadn't been much light. Now she saw them clearly. Now she saw the truth of my unworthiness. How had she let a foul creature such as me get anywhere near her soft skin? How had she let an unworthy beast get close enough to taste her flesh?

"She did this to you?"

There was a growl in her voice. A low rumble that made my panther sit back on its haunches and look up. Its tongue lolled out of its mouth as it regarded the object of its devotion.

Stella wasn't looking into my eyes. She was looking at my abdomen. With her bare hands—and maybe a touch of magic—she tore apart my shirt to expose the rest of my ravaged skin.

I'd always been cautious about revealing my scars. Never fucked a woman with my shirt off. I doubt I'd even taken my pants all the way off. There'd never been a need, or a desire, to be naked with another person. Until now.

A little voice in my head told me to cover up, to hide my wounds. It was the voice of the scared cub I once was. It looked out through my eyes now at the anger on the face of the woman who reached a fingertip toward my ragged skin: five claw marks, the middle two just as deep as the others. She had wanted it to hurt.

"How'd she die?"

I inhaled deeply. The oxygen reached down deep into my belly, where the pain of my mother's wrath still rested. The breath called it to stir. It was the cub that answered.

"She succumbed to the Call of the Wild."

"The sickness when the god of Arcadia went insane?"

I nodded instead of explaining the details of shifters being locked into their half-shifted animal forms for years. Even though the portal between Earth and Arcadia had been closed for decades during Pan's insanity, a few Arcadians had managed to slip through the cracks between worlds. So the people here had heard of the strife we all went through but were powerless to do anything to help until a woman from this world got through to our world and our god.

With her unique beast, Adora had been the only being able to get through to Pan, the mad god of our world. Because she had been able to reach his heart, the madness had been healed. Not only in him, in but all of us. Their story showed proof that love moved mountains and healed monsters.

I realized I'd been holding myself stiff, bracing for a reaction of disgust or pity from Stella. It never came. What did come was that fingertip finally landing on the raised skin of my childhood wounds. Only to be jerked away just as quickly.

"Did I hurt you?"

I'd gasped at her touch. Better that than the moan that was now rising up my throat. The sad cub in my gut was long gone. In his place was a touch-starved panther who wanted to sink its teeth into this woman who constantly assaulted him with her gentleness and care.

My hands snaked out to snatch her wrists. My grip was firm. She had to understand there wasn't much gentleness in me.

Stella stepped closer. Instead of just one finger, she set all five of one hand on my abdomen, covering the deepest of the scars. When she placed the palm of the other hand against the shallow end of the scars, I was undone. But she wasn't finished.

In a gesture that took my breath away, she leaned in and kissed the wounds. Each kiss was a tingling whisper against my skin. I'd forgotten over the years that I was in pain. The pulls and tugs of the torn flesh had been nothing but background noise in my head, easy to ignore when I was more concerned about food, or shelter, or safety.

Now I looked down to see if she was using her magic to knit the skin back together. She wasn't. Not with any witch's magic. It was the power of her as a woman who thought I belonged to her.

I did belong to her. I was bound to her. I would do anything for her. If all she wanted was for me to bathe her, then that's what she'd get.

The cramped bathroom, the rundown hotel, the noise and chaos of the settlement outside—it all faded away. There was only Stella and me. I wrapped my arms around her, pulling her close.

"No one will ever hurt you again," she vowed.

I pressed my lips into her hair. Up close, that warm, sweet scent of hers was an aphrodisiac. I was already high. I had an endless supply of her standing in my embrace.

Bending down, I turned on the faucet over the tub. A gentle rushing sound filled the room as the water splashed into its depths. It was inviting and soothing, like an embrace. Like the woman whose body I wanted to return to.

I went back to Stella and carefully removed her shirt, making sure not to let it slip from my grasp. She valued her clothing, and I didn't want to risk damaging it. As I unclasped her bra, my mouth went dry, and I licked my lips in anticipation. Her caramel-colored nipples were exposed. A surge of desire took hold of me at the sight.

Her eyes met mine, and in that moment, there was no denying the intense chemistry between us. I pulled her closer to me. I trailed kisses along her jawline. Down her neck. She moaned softly and tangled her fingers in my hair, urging me on.

My hand slid down to the waistband of her pants, unbuttoning and unzipping them with ease. They fell to the ground, revealing her lacy underwear. I couldn't resist running my hand over the soft fabric. Stella gasped and leaned into me, her body trembling. In one swift move, I lifted her up and carried her over to the bath.

There was a delighted grin on her face as she laced her fingers behind my neck. "Third time."

She didn't need to explain. That was happening more and more. I knew she meant it was the third time I'd swept her off her feet.

I carried Stella's weight with ease, her soft curves fitting perfectly against me as I lowered her into the warm bathwater. She sighed contentedly, leaning back and closing her eyes as the water enveloped her. I watched her with a tenderness that surprised even myself.

Leaning over her, I began to wash away the grime and dirt of our journey. My hands moved gently over her skin. The water shifted and rippled, reflecting the glow in her eyes as she looked up at me. Her trust in me was an unimaginable gift, the connection that hummed between us an invisible thread whose knot I felt tightening.

I did not resist.

"Is this a preview of what I can expect in palace life?"

The soap slipped from my hand. Her casual mention of looking forward to palace life, to being tended to in luxury, jolted me back to reality. Did I even have a tub in my quarters? I had no idea because I spent most of my time in a cabin at the edge of the palace grounds.

Dion aside, Stella was destined for a life of luxury. I couldn't bear the thought of letting her go. My panther and I were in agreement—Stella was ours. But that acknowledgment came with a heavy burden, the knowledge that in keeping her with me, I would be holding her back from a life of royal splendor. She deserved to be a queen, not just the princess she was in my heart.

"I want you here with me, Oz. Get in the tub."

"No," I said, lifting her from the tub. "I'm taking you to bed."

CHAPTER 29

Stella

I think I was born without shame of nudity. I saw the other girls in the girls' bathroom and at sleepovers. How their bodies were different from mine, slimmer, leaner. They had all looked like sticks to me, like dolls with bendable, breakable parts. I'd never been attracted to skinny men, and I'd never wanted to be a skinny woman. I liked food too much.

I liked sex, too.

When Oz laid me down on the bed, still dripping wet from the bath, I spread my thighs shamelessly. He stared for a moment. And then stared some more.

I was starting to feel self-conscious until he licked his lips. That was a signal I knew all too well. What man could resist the sight of wet and waiting vagina? Not any—

Oz turned on his heel. He marched toward the door. His hands fisted at his sides.

"Oz?"

He didn't respond. He reached for one of the wrapped sexy toys. I couldn't see which one he grabbed. When he turned to come back to me, I saw that a spot was empty in the line of packaged dildos.

He tore through the packaging, letting the cardboard and plastic fall to the ground like snow. Christmas wasn't really a thing in the Crossroads. I loved getting gifts at any time of year.

"I want to watch you." Oz held up a thick purple dildo with a curved end and an on switch that signaled there was a motor inside.

Yes! My mate was kinky. I had to be the luckiest girl in the—"Oh!"

The buzz of the vibrator jolted my legs back apart. My eyes went wide. Not with surprise. I was the proud owner of many sexual aides during the time when I didn't have a partner to assist me. I had just never had a partner assist with my sex toys.

The vibrator hummed against my inner thigh, but I felt the reverb pulse through my entire body. Oz pressed the dildo just to my entrance. The bulbous head rested below my clit. I let out a little whimper as I met Oz's gaze. He was doing just as he said. He was watching me.

"Tell me what you like, Stella."

"I like everything you're doing," I whispered, my voice shaking.

My eyes locked onto his, and I saw the hunger in them. I licked my lips. He tracked the movement. First with his eyes. Then with the vibrator. He ran the head around my entrance, ending the journey right on top of my clit.

My hips jerked off the bed.

"Shhhhh," he soothed. "You'll have to hold still so I can get this in."

He said it with a smirk. That smirk grew wider as he pushed the vibrator inside me slowly. A keening sound came from my throat as the buzzing sensation filled me. I arched my back. My entire body trembled with the pleasure of it.

It wasn't just the vibrations or the sensation of being filled by the dildo. It was mostly Oz's eyes, watching my every twitch and blink and gasp.

"Please," I begged.

"What do you want, princess?"

"I want you."

"You have me."

He bent his head and kissed the inner thigh of my right leg. Then the same spot on my left leg. Back and forth he went, higher and higher. All the while, he kept the vibrator inside, not thrusting. Instead, he tilted the device forward so that it pressed against the front of my core, right over the spongy patch of nerves that I knew would make me erupt.

No man had ever found my G-spot. Not only did Oz know exactly where it was, he knew exactly what to do with it.

His lips made their way up my legs. His gaze never left me as I trembled under his machinations. All I could feel was his breath on my skin. His eyes on my flesh. I'd never felt more turned on in my life.

"This is how a goddess deserves to be worshiped."

Those were the last words I remembered understanding from his lips before they wrapped around my clit.

I jackknifed off the bed, but I didn't get far. Oz's big body covered my thighs, not letting me wiggle too much. His free hand pressed against my sternum, holding me in place as he lapped at my bud while buzzing my core with the vibrator.

It was too much.

It was just perfect.

I needed a breather.

I never wanted him to stop.

I don't remember when I started coming. I don't remember when I stopped. I might have even left my body for a few seconds or years.

When I came back down from that high, Oz's lips were no longer on my clit. They were on my mouth.

I tasted the musk of my essence. Mixed with the masculine scent of him, it was the best delicacy my palate had ever experienced. I wanted nothing else on my tongue for breakfast, lunch, dinner, or snacks.

The touch of his lips was both gentle and intense, a prayer and a promise. I felt worshiped. I felt safe. I felt loved. Even though he hadn't said it yet, I knew he felt it.

My only regret was that he hadn't entered me himself. Probably because I'd passed out with what my man obviously considered foreplay. I was ready now. Before I could tell Oz to come hither, a vision came for me.

I saw us, Oz and me, soaring through the sky on a magnificent winged horse. It wasn't the black kelpie. It was a Pegasus.

Its powerful wings beat rhythmically against a backdrop of fluffy clouds and a boundless azure sky. The sensation of the wind in my hair, the exhilarating freedom of flying, the closeness of Oz beside me—it was surreal, breathtaking. I was lost in the wonder of it, unsure if it was a hallucination brought on by the intensity of my orgasms or a genuine glimpse into the future.

My first sight of a horse had been a warning. Could this

be the same kind of message? My answer came at the sound of a click at the door.

Oz's lips left mine. He rolled over and off me in an instant, every muscle coiled and ready.

The atmosphere in the room shifted instantly. The pleasurable petting and languorous kisses all faded. The previously dull sounds of the hotel—distant conversations, the hum of the old air conditioning unit—now felt ominous and foreboding. Oz's gaze was fixed on the door, his protective instincts in full force.

I sat up in the bed, covers pulled up to my chin to hide my nudity. Oz moved forward with quiet, controlled urgency. His body was a silhouette against the dim light, a figure of strength and readiness. The sense of safety I felt in his arms moments ago was now replaced by a surge of adrenaline, a readiness for whatever or whoever was on the other side of that door.

CHAPTER 30

Oz

I was pleasure drunk on Stella. But my senses weren't dampened; they were heightened. As the sound at the door escalated from a suspicious click to the unmistakable noise of someone trying to force entry, my instincts kicked in.

"Get dressed," I ordered.

Stella didn't argue. She moved into the bathroom, taking her clothes with her.

I positioned myself between Stella and the door. My muscles tensed. Whoever was on the other side wasn't making a strong play at stealth.

My hands curled into fists, claws pricking the center of my palms. But I didn't feel the pain.

Could it be Dion at the door? He had foresight. He'd seen Stella. Had he seen me with her, marking the mate that was supposed to be his? Pleasuring her to within an inch of her life with my full attention? Not even a thought of entertaining another woman.

The panther within me growled with ferocious intensity. Its instincts urged me to protect what was mine. Stella was mine. The bond between us pulsed like an explosive charge, just waiting for a match strike.

I yanked the door open, and a body crashed in. In the darkness, I could barely make out the figure of the intruder. It didn't matter. With a snarl, I lunged forward.

I seized the idiot assailant by the collar, pinning him against the wall. With my claws at his throat, his body sagged in surrender. Needless to say, this wasn't the panther king.

A thin body dangled in the air. His youth was evident in the uncertainty that flickered across his face. His features were unremarkable. His appearance would have blended into the background of any bustling city street. His scent held no distinguishing markers, no traces of magic or supernatural essence. He was a human, the original inhabitants of this world who were near extinct these days.

"You picked the wrong room, kid."

"I... I didn't mean no harm, mister. I was just... trying to..."

"Steal from us?" I finished his sentence, my tone tinged with irritation.

"You were supposed to be asleep. Most of them are asleep after..." He waved his hand at the bed.

The rumpled sheets were evidence that something had happened there. Unlike other wham-bam-thank-you-ma'am men that must frequent this establishment, I had only been warming up my princess. I'd been waiting patiently for her to return to consciousness so that I could start the next round.

"I'm sorry, sir. I won't do it again, I swear."

He was lying, of course. But he wasn't my problem. The kid from the boat with the ball still had that fresh, just into the world smell. This kid stank of the streets and neglect. He wasn't going to change.

"Here," said Stella.

She walked up behind me, but I blocked her so that she couldn't get within arm's distance of this delinquent.

"Oz," she humphed.

I didn't move or loosen my hold on the kid.

"Fine." She held out her hand to me. "Will you give this to him, please?"

It was a wristband. I had no intention of handing it over to the thief. Not because I cared about his state of poverty. Because I didn't want anyone to have anything that belonged to my mate other than me.

"It was a gift from Ken."

I dropped the bracelet into the kid's hand and shoved him out the door. I didn't miss his toothsome grin as he looked down at the bounty. It wasn't worth much, but it might get him something to eat and maybe a new shirt.

"We have to leave."

Stella didn't argue with me. In fact, she probably had foreseen it because she was fully dressed and had her bag slung over her shoulder. She was stunning, as always. Not a hair out of place. Not a wrinkle in the clothing she'd worn for three days now.

She handed me my shirt. I tugged it over my head. As I pulled the fabric down over my chest, I felt her hands on me, helping me.

I'd never had a woman dress me. Never had anyone make sure my collar was straight and the tails of my shirt tucked in. Stella did all of this for me. Then she smoothed the wrinkles, brushed away the smudges of dirt, even did something to the armpits that lifted the funk of three days off me.

When she was done, she smiled down at her handiwork, then up at me. I knew it was a kiss she wanted as payment for making me over. I was going to pay up. First I took a moment to admire the gift I'd been given in this woman.

I didn't have the right to say those three little words. If she listened closely, she would hear them coming from every pore in my skin. In the pounding of my fool heart. In the center of my eyes that refused to stay from her person.

I bent my head, brushing my lips against hers. The musky taste of her core was still on my tongue. Mixed with the sweetness of her lips, it was enough to bring a man to his knees.

Once again, we held hands as we walked out of the room and down the hall. The hotel owner was conspicuously absent from the front desk as we made our way out. I'd heard the shuffling of feet and the quiet snick of a door as we made our way down the hall. He knew what kind of establishment he was running. All I wanted was to get my princess out of it.

Stepping out into the cool night air, the change in atmosphere was immediate. The city's night sounds surrounded us. I heard what sounded like tribal drumming. Chatter spilled out from seedy night clubs. The scents of street food that could have only come from the swampy river water mingled with the urban smells of crowded, unwashed bodies.

As we quickly moved away from the hotel, my mind raced with thoughts of where to go next, of how to keep

Stella safe. I had no idea how we were going to get out of here and to Chicago for the train.

I felt the weight of stares on us, the predatory glances of those who saw us as easy prey. Criminals had a keen sense for those who lacked direction. They saw Stella and me as lost wanderers ripe for exploitation, or worse.

Another confrontation was the last thing I needed right now. I made a decision to go left. Stella had stopped walking in the middle of the street. Her gaze was fixed on something above us, her expression filled with wonder and awe.

"It's a Pegasus."

"Pegasus?" I followed her gaze to a sign—a man riding a winged horse.

"It's the way we're going to get out of here."

There were horse shifters. There were even dragons. But there were no such things as unicorns. At least, I didn't think so.

"I saw a vision. I think that's how we get out of here."

I looked again at the sign. Beneath it was a run-down building. It looked like it was open for business. Whatever it was, it was a direction. I steered us toward it, leaving the gang of thugs behind.

Five minutes later, we stepped into the shop, a place that seemed more like a junkyard than a store. Piles of mechanical parts and odd contraptions were scattered haphazardly around the room, creating a maze of techno-logical debris.

Stella's hand was clasped tightly in mine as we navi-gated through the clutter. There were fire hazards at each turn. A deep, bellowing growl shattered the calm. I pushed Stella behind me and faced the door, certain the vagrants from outside had followed us in.

It wasn't vampires looking for a quick bite. It wasn't witches itching to cast a spell. Or fairies hoping for some carnal fun. There, prowling toward us, was a beast with a golden coat of fur, dark eyes that gleamed with malice.

My king had come to kill his best friend and claim his mate.

CHAPTER 31

Stella

The air crackled with energy. The texture of it wasn't magical. It sizzled like electricity. The scent of metal and oil filled my nostrils, intermingling with the faint aroma of herbs and incense that lingered in the air. My skin prickled with anticipation.

I knew we were being watched. I couldn't tell from which direction. The watching didn't feel unsafe. It didn't feel dangerous.

Out of the corner of my eye, I caught a glimpse of movement from the shadows—a flicker of golden fur catching the faint glow. Oz shoved me behind him. But there was no hiding what was advancing on us.

A jaguar, golden and majestic, emerged from the darkness. Its sleek form moved with a silent grace that sent a shiver down my spine.

Peering over Oz's shoulder, I was captivated by the

beast's beauty, by the way its muscles rippled beneath its golden coat, by the fierce intelligence gleaming in its eyes. It felt familiar to me, like an old friend returning after a long absence.

But then, in an instant, its friendly façade melted away. It bared its canines in a menacing snarl. Its gaze fixed on Oz with an intensity that sent fear coursing through me.

Oz's muscles tensed beneath my hands. A wave of apprehension washed over me. He was poised to confront the panther, his instincts urging him into action. As his grip tightened once, a vision seized hold of my mind.

The shop faded away, replaced by the imposing walls of a castle. Oz stood before me, transformed into his sleek panther form, his fur glistening ebony in the dim light. Across from him, a golden jaguar loomed, its eyes gleaming with a feral hunger.

"I believe my best friend has come to challenge me for your hand," said the jaguar in a deep baritone.

In a blur of motion, violence erupted, blood staining the pristine floors of the castle. I couldn't see the carnage, but I knew in my heart that the victor was not Oz.

I snapped back to reality just as Oz moved to strike. Bile was in my throat, the acid robbing me of words. This wasn't a castle, but I knew the outcome would be the same. I reached out with my magic, reasoning that fur was like thread. Maybe I could tighten the beast's hair until it felt like a snatched weave?

I raised my hands. Magic flowed to my fingertips. And stopped there.

To my surprise, the jaguar was not flesh and fur. It was cold metal; a construction of gears and wires fashioned into the shape of a fearsome predator.

I looked down at the ring on my hand. I'd bought it at

the local market years ago. It had been too small then. But just as my magic allowed me to tailor thread, I'd been able to manipulate the metal until the band fit me perfectly.

Raising my hand at the advancing metallic behemoth, I felt the pulsing energy of the machine course through me. Holding my fingers out and erect, I halted its advance, freezing it in its tracks. Then I brought all five of my fingers into a ball, unleashing a torrent of magic, twisting and contorting the metal until it crumpled and buckled under my command.

Slowly, Oz lowered his fist. He cocked his head to the side as he looked at the fallen enemy. Then he looked over at me. A small smile played at the corner of his mouth. It grew as he assessed me anew.

I'd never felt sexier in any outfit than I did as he looked at me. Not at what I wore, but what I'd done. Seeing pride in my man's eyes was hotter than seeing desire.

"Look at what you did!"

In an act of déjà vu, Oz once again swept me behind him. He placed me closer to the defunct metal jaguar and faced off against the darkness. What emerged from the dark was a lanky man. He was tall and wiry. A cap on his head gave him more height with the gizmos coming out of it; a monocle, a pair of tweezers — was that a laser gun?

The man's hands were stained with grease. His clothes were pristine, covered mostly by a dingy smock. The best word to describe him would've been dapper. He looked like he'd come out of an early nineteenth century sepia toned film.

"All that hard work now a heap on the floor." He glowered at us, censor on his face like he was scolding disobedient children. "Where am I going to get the metal to prepare him?"

"I'd be more worried about keeping my head on my shoulders if I were you." Oz's voice was low and menacing.

I wondered if the man had heard it. He held a controller of some kind in his hand. His fingers flicked and switched at the gears.

"I'm a human living in No Man's Land with no affiliation. That was my security system."

"It was about to attack my mate."

The man gave a huff and marched toward the defunct jaguar robot. Oz snaked a hand out to grab him, but I caught his forearm. Just as I'd gotten the sense that the jaguar was harmless, I got the same sense about the man.

To prove me right, once the man reached his metal creation, he pried open its mouth to reveal a hollow cavity. "It was all for show. You were in no real harm."

We might not have been in harm, but this human was. The growl that came from Oz was low and out of patience. I wrapped my hand tighter around his biceps. All fear was gone from my person. I was too busy grinning that he'd just told another living soul that I was his mate.

This was the first time I'd been claimed so publicly. Ken preferred to spend our dates indoors. Preferably on my couch, eating my snacks, eyes glued to my entertainment center. We'd never gone out dancing, unless it was at the club—and very rarely at that.

"It's fine. He's fixable," said the human, brushing oil off his hand before extending it to Oz. "Name's Perseus."

Oz looked at that hand like he wanted to bite it off.

"I'm Stella, and this is Oz."

Oz rounded on me. His eyes were like cut glass as he glared at me. I knew without him saying that I shouldn't give strangers our real names. He was right, of course. But honestly, I was too thrilled that we were doing the silent communication thing that long-time lovers did.

"Stella, Latin word for star. Often associated with brightness and guidance, much like a constellation in the night sky."

In response, I giggled. Perseus was a charmer. A charmer who was about to have his head bitten off by a grumpy panther shifter.

"We're looking for a way to get to Chicago," I said before Oz could open his mouth.

Perseus responded with a crooked smile. He beckoned us toward the back of the shop. Oz stepped in front of me, his trust in the quirky human a faint line. Until he saw what was behind the curtain.

The Pegasus stood before us, a marvel of mechanical ingenuity and fantastical design. Its form was a maze of intricate gears, shimmering wings, and powerful engines, blending together in a mesmerizing display of craftsmanship. It was exactly as I'd seen it in my head.

CHAPTER 32

Oz

My fingers trailed along the frigid, metallic surface of the Pegasus flying contraption. I'd hoped the metal would ground me. It didn't. My panther remained close to the surface.

It didn't feel the need to stalk Stella at the moment. She stood chatting with the human inventor. I had to acknowledge that the man was smarter than he looked. First with the metallic panther security system then to the flying horse that would carry us away shortly. What clinched Perseus's intelligence for me was the distance he kept between himself and Stella. Though only human, apparently the man knew a shifter male in the throes of the mating dance when he saw it. Plus, I could still snap his neck with little effort, if necessary.

No, the panther was on edge because of the calm that had settled over me. Less than an hour ago, I'd been resigned to slaughter my king, my best friend, as I thought he prowled toward me and what was mine. Even after I'd seen it wasn't Dion, I still felt no remorse for my intended actions.

For the second time in as many days, Stella had saved me. If I were keeping score, we were even. She was the only other person in this universe who had stuck her neck out for me.

And now, in just a few days' time, I would be delivering this bright treasure into the careless arms of a man I knew would break her heart. That would be, once Dion emerged from his slumber, likely entangled with the women who shared his bed for that night.

That was why I felt no remorse, I told myself. Dion was going to hurt Stella. He would be another in the line of men who had cheated on her, lied to her, and used her.

Inside my belly, my panther growled low. I hung my head, knowing the meaning of that growl. I was lying to her right now by omission.

What if that truth never got to see the light of day? What if I could keep her to myself? It was devotion she wanted. I seriously doubted my king could give that to her. I knew with a certainty that I could. That I would.

"You two are lucky to have made it out of the Cross-roads when you did," Perseus was saying. "The seal to Tartarus was breached."

Tartarus was the home of Pandora's Prison, where shadow shifters resided. If the shadow kind had come into this world, then Earth had a whole new slew of problems to contend with. Maybe Arcadia was safest for Stella after all.

"I heard that shadow shifters flooded into the Cross-roads. Those who were present at the time of the portal's opening, they... changed. Humans and supernaturals alike developed abilities with death-related powers. Some supernaturals found their existing powers heightened beyond what they were born to do."

The implications of Perseus's words sank in like a lead weight. We had been there just as the portal had opened. I doubted any of the magic had touched me. But Stella had said her visions were stronger.

She sauntered toward me now. I allowed my gaze to linger over each of her curves. As always, she was polished and pristine, as though she'd stepped right out of my dreams. When she reached me, she put her hand to my chest. My fool heart leaped toward her, as was now its custom.

The organ had shifted from a blood pumping mechanism into a dog. I was Stella's pet, wagging its tail excitedly for any morsel of attention.

She rose on her tiptoes and planted a quick kiss at the corner of my mouth. It took everything in me not to sink my claws into her and pull her closer. I wanted to—needed to—devour her.

"Perseus said there are snacks inside the shop. You want something?"

I shook my head. She pressed another kiss to my mouth and then disappeared into the shop, leaving me alone with Perseus and the looming contraption that was going to carry us to Chicago. The inventor bustled around the Pegasus, his hands moving deftly as he made last-minute adjustments. The metallic beast loomed over us, its gears whirring like a conspirator in my and Stella's escape plan. As it looked down at me with glass eyes, I got the sense it knew of the alterations I was making to that plan.

"What do you know about the House of Earth and Emerald?" I aimed for a disinterested tone, but any shifter could've scented my urgency at the inquiry. Luckily, Perseus was human.

"The House of Earth and Emerald? It's a sanctuary of sorts, hidden away from prying eyes. Mostly made up of shifters. More independent than pack mentality. They only unite for big things and won't take on people who'll cause *problems*. It's popular for its lack of rules or restraints."

I didn't miss how he emphasized problems. It was clear, looking at the two of us, that Stella and I were running from something. We were actually running from a number of somethings.

I didn't want Stella to spend the rest of her life running. I wanted her to have the house she'd dreamed of. It wouldn't be a palace. She'd said she'd stay in the shack with me. I could offer her more than a shack. First I had to find a House that would take us in.

"The female chancellor that presides has three mates," Perseus continued. "The House is headquartered near New York City. Not too far off from Chicago for Peggy to get you there. For a slightly higher price, of course."

Of course. No matter where I was in this universe, there was always a price to be paid. If that was all it took to keep my mate safe and by my side, I'd pay it.

I was protecting not only my mate's physical safety; I was protecting her heart, too. If we disappeared into another House, we would have protection from Ken and his vamps. But we would also have sanctuary from the panther king.

CHAPTER 33

Stella

"This lever here controls your ascent and descent. Pull up to rise, push down to lower. Keep it smooth, or you'll get a jerky flight."

Oz nodded, his eyes following every one of Perseus's movements, committing them to memory. His jet-black hair framed his chiseled features, casting shadows that accentuated the intensity in his eyes. Those eyes, like molten gold, were entirely focused on the task at hand. When he looked up at me, I saw the panther inside him. The corner of his lips quirked up ever so slightly. It was all cat, a feline smirk that told me I was the ball of yarn he was looking forward to playing with.

I pressed my thighs together, eager to get up in the air so that I could be alone with my panther. Perseus continued, pointing to a series of buttons and dials.

"These dials control your speed. The Pegasus can go fast, but I'd start slow until you get the hang of it. And this button here"—he tapped a red button on the dashboard—"is your emergency stop. Only use it if you absolutely need to—it's got a bit of a jolt."

Oz grunted in response.

"And keep an eye on the fuel gauge. If it hits red, you'll need to land immediately or risk crashing. Magic can only do so much in this world."

"What's this do?" I pointed to what looked like a hand-sized television screen.

"It's for communication. But it's defunct." Perseus clapped his hands together. "All right then, you're all set. Safe travels, and maybe keep the flying to the clouds, huh? Draws less attention."

"Thanks, Perseus," I said. "For everything."

He opened his mouth. Then appeared to think better and closed it. Instead, he opened his arms and gave me a squeeze. I squeezed him back. Perseus let me go and turned to Oz. Once again, he spread his arms wide and gave Oz a sultry grin. I'd caught the inventor checking out my man's ass a couple of times in the last few hours.

Oz grunted and turned away. He reached out a hand to me. I looked at his large palm. There were calluses and cuts spread out along his life line. My fingertips landed on the end of that lifeline. I reached until I was at the beginning of the line. Then Oz's hand clamped around mine.

The wicker basket beneath my feet felt surprisingly sturdy as I settled into the belly of the Pegasus. From above came the gentle warmth of the burner flames that would fly the contraption. The burner ignited with a soft whoosh. The ground beneath us slipped away as we ascended into the sky. With each passing moment, the world below grew smaller, the distant horizon beckoning us onward.

And then we were flying.

For effect, Perseus had the horse's wings beat, though they were completely ineffectual as part of what made the machine fly. It was all gas and sparks and gears, things I didn't know about. Not because I was a girl; because I was a witch. Magic ruled everything around me.

The view took my breath away. No Man's Land stretched out beneath us, a tapestry of human ruins and natural beauty, its scars and rough edges softened by the distance. From up here, the world was peaceful, serene, a contrast to the dangers and struggles we'd faced on the ground.

I leaned back, allowing myself to be mesmerized by the vast expanse of sky around us. The air was cooler up here, a refreshing change from the stifling atmosphere of the city. It was a rare moment of tranquility, a brief escape from the chaos of our lives.

Up here in the clouds, every worry fell away. Oz's black hair danced in the breeze. Had it grown longer in the few days that we'd known each other? The stubble on his chin certainly had darkened. It made him even sexier.

He turned from the controls and prowled toward me. I inhaled with anticipation, ready to pick up where we had left off in the hotel room. There was no way we could be disturbed by someone picking the locks or coming after us now. I was finally going to sink my teeth into my panther.

Oz reached for me. Then past me. There was a strap behind the seat. He pulled it forward and over my torso. I heard a click. I was trapped in place by the seatbelt.

"Kinky," I purred.

"I want to make sure you're safe." His voice was barely audible over the hum of the engines.

"We're in the air. No one can even reach me."

There had been a dragon in these parts not long ago. But that fire breather had been closer to Portland. And I didn't think it ate people... on purpose.

Oz smiled as he sat down beside me. He didn't buckle himself in. His gaze returned to the horizon. The weight of his responsibilities remained heavy on his shoulders, even though we were airborne.

"Hey, Oz? Wanna join the mile high club?"

"Stella," he warned.

"It's a full moon tonight. I'll be in heat. Figured we might as well get a head start."

He turned to me then. His index finger traced my brow. There was barely an inch between us. I moved to close the distance but was thwarted by the seatbelt.

Oz grinned.

"You are a kinky bastard, aren't you?"

His grin mellowed as he traced from my cheekbones down the slope of my nose. "I've been thinking about that."

"The kinky things you're going to do to me?"

"We won't make it to Portland before you go into heat."

"*If* I go into heat. I've never shifted."

"You've been in heat since the moment we met."

"Hey!" I swatted at his chest.

Oz caught my hand and pressed a kiss to each fingertip. "What if we went to Earth and Emerald instead?"

I shrugged, savoring the feel of his lips against my fingers. "You're in charge of the destination. All I care about is that I'm with you."

There was a look I had never seen on a man's face

before. Oz brushed the hair out of my face, then cupped my cheek. "I'm going to spend the rest of my life deserving you, Stella."

"I'm going to spend the rest of my life trying to make you smile."

Miracle of miracles, a small smile landed on his face. It was big and wide and beautiful. I was instantly addicted to it. I was going to do whatever it took to get myself a hit of his smile every day.

I gasped dramatically. "There it is. I'm winning already."

He chuckled. It was the first time he'd laughed. It was a wonderful sound. And I would get to hear it for the rest of our lives. I was a lucky girl. So, of course, that's when the Pegasus jerked sharply.

Oz was flung to the side. I remained exactly where I was, held in my seat by the belt. Oz quickly righted himself and grabbed for the controls. His features went from concern to frantic. I could feel why. The horse was now flying in a different direction.

As Oz struggled to regain control of the Pegasus, the flying machine's behavior became increasingly erratic. There was a flicker and a pop emanating from the defunct television screen. Perseus appeared in a flurry of static.

"Stella, Oz," Perseus's voice crackled through the speakers, his expression grim. "I'm sorry, I really am. There's a bounty out for the two of you. The Crimson Roses will be waiting for you just outside of Chicago."

The words hit like a physical blow. The mix of betrayal and shock was a gut punch. I'd thought we were safe. What good were my visions if they led me directly into danger?

Oz's hands tightened on the controls, his jaw clenched in anger. "I knew I didn't like you."

"Well, I like you," said Perseus. "So I put in a failsafe. There's a manual override. It's under the main control panel. It'll let you land the Pegasus a few miles away from where I told them you'd be dropped off. It's the best I can do."

CHAPTER 34

Oz

The ground rushed toward us at a terrifying speed. I worked the manual override, trying to steady the Pegasus for a less catastrophic landing. The whir of gears and the roar of wind were deafening. Through it all, Stella never cried out. She never whimpered.

The seatbelt held her tight. Her gaze never left mine. I felt more than saw the trust in her eyes. She didn't doubt me. My heart pounded against my ribcage, each beat a thunderous echo of the adrenaline surging through my veins.

I made a split-second decision. As the ground loomed closer, I shifted into my panther form. My body contorted and expanded. Fur bristled along my spine. Wrapping my body around Stella, I shielded her with every ounce of my being. We braced for impact.

The ground met us with a bone-jarring thud that reverberated through my entire body. The world became a blur of motion and noise as we tumbled. The Pegasus crashed around us, breaking metal and shattering glass.

Everything was still, save for the pounding in my head and the labored breaths escaping my lungs. Stella was nestled against me, her body unharmed against my fur. Relief washed over me, followed swiftly by a surge of protective urgency.

But there was no time to savor our survival. The sound of boots impacting the ground cut through the haze of my disorientation. The vampires were moving in fast. Ken and his men were coming for us.

With a growl rumbling deep in my throat, I shook off the impact. My senses were heightened, each sound and smell acutely clear in the aftermath of the crash. The scent of damp earth and crushed foliage mixed with the more ominous odors of sweat and the iron of blood—the unmistakable signs of our pursuers.

Stella stirred beneath me. Gone was the trust in her eyes. Now there was fear.

"They're coming."

We were exposed, vulnerable in the wreckage of the Pegasus. The ground beneath my paws was soft. The metallic tang of the gun held by one of Ken's men cut through the natural smells of the forest.

Seriously? Someone brought a gun to a supernatural fight? Now I was pissed.

Ken's voice broke through the tense silence. "Set it to stun," he commanded. "We can bleed him and make a fortune off his blood."

My growl made the ground tremble. They were stupider than I figured if they thought they could stun a panther with a human weapon. I was stronger than a natural born animal. There was magic in the blood they planned to make a fortune from.

Stella's presence behind me was a constant reminder of what was at stake. Like hell they were going to take me. They would have to kill me before I'd leave her unprotected. Pity for them that I wasn't easy to kill.

I crouched, ready to spring. My muscles coiled like tightly wound springs. Every fiber of my being was focused on the man with the gun. But my canines ached to take a bite out of Ken.

The gunman aimed the weapon at me. His finger tightened on the trigger. I didn't hesitate. I pounced.

I became a blur of speed and power, hurtling toward him with all the force of my beast. The gun went off, a sharp crack that pierced the air. Stella's scream echoed through the trees, a sound that cut to my core. I realized my mistake halfway through my pounce.

It wasn't a human gun. There was magic in the barrel. It smelled the same as the spell the boat witch had cast.

It was going to happen again. I was going to be left paralyzed and powerless.

But somehow I was still moving. I wasn't stunned. My claws struck home. The gun fell to the ground, along with the hand of its wielder.

One by one, the triumphant smirks fell from the faces of our attackers. A few even took steps back. Ken's jaw was tight as he regarded me. His glare lifted to Stella.

Stella. She was standing now. Her pristine blouse ripped after our fall from the sky. Her elegant shoulders were on display, as was the bite mark I'd given her.

The bite mark. The tang of her blood on my tongue. That's why the stun gun and the spell housed inside of it didn't work on me.

Now it was the taste of adrenaline on my tongue. With a low growl, I lunged into action. The rest of the men surrounding us were armed with fangs and speed. But so was I.

I engaged another attacker, the rush of combat fueling my movements. The man swung at me with a club. I dodged, swift and agile, closing the distance between us in a heartbeat. My jaws clamped down on his arm, the force of my bite sending him sprawling to the ground with a cry of pain.

But I was outnumbered, ten to one. For every man I took down, two more took his place. They circled around me, like a pack of hyenas trying to corner a lion, their snarls and hisses the soundtrack to this battle to the death.

I moved like a whirlwind, darting in and out of their reach, always keeping Stella at my back so that no one could pass. Each hit I landed was a message—I was not to be trifled with. And I would not be stolen from.

Stella was mine.

I launched myself at another assailant, taking him down with a powerful swipe of my paw, which was the size of his head. The crunch of bone was a satisfying sound. But the men kept coming, relentless in their pursuit.

The strain of the fight was beginning to take its toll. My muscles screamed along with my victims. My breath came in ragged gasps. But I didn't relent. I couldn't. Stella's safety, our future together, hung in the balance.

It was this divided attention that gave Ken his opening. Out of the corner of my eye, I saw him make a beeline for Stella.

CHAPTER 35

Stella

Ken's hands clamped down on my arms, his grip iron-tight and unyielding. I struggled against him, trying to pull away, but his strength was overpowering. The smell of his cologne, once familiar and now repulsive, filled my nostrils.

I needed both my hands to conjure my tailoring spell. Not that it would've done much good on him. His clothes were already too tight. Even if I squeezed the crotch of his pants, it wouldn't do much to disturb his little dick.

With my free hand, I reached into the purse that was still slung across my shoulder. There were two weapons in there. I grabbed for the first and slammed it with all my might into Ken's chest. Unfortunately, the broken heel wasn't sharp enough to pierce the empty cavern of his heart. All I got for my efforts was a snort from him.

"Let go of me, Ken." Anger clawed at me from the inside.

"Don't be like that, babe. Remember how good we were together?"

"Good? You cheated on me."

"I never cheated on you." He laughed, a cold, hollow sound that echoed through the trees. He twisted my arm. I pressed closer to him in search of relief. "You were always the other woman, Stella."

How had I not noticed how greasy his hair was? How had I missed the plastic look of his brows, like he'd had an old-fashioned human surgery to even out wrinkles? How had I not realized his skin looked sunburned, even though he was a hundred-year-old vampire who stayed out of sunlight?

"Now that I know the real value of your blood, you're going to be working for me in a... different capacity."

His glance went over my head. Oz was fighting a vicious battle against three vampires. He was holding his own, but there were another three vamps surrounding the fight. He wasn't going to last long.

Ken's laughter was maniacal, like a villain in a bad movie. I shuddered at the sound, my skin crawling at his touch. How could I have ever thought I loved this vile creature?

"At least now Uziah won't make me fuck you to get you to comply. That'll keep Peaches happy."

Peaches? The hairy Neanderthal? It was the thought of that woman's hairy hoo-ha more than anything that made me snap. And by snap, I meant bones and muscles and tendons.

Ken must have heard it, too. He let go of my arm. His eyes went huge as he took a step back from me.

The other vamps jerked like they'd heard a dog whistle. All of their gazes snapped to Ken, and then to me. I was elated, as this would give Oz the advantage. But Oz held still, his gaze transfixed on me as well.

It was then I thought it prudent to focus on myself as well. Because something was happening to me.

It began with a sensation of nausea swirling in the pit of my belly. I heaved, my body convulsing with the effort to vomit up the overwhelming force building within me. I regained my composure, only to be struck by another wave of intense discomfort. Doubling over, I clutched my stomach.

Through the haze of pain, I felt more than heard Oz's growl of concern behind me. I tried to open my mouth to reassure him, but the words caught in my throat. Something was happening to my mouth. Something was happening to my hands, to my legs, to my whole body.

"Let it happen, goddess."

That was Oz's voice in my head. I heard him clearly. Logically, I knew he hadn't spoken those words out loud. He was in his panther form.

My bones broke and bent. Muscles twisted and reformed. Each movement was accompanied by an agony that threatened to consume me whole. It was as if my very essence was being torn apart and remolded into something new, something wild.

The pain reached a fever pitch. And then, as swiftly as it had begun, it was over. In its wake, I was disoriented. I lifted my gaze, and the world didn't look the same.

The forest was no longer green. Everything looked gray. Except for the tops of the wildflowers sprinkled around the clearing. Those were the most vibrant yellow I'd ever seen in my life. The sky above was bluer than I had ever known it to be, even though it was the moon that was high and not the sun. The canopy of trees was all shadows and light, its intricate patterns woven in shades of charcoal and slate. The ground beneath my paws was a patchwork of earthy browns and soft, sandy yellows, punctuated by the occasional splash of gray from fallen leaves and branches.

Wait. Paws? Yup, those were paws on my feet. My hands, too. All around me, my pink outfit lay in tattered shreds. I doubted my magic could put that back together.

She was finally here. My cat. I saw the golden sheen of my fur. But I couldn't make out any spots. Shouldn't I have black spots? My mother had told me my father's animal form had both gold and black spots.

I wanted a mirror. I wanted to run to the lake I could scent in the distance. I wanted to see all of me. Of course I did. I was still vain when it came to appearances. But there was still the matter of the battle going on around me.

It had paused for my transformation. Now that my jaguar was out, the vamps were shaking off their shock and reforming their ranks.

I wasn't a fighter. At least I hadn't been before that portal had opened and wreaked havoc on my world. Ken had taken my self-worth from me, but I'd be damned if he would take my fated mate.

I sprang forward, testing my new form. All I felt was strength and power coursing through my muscles as I easily took down one of the vamps who had been moving in on Oz. My second kill was done with the same fluid grace, each movement instinctual and precise. This was easy, the fighting as well as the killing.

From my peripheral, I saw that Oz had stepped back, letting me take down each and every vamp. His maw looked like it was stretched into a feline grin of pride as he watched. Then his paw struck out. He caught Ken by the shirt tails as he tried to run. With one massive paw, Oz pinned the coward in place until I was ready for him.

The forest, once filled with the sounds of confrontation, now echoed with their retreating footsteps and panicked breaths of the one who got away. That one was not Ken.

I prowled up to my former lover. He pleaded with his eyes, with his voice. None of it penetrated to the woman inside my beast's belly.

In the end, I did show mercy. I made it quick.

CHAPTER 36

Oz

The smell of Ken's blood was foul. The sight of it made me grin. My girl looked fearsome standing over his decapitated carcass. The blood on her mouth made her far more beautiful than any of the cosmetics she painted on her face. I wanted to wipe the vamp's blood off and replace it with mine, then kiss her senseless.

I took a step toward her... and promptly crashed into the forest floor.

My nose fell into the armpit of a dismembered vamp. I couldn't remember if the limb had been torn by my canines or Stella's. The battle was all a blur. And now that she was safe, my injuries caught up with me.

Lying there on the forest floor, battered and bruised from the fight, my gaze fixed on her. In her jaguar form, Stella was a sight to behold, a breathtaking blend of power and grace. The moonlight filtered through the canopy of trees, casting her sleek, spotless fur in a luminescent glow. The golden highlights of her fur danced and shimmered with a life of their own.

I must be dying. I didn't notice things like shimmering light. I did notice everything about this woman, both in her human and animal forms. The undeniable fact about my fated mate was the uniqueness of her spots, or rather lack thereof. Her coat was identical to Dion's. Their royal spotless coat was a mark of lineage and destiny. It was irrefutable proof that she was more than just a witch with rare powers; she was destined for the throne, born to be a queen.

Stella padded over to me, her movements graceful despite the traces of vampire blood marring her fur. The same blood matted my fur. It was her animal's first time meeting mine. I wondered if she'd recognize me in this state. Even if she didn't and decided to take me out, I'd go willingly. I was dead serious when I said I would die for this woman.

She bent her head toward me. I wanted to tell her that she was a queen, a goddess among our kind, that she bowed to no one.

She nuzzled the side of my face, clearly sniffing me to see who I was. Decision made that I meant her no harm, she licked at the blood on my maw. Her face crumbled and puckered, much like in her human form when something displeased her. In a very human gesture, she spat out Ken's blood, her rejection of her ex complete.

I wanted to chuckle at the sight, at her defiance in the face of danger. Maybe I did chuckle, but the laughter caught in my throat as I tasted my own blood, nearly choking on it.

Magic filled the clearing as she shifted from animal to human. She was completely nude under the moonlight. I did choke then, nearly swallowing my tongue this time. I made the beast recede and took back my human form.

This was not how I planned to be naked with this woman for the first time.

I could barely speak, let alone move. Every part of my body ached. Even my eyelids. Now that my body was flesh again, I saw where the damage had been done.

My chest rose and fell with labored breaths. There was a puncture wound in my chest from vampire fangs. I felt the pulsating agony in my torso where the flesh was ripped. My arms lay heavy at my sides, ripped to shreds by vampires' claws. I tried to sit up, but my abdomen protested with a sharp twinge, the tender flesh a battleground of cuts and bites inflicted by my dead adversaries.

Both of my legs ached. There was no way I could get up. No way I could run. No way I could protect my mate from the next battle. Because there would be more. At least one had gotten away. I knew Ken wasn't the one in charge. His boss would send more now that they knew what Stella was.

"Shhhh," Stella soothed. "I've got you. I can fix you."

My lips stretched at the thought. I'd always been broken. Since the moment I'd been born, things hadn't worked out right for me. This last battle, this had been what my life was leading me to: to her. I just had one more thing to do in this world, and that was to get Stella to safety.

Warmth flooded me when her fingers touched my skin. I was feverish for her. But the heat wasn't filled with desire. It didn't set off the alarm bells of death. It felt rejuvenating.

Magic flowed between me and Stella. I watched as her fingers hovered over me, knitting my wounds back together. The pain was a dull throb. Then pretty soon nonexistent.

"Those wounds were mortal." My voice sounded like gravel being put through a glass strainer.

"And now they're mended."

Stella ran her hands down my chest. The gashes that had given up pints of my blood were now closed. She hesitated over the scars my mother had given me. There was a question in her eyes. She didn't ask it. She moved her hand from my chest and cupped my cheek.

"I'm not letting anyone take you away from me."

The fierceness of her words replenished me more than a blood transfusion. I sat up and pulled her toward me. She wrapped herself around me, holding me tightly.

"You're mine." Her words were an incantation. They wrapped around me like a spell, binding us even tighter.

"I'm yours," I swore.

"I don't want you to die for me. I want you to live with me. Do you understand me?"

I smiled into her neck, breathing her in. "Whatever you wish, princess."

She pulled back, her features stern. Stern Stella was hot. The determined set to her lips made me want to bite them.

"I'll scrounge us up some clothes," she said as she climbed out of my embrace.

I watched her lush ass as she moved through the clearing, peering down at the dead bodies. She grabbed a pair of jeans from one guy. She slipped into them and then used her magic to mold them to her form. Next she reached for a shirt, but when I saw who it came from, I growled.

"What?" she said, holding up Ken's silk shirt—really, what man came to a battle wearing silk? "I picked this out for him. Might as well take advantage of it."

"I will not allow my mate to carry the scent of an asswipe."

"Fair point."

She scrounged around some more until we were both clothed and then used her magic to do away with the blood and dirt and tailor the fit.

"We can't go to Earth and Emerald," I told her once we were dressed.

She didn't even look up. She simply shrugged her shoulders. "You're the captain of the ship. I'm simply the cruise director."

"The activities that keep happening around us is why we can't stay here. I need to get you off world. I need to get you to Arcadia."

I purposefully didn't say to Panthera. Though how we'd live in the realm while staying out of the claws of the panther king, I had no idea. Stella's safety remained my number one priority. I might not keep her in luxury, but I would keep her. And I would never break her heart.

CHAPTER 37

Stella

It felt like a bullet being fired out of a gun. The world was a blur of colors and shapes, streaking past in a dizzying whirl. I braced myself in my seat. Not because I was afraid, but because I had the suspicion that she could run faster.

The animal inside me huffed that she could. All my life she'd lain asleep in my belly. I'd felt the phantom of her whiskers twitch, heard her sigh, even felt the velvet of her tongue loll out a time or two. Now she sat up, itching to break free and run.

I kept rubbing at my skin, certain there was still fur there instead of flesh. Everything was brighter and duller at the same time. The contrast of colors was sharp, but the saturation was off. The blues and greens of peoples' outfits looked like they'd been dyed straight from the sky and fields.

A woman strolled through the train car. Her outfit was tailored to fit her body. The fabric was quality. The sneer she sent down from the slope at the top of her nose told me she thought herself important. The raised brow she gave me and my ensemble told me she found me lacking.

To her credit, I was dressed in men's clothing. Even though I'd done my best to fit them, I was sure I looked like I was wearing my lover's clothing after a walk of shame. When I saw my lover walking toward me, all I felt was heat and desire and gratitude, all rolled into one.

There was no room in my heart to deal with the shame or the shade from Ms. Hoity Toity. The love I felt for Oz was too big. The love I saw reflected back at me from his gaze blinded me to anyone else's judgment.

The man who walked behind the woman judged me much differently. His once-over became a twice-over, his glance lingering on my bare shoulder. The bite of his lower lip was a clear offer.

He looked me up and down a third time, then winked. It was a bold, uninvited gesture. One that I did not return. Before I could react, Oz's low growl filled the space between us. It was a protective sound that made the guy look away quickly, his momentary bravado faltering under Oz's intimidating stare.

"Are you going to do the whole growly *you're mine* thing now?"

"No," Oz said, holding out his hand to me. "Because I am yours."

He tugged me to standing. Brushing first a kiss to my temple, then to the side of my mouth, Oz pulled me close and whispered in my ear, loud enough for the man in the next seat to hear. "I sensed you were about to bite his head off, anyway. I did him a favor."

That was true. Especially after what I did to my last ex. I knew Oz was thinking exactly that by the grin on his face. I kissed that grin full-on.

The whistle of the train was a sharp, piercing sound that cut through the hum of conversations. It was an express train, a straight shot to Portland, our temporary sanctuary before we journeyed onward to Arcadia.

Inside the train's dining car, the atmosphere was a blend of the functional and the comforting. The car itself was a long, narrow space, with tables lined up along the windows. Each table was draped with a simple, clean cloth, the minimalistic setting providing a sense of order amidst the chaos of our lives. The lighting was soft and subdued, casting a gentle glow over the passengers, many of whom were absorbed in quiet conversations or lost in their own thoughts.

At one end of the car was a small counter where a barista worked efficiently, the sound of steaming milk and the clink of cups like their own conversation. The array of pastries and sandwiches on display added a visual appeal, their colors and textures promising a taste of normalcy. It was more civilized than most of No Man's Land. Had I known I would be treated like this, I might have opted to spend my days riding the rails.

Passengers sat or moved around, some gazing out of the large windows at the passing scenery, others engrossed in books or digital devices powered by magic or the sun. There was a hum of subdued activity, a collective sense of being in transit, of being between places and perhaps even between destinies.

Our table, positioned near the window, offered a view of the ever-changing landscape, but my focus was entirely on Oz. The man was slicing my food with meticulous care, his movements precise and deliberate. Each cut of the knife through the food was a small act of tenderness, a silent expression of his care for me.

"Where did you go?" I ask.

"I sent a message to the king to let him know of our imminent arrival."

"Why did the king send you to get me?"

Oz pressed his lips together, his concentration on the fork in his right hand as he stacked the perfect bite for me.

"Is it because of my father?"

Oz glanced up at the same time that he lifted the fork to my mouth. I ate obediently, my gaze widening slightly at the flavorful bite. Oz smiled as he watched me chew and then swallow.

"My father died when I was very young," I said as he built me another perfect bite. "He was murdered."

The sound of metal against porcelain made me wince. Oz gripped the fork tighter and then began rebuilding the perfect bite for me.

"My mother said it was because of his blood. I didn't understand it when I was younger. But now I think I do. There's something about my blood, isn't there? It's resistant to magic."

Oz lifted the fork to my mouth.

I ate dutifully, chewing the food as I mulled over the possibilities. "I really am a princess."

He didn't confirm it. But he didn't need to.

"Ken never drank from me. None of my vampire boyfriends did."

Oz growled low in his throat.

I took the fork from him and began building him a forkful. The delectable piece of grilled salmon should be shared. The vegetables accompanying the dish—crisp green asparagus, bright yellow bell peppers, and cherry tomatoes that glistened like little rubies—were vibrant as well as delicious. I lifted the fork to his mouth, and after a moment, he opened for me. I knew he liked it when his brow raised.

"Sometimes I think humans had the right of it with using paper and metal for currency. We're barbarians here using blood and teeth and hair."

In response, Oz poured a sample of wine into his glass, tasting it before filling my glass. It was a deep red, the color of passion. It swirled in the glass like liquid velvet.

"Are you trying to get me drunk?" I asked with a playful smile, the tension of our situation momentarily forgotten in the warmth of the moment.

"No, I'm just making sure you have everything you need."

I looked into his eyes, those deep pools of sincerity and strength. He was always putting me before him, even in this small way of feeding me and making sure I had something to drink. No, not just something to drink—the best.

"I have everything I've ever wanted." The wine tasted like a promise, a vow of shared futures now that the battles were over. I reached across the table, taking Oz's hand in mine. The connection was electric, a current that ran between us, unspoken but deeply felt. "Let's go to our sleeping compartment."

He swallowed. His throat worked, like he was trying to come up with some excuse and failing.

"You said you're mine. You claimed me." I fingered the mark on my shoulder. "I want to claim you."

CHAPTER 38

Oz

The quiet snick of the door closing was like the bell tolling. I knew my time was running short. In the days, the hours, the moments I had left, I'd determined I would spend every second worshiping the woman standing at the edge of the narrow bed.

Stella disrobed in front of me as though it was the most natural thing in the world and not the exquisite gift that it was. First, her shoulders were revealed along with my claiming mark. The scar had looked angry when I'd first left it there. Now it blended perfectly with her honeyed skin, like she'd been born with the mark.

The silk fabric of the shirt slipped from her body. Her lush breasts with the caramel tips greeted me. The nipples looked more like fingers beckoning me closer, closer. I stepped toward her, no longer able to keep away.

She wasn't sin incarnate. I was. If anyone would have to

pay for what was between us, it would only be me. I accepted my fate.

As I advanced on her, my gaze traveled down her curves to her stomach. I bit the inside of my lip at the sight of her belly button. I couldn't wait to dip my tongue in that hollow divot. I wondered if she would giggle or moan. Soon, I'd find out.

But first, I wanted another taste of her real treasure. She was bare between her thighs, which gave me a view of the dusky pink heart of her. I needed to swallow. And then swallow again. Didn't matter how many times I did it, I would never cease wanting to taste this woman.

This princess of my race.

This goddess among women.

Stella stood before me, completely nude. My legs went wobbly prepared to give her her due. I should be on my knees.

I let her pull up my shirt. She saw my scars and ran a hand and then her lips over them. I hissed at the contact. It was as though those wounds had never hurt. As though they'd been put there for her pleasure.

She undid the buttons of my pants and bent as she shoved them down. She stayed down on her knees, which bothered me at first. I was the one meant to worship her. But when she took me into her palm, I decided to give my goddess what she wanted. But not in this way.

I reached down and pulled her up. "Not on your knees."

"But I want to."

"You bow before no one. Do you understand me?"

She nodded. And then her lips were on mine. She kissed me, her lips warm and insistent. Her hands tangled in my hair as she deepened the kiss. My head was spinning with want, my body reeling with the knowledge that it could have.

Right now, she was mine. When we got to Portland, she might choose me still. Even if she didn't, I would be hers until my last breath. I would love her until my heart stopped. There was nothing and no one who could take that away from me.

Our tongues danced together, which was funny since I had never danced a single step in time to a beat in my life. But that's what we were doing together. The music was the pounding of my heart. It wasn't racing. It didn't feel rushed or forced. It felt natural and right. It felt as if we had always been meant to be together.

I broke the kiss, looking into Stella's eyes. In them, I saw the reflection of the rising moon. There was a small voice in the back of my head that wondered if this was all an effect of the moon's pull on her animal nature. I was sure that had something to do with it. But not all.

"I love you," I said.

Her smile was the most beautiful thing I'd ever seen in my life. It took her a couple of times before she could get the words past her throat. "I love you, too. I mean, I really do. Not because I'm supposed to because we're fated and all. Because I actually like you as a person. You're strong and brave. And so thoughtful. I love how you take care of me in the simplest ways. No one's ever done that for me. And you're so fucking sexy. I can't wait to have you inside me."

I ran my knuckles down the side of her face, cherishing each of her features from her eager eyes, to her flaring nostrils, to those supple lips.

"And you're loyal. I don't doubt for a second that you would turn your back on me."

Now it was my turn to choke out the words. "I was loyal to the king. Now all my loyalty is to you."

She smiled, then went up on her toes to kiss me again.

I pressed my index finger to her lips. "Remember that. Promise me, you'll remember that."

"I will. Can I jump your bones now?"

"Yes. You can jump my bones now."

"I'm gonna start with this one."

She wrapped her hand around my erection. Now it was her giving the tug, and I was the one following. She led me to the bed and shoved me down on it.

Stella's body was a masterpiece. I admired every inch of it as she towered over me, completely naked. I had killed for this woman. I would do it again. In a heartbeat.

Her hands trailed up and down my erection. I groaned at the sensation, closing my eyes and letting myself get lost in the pleasure. It was all happening too soon. I didn't want it to be over just as it started. It had been a while for me and never this good.

Just as I thought I had myself under control, she licked my tip. I jackknifed off the bed, taking her with me. But my woman was strong. Or maybe that was the cat peeking out of her eyes.

She pressed me back down on the bed. I fought for control. It was a losing battle because Stella wasn't playing fair.

She had a tight grip on my length, her mouth at the tip. The other hand cupped my balls. There was no way I could win. I was going to have to surrender. That's when her teeth nipped at my flesh.

"You said I could mark you."

My brain was not working. Neither was my throat. The only thing I could get past my lips were moans.

With her fingers still stroking my length, she lifted my ball sack. I felt her lips on the underside of the skin there. And then her teeth.

The pleasure started where her teeth marked me as hers. Then my balls swelled, preparing for release. Only somehow I didn't blow my load.

My mind was so focused on that spot where she had marked her claim on me. All the ecstasy was concentrated there. It was pure joy that went in a loop from her bite to my balls to my cock and back again.

On and on it went like the world's longest orgasm. I don't think I noticed when she lifted her face from my crotch. She let go of my cock, forcing another groan from me. The pleasure was, at this point, becoming painful. Then she sank that lush body down on me, and I came to understand the word nirvana.

Everything faded away. For a brief second, even Stella left my consciousness. What remained was only sensation. Her warmth surrounding my cock ignited every nerve ending inside of me.

It was as if I had been searching for something my entire life, and I had finally found it. There was a sense of completeness, of wholeness, that washed over me. It was more than physical pleasure; it was an ascension. I'd touched death and understood what it truly meant to be alive. All worries, doubts, and fears melted away, replaced by an overwhelming sense of peace and contentment.

I saw stars. It was fitting. Because Stella was now my true north.

CHAPTER 39

Stella

The steady rhythm of the train's movements lulled me into a sense of security. That and the multiple orgasms I'd had made it impossible for me to keep my eyes open. I couldn't tell the difference between the aftershocks of pleasure and the gentle rocking of the train as it made its way across No Man's Land.

Oz's arms around me felt like a shield against the world. His big body offered warmth and protection that no blanket could match. Contentment washed over me, a feeling of safety and belonging that I had never known before.

I felt like I'd won a marathon and received a gold medal. Like I'd done an excellent school report and received an A+. Like I'd solved world peace and was getting a prize.

Because I'd done it. I'd accomplished the dream I'd never dared dream. I'd found a good man with a good heart who would set me on a pedestal and not leave my side.

As though to punctuate that assertion, Oz squeezed me into his side. He nuzzled his nose into my neck and inhaled. I was fast asleep, but I knew this was happening in reality. My dreams were lucid. The connection between us was strong. So it didn't surprise me when I saw him inside my mind's eye.

I found myself in a vast, shadowy space. Unlike the tranquility inside our train car, the air in the dream was thick with tension. Oz was on his knees, his head bowed in submission. Towering over him was a massive jaguar, its fur gold as the sun, its eyes burning with a fierce, angry fire —the pupils black coal.

King Dion.

I'd never met the man. Never seen his face except... in another vision. He was the same man who'd smiled at me in welcome in that other vision. He wasn't smiling down at Oz.

There was a palace in the background. The one I'd seen before, where Oz had taken me in another vision. The two of them were outside the gates. The scent of the forest, damp and earthy, permeated my mind, mingling with a hint of something wild, something primal. The silence was palpable, broken only by Dion's deep, resonant voice.

"What did I tell you about Stella?" King Dion's words were like a thunderclap, echoing around us. The golden jaguar moved his lips. The voice that came out was part man, part animalistic growl.

I knew I was dreaming while lying secure in Oz's arms, but the sound of the panther king's voice held so much command that I felt my knees buckle back in reality.

Oz's voice when he spoke was subdued and tinged with regret. "You told me to take care of her."

It took me a minute to realize that it was my name that

had come out of the king's mouth. They were talking about me.

"Is this what you call taking care of her?" Dion's tone was sharp, cutting through the air.

"Sorry, sire," Oz replied, his posture one of contrition and deference.

"I trusted you with her," Dion continued, his disappointment evident.

The words struck a chord in me, resonating with a haunting familiarity. This conversation was eerily similar to what I'd overheard between Uziah and Ken. The same possessiveness, the same sense of being a pawn in someone else's game.

"Stella is too important." Dion's voice was a low growl.

"I know I screwed up," Oz admitted.

This wasn't a dream. I tried and failed to convince myself it was a nightmare. It was a vision. Deep down, I knew that. What I was seeing in my mind right now was going to happen.

Maybe. Not definitely. I'd been wrong before. Many times.

I wasn't wrong about Oz. I didn't doubt that he loved me. That he would fight to the death for me.

It was my fear, my hangups about my past relationships that were mixed in this vision. There might have been some morsel of truth in there. Perhaps the king was angry with Oz over what had happened to me. A lot had happened over the past few days. But Oz wasn't using me.

He wasn't.

I made myself toss and turn, trying to break out of the vision and wake myself up. The tendrils of the dream had dug in. Getting my eyes to open was a battle. But I was strong now. I had a jaguar awake inside of me.

I woke with a growl in my throat. The battle to wake was so intense that the roar came out as a whimper. That whimper died in my throat when I saw that I was in bed alone.

I swore I heard fate laughing as the dream dissipated like mist in the morning sun. The compartment was dimly lit. The soft glow of the early morning light filtered through the curtains. Oz's absence was a cold, empty space beside me, filling me with a sense of unease.

I sat up, wrapping my arms around myself, trying to shake off the remnants of the vision. There was no need to panic. Oz was not using me. The king was likely upset about all the time it was taking to get me to safety.

That wasn't Oz's fault. He'd gone above and beyond. I'd make sure King Dion knew that. He'd said that I was important. He had to listen to me.

The train continued its relentless journey, the sound of the wheels on the tracks a constant, unyielding reminder that we were moving forward, toward an uncertain future. Oz's absence, his silent departure, added to the growing sense of foreboding.

I rose, moving to the window, watching as the world outside came to life with the dawn. The landscape was a blur of colors and shapes, a fleeting glimpse of a world in constant motion.

Then the landscape became more distinct. The train was slowing down. We weren't in Portland. I knew what I was seeing outside the window was still No Man's Land.

Ruins dotted the horizon, the skeletal remains of buildings and structures long abandoned to nature's reclaiming grasp. Vines creeped up crumbling walls and trees growing through shattered windows. The remnants of civilization lay in ruins, overtaken by the unstoppable forces of growth and decay as humanity went extinct and supernaturals pledged themselves to Houses at the outskirts of the continent.

There was an awful sound of nails on a chalkboard. Except it was iron screaming against iron. The train was coming to a halt.

Looking out the window, I saw why. There was a cloud of dust up ahead. It looked like a tornado. But tornados didn't move like that. They didn't advance in a straight line.

I dressed quickly, for the second time in my life, not bothering to tailor my ill-fitting clothing, and made my way out of the compartment. The narrow corridors of the train were a scene of frantic activity with passengers rushing around, their voices raised in alarm and confusion. I pushed my way through the throng but still got jostled around.

Someone reached for me and got hold of my upper arm. My mind told me to strike out. But my heart knew who it was.

I turned into the face of the man I loved, a smile growing.

Oz wasn't smiling. There was a hint of panic in his golden eyes. "They're coming for you."

CHAPTER 40

Oz

We were so close. Portland was only twenty miles away. I should've known it wouldn't be that easy. Nothing had been easy since the first moment I saw Stella. But every moment, every drop of blood, every scar I'd earned from protecting her had been worth it. If they—whoever they were—thought I'd stop now, they were idiots.

The security guards at the front of the train shuffled and armed themselves, their movements tense and hurried. The metallic clicks of their weapons loading punctuated the screech of the train's wheels. The thundering of whatever was moving toward us kicked up dirt in its trail.

When the cause of the dust was revealed, there was a collective gasp all around the train compartment. Through the window, the world outside was overshadowed by an incredible sight—a pirate ship sailing on sand. Its dark silhouette sliced across the landscape. Its looming presence bore down on us like a behemoth as it emerged from the sandstorm.

The ship's massive sails billowed in the arid breeze, their tattered edges fluttering like the wings of a predatory bird. Each gust of wind stirred up clouds of sand, obscuring the ship in a haze of gritty particles. The hull of the ship rose high above the ruins, casting a long, ominous shadow across the barren landscape. Cracked and sun-bleached wood adorned with rusted metal fittings formed the skeleton of the vessel.

I wasn't from this planet, so I wasn't sure if a land ship was a normal occurrence. A look around at the gaping passengers told me it was out of the norm. Witnessing the tremor in more than one of the security guards told me that we were outmatched.

"It's her," said Stella.

I was about to ask who when I saw a flash of moon silver hair at the bow. It was the boat witch. Even from this distance, I saw her rotted teeth as she grinned.

"She's after me, isn't she?"

I pulled Stella tighter to my body. In another time, I might have laughed at the baffled look on her face. Stella couldn't understand why the witch kept coming. Why the vamps wouldn't let her go. She didn't know who or what she was.

A panther shifter with the blood of a witch, and quite possibly the blood of the gods. I'd seen her coat when she'd shifted. Only royals were spotless. And royal cats had a direct line from the original feline god. A pint of her blood would set someone up for life. If they managed to possess her fully, they would live like kings and queens for generations.

With a thunderous crash, the ship dropped its massive anchor just above the train tracks. The sound was deafening, a violent interruption that sent a shiver down my spine. The anchor's chain rattled and groaned under its weight. There was no way the train would move forward if its path was damaged.

Stella's grip on me tightened, her body tensing in my arms. I felt her heartbeat quicken, a rapid drum against my chest. The air in the compartment grew thick with apprehension. Tangible tension suffused everything around us.

"Attention, conductor of this train." The witch's voice boomed from the pirate ship, magnified and distorted through a loudspeaker, slicing through the chaos. "We have reason to believe you have a woman on board. A witch."

Interesting—she'd called Stella a witch and not what the witch knew her to be. Clearly, she didn't want any competition on what she knew was her treasure.

"If you send her over to us, we'll pull up the anchor and be on our way. Refuse, and you'll have to walk the rest of the way to Portland in the middle of No Man's Land. That should be fun."

People looked around at the women gathered on the train. It was clear they would turn over each and every one to save their own hides. Even the guards were looking around at the passengers.

Not only would we have no help, we were outnumbered. There was no kelpie to come out of the water and save us. There was no flying Pegasus to take us away. Even if both Stella and I shifted, there were too many pirates and too many supernaturals looking out for themselves.

We were doomed. But like hell was I giving up. Looking into Stella's eyes, I saw the exact same determination.

"Ride or die," she said with steely determination.

The choice confused me. It didn't sound like a question. It was a statement. We were about to do both: ride out onto the sand and likely die.

The air carried the sharp scent of fear mingled with the metallic tang of imminent conflict. I braced myself, muscles coiled, preparing to shift into my panther form and confront first the dozen guards before facing the true danger outside. Stella's flesh bristled with the oncoming change. I wanted to tell her to hold back, to stay behind me.

She wasn't going to stay back. She was coming with me. We'd ride this out together. If it came to it, we'd die together.

Before I could act, I saw something unfolding beyond the dust from the pirate ship. Something else was moving in fast. Faster than the ship had traveled.

There was no mast, no sails. There was no swirling tornado. It cut a straight path toward the ship on four massive paws.

Those paws struck the ground louder than thunder. More like bombs exploding. The golden beast was so bright it blocked out the sun. Everyone onboard the ship, onboard the train, sheltered their eyes as they witnessed the fury of the panther king.

With the blood of the gods running through his veins, Dion's beast was nearly as large as the ship. His roar was a thunderous sound that reverberated through the air, a primal declaration of his presence and power. It was a sound that spoke of ancient strength and untamed wildness.

The security guards froze in their tracks, their resolve

faltering at the sight of the king. A stunned silence fell over the train and its occupants. The witch's voice over the loud-speaker cut off abruptly as she retreated toward the back of the ship.

With a massive paw, Dion swatted the anchor away like it was a ball of yarn. Then he opened his mouth and let out a deafening roar. The sound shook the ship, sending it hurtling away. The pirates spilled out and fell to the ground, making a thud and crunch as many died. Those who didn't became a snack for the king's beast.

Licking the blood off its maw, the panther king turned back to us. I dropped to my knees, pulling Stella down beside me. I knew my time was up. I also knew that she would forever be safe. It was more than I could ask for. I just hoped my death would be as swift as the pirates'.

CHAPTER 41

Stella

Blood and Beryl was a different world from a different era. I'd grown up comparatively wealthy in the Crossroads. There was always a roof over my head that didn't leak. I had at least one meal a day. My clothes were never rags, and not just because of my power.

In the Crossroads, I'd walked each day on broken cobblestones and pavement that bore the scars of war. If people didn't watch where they stepped, they could easily become a casualty. Most structures were dilapidated, if they stood erect at all. There was hunger in people's eyes back in the Crossroads, and they just might cross the street to take a bite out of their neighbor if they thought they could get away with it.

Here in Blood and Beryl, the structures stood tall and proud, reminiscent of photographs from a century ago when humanity thrived and order reigned supreme. The homes and businesses along the streets bore none of the scars of decay that plagued the outside world. There were no broken windows or crumbling gutters. Instead, the buildings boasted a pristine appearance, as if they had just received a fresh coat of paint. There was an air of cleanliness and prosperity that permeated the atmosphere, a bright contrast from the dark squalor and desperation of the streets of No Man's Land.

Even the people appeared healthy and well-fed. Their faces bore none of the gauntness or weariness that those living beyond the House's walls wore. If the common folk lived in such luxury, then surely those in positions of power must lead lives beyond imagination.

I'd heard about the Vampire King and his shifter queen, whose animal walked beside her at all times. Niamh would gossip about their love story, looking dreamily off into the distance. Before Danni became consort to the king, she had rejected the cruel vampire prince of another House. Elias had born witness to that rejection, and when the prince's father would've had Danni killed, Elias offered her sanctuary at Blood and Beryl. Then, soon after, he claimed her as his own. It was supposed to be a love match. I couldn't wait to see for myself so that I could tell Niamh.

At least I hoped one day I could tell Niamh. And Tori. I had to believe my girls were okay. They were both smart enough and tough enough to make it through the portal opening alive.

"I'm sorry for the threats to your life, Stella. I should have come for you myself once I realized who you were."

The King of Panthers looked down at me. His eyes, dark and intense, held the weight of centuries, but he couldn't have been too much older than me. Though looks could be deceiving with supernaturals. Vampires lived for hundreds of years without aging a day.

Dion looked like he was in his prime. Golden strands of hair framed his face, catching the light in a halo of radiance that accentuated his regal bearing. His eyes were pools of darkness that threatened to suck me in. Except I didn't feel even a pinch of fear as I met his gaze.

There was an echo of his beast that lingered around him. Like a golden aura pushing off his shoulders. I could still see traces of the giant jaguar in the curve of his mouth, in the way his muscles tensed beneath his skin, ready to spring into action at a moment's notice.

Supernatural physics was weird. How could a beast that big fit itself into this man... who honestly was still very, very big.

Despite Dion's massive size and undeniable strength, I knew he wasn't a danger to me. Something inside me told me he was safe. He was shelter. If I wanted, I could crawl into his lap and he would hold me. He'd tell me everything would be okay. And I would believe.

Except I didn't want to crawl into his lap. I was happy right where I was. Next to Oz.

"That's okay," I told the king. "Oz took care of me."

I glanced over at Oz, but he was avoiding my gaze. His jaw was tense, his hands balled into fists. He was stewing. Likely not just over the latest battle he'd nearly lost me in. He was probably thinking back on all our mishaps and how he would give an accounting to his king.

"He never let anyone hurt me. He put himself between me and danger every time. And we made it through safely."

Oz did look at me then. The turmoil churned in that golden gaze that I loved. I wished we were alone so that I could kiss and soothe him. But I doubted that kind of behavior would be appropriate in front of the king.

"I never doubted he would," said Dion. "Once you're on Panthera, I can assure you there will be no more threats to your life in the palace."

"Can't say I'm not looking forward to palace life." I grinned as I imagined the luxury, and by luxury, I meant a warm bath and a decent meal. A new outfit didn't even cross my mind... at first.

"It is what you deserve," King Dion was saying as I was fantasizing about bedsheet thread counts. "I'm sorry I couldn't get to you sooner. I didn't see you until we were here on Earth and the portal from Tartarus opened. Had I known where you were, I would've found a way to get to you. To bring you where you belonged."

Dion's gaze was so earnest. His words were so sincere. I reached out and put a hand on his shoulder. When my fingertips brushed his bare skin, I felt... something. It was a connection, but it was faint. Like the power lines had been set, but never charged.

The hum between us grew louder. I felt the vibrations start low in my seat. The huff of air lifted the tendrils of my hair from the back of my neck. Dion glanced past me, a brow raised as he looked at Oz.

Instantly, I took my hand away. Belatedly, I remembered that newly mated males did not take kindly to others touching their woman.

King Dion was entirely unfazed. In fact, he looked amused. A mischievous glint tugged at the brow he had raised. "You are breathtaking. Too beautiful to be wearing rags like these. Let's see about getting you out of these clothes."

There went the rumbling again. Dion was playing with

fire, and he knew it. Another time I would've gone along and roused my man. But Oz and I had just been through so much. The man's nerves couldn't take much more.

I sent Dion a look. He got it immediately. I knew he did. The look he sent me back was one of reluctant agreement, like I was asking him to give back a toy he wasn't done playing with. I couldn't help but grin at him. I'd never had such an easy connection to someone.

Well, except with Oz. But Oz's displays of affection were hard won. Dion's were easily given.

This king wasn't like the small leaders who ruled by fear. He was open and friendly. He was the kind of man that made his subjects want to lean in, not cower away in fear. But maybe I was reading him wrong. I'd always read men wrong.

Except for Oz.

Well, except for now. Oz seemed a shell of the man who had been prepared to run head first into danger to protect me just an hour ago. Now he couldn't seem to lift his head to even look at me.

Dion took my hand. There was a warmth there. It tingled like he was someone familiar to me. The way his eyes sparkled as he looked at me made me feel cozy inside. The way he smiled at me made me want to tell him my secrets and know that he would keep them all to himself.

Letting go of the king's hand, I turned to my mate. Oz's gaze was locked on my hand, on the spot where Dion had held it. I leaned into Oz and pressed a kiss on his cheek. He jerked as though I'd startled him back to life. His gaze connected with mine and, for a second, he was completely unguarded.

I saw all the love and longing, all the desire and yearning. It was all for me.

"Find me later?" I said to him.

Oz parted his lips. Nothing came out except a choking sound. I slipped out of the Jeep that had pulled up to a sprawling mansion. The kind that I'd only seen in old movies and books. Walking beyond the gates, I stared in awe at the manicured lawn and massive house. I never thought it real that people actually lived like this.

"You must be Stella."

The first thing I saw was the white wolf. The animal looked at me impassively with intelligent eyes. I should have been afraid, but once again, I wasn't. The animal inside of me was awake. It nudged at my belly, wanting to come out and play. I got the sense that that was what the wolf was sensing: a potential new running mate.

I got the sense that the woman standing beside the wolf was deciding if I might be a new friend as well. "Do I address you as my lady or your Highness?"

The snort that burst from her nose was very unladylike. "You can call me Dani. And this is Nova."

"Nice to meet you both."

"I'm glad you made it out of there safely. The portal opening is causing a bit of a diplomatic nightmare."

"What came out of it?"

Dani shrugged. "Nothing we can't manage. The House leaders are working to get it all under control."

"Will I be able to make a call to the Crossroads? I have friends there I want to check on."

"You should be able to reach them now. The magic that poured out is settling, and things are getting back into working order."

That was a relief. I wanted to check on Tori and Niamh before I sunk into a bath and wardrobe change.

"I spent a little time in No Man's Land when I left my house," Dani said as we entered the grand house.

I was so overtaken by the opulence of the place that I didn't watch my tongue when I spoke. "I heard about that. It was right after you rejected your first mate."

I scrunched up my face and balled my fists, wishing I could tailor the words I'd just said. A glance at Dani told me she was amused and not the least bit offended.

"Best thing I ever did. Though I don't recommend it for you. King Dion is a good man."

"King Dion? My mate is Oz."

Dani's brows went up in surprise and then lowered in confusion. "I thought Dion sent Oz to the Crossroads to fetch his fated mate for him?"

I went stock still. Even my heart stopped beating. I should've laughed. I should've found those words amusing. But they rang with a truth so loud that my entire world tilted.

My brain was like one of those media players that was able to rewind video or audio. There was a whirring sound in my head as I turned back everything that had happened to me over the past few days, everything that Oz had said and done. His reluctance. His denial.

"Would you excuse me for a moment, Dani? I forgot something in the Jeep."

I turned on my heel and headed back down the hall. Back through that grand entryway. Back toward those massive doors. But I didn't need to go any farther. Oz and Dion were just outside.

"What did I tell you about Stella?" King Dion's words were like a thunderclap, echoing into the house.

Oz's voice was subdued, tinged with regret. "You told me to take care of her."

"Is this what you call taking care of her?"

"Sorry, sire."

"I trusted you with her."

The words struck a chord in me, resonating with its haunting familiarity. I'd dreamed this. Then seen it play out between Ken and Uziah. Then dreamed it again. This could not be happening to me again. I could not have fallen for the same game twice in one lifetime. Hell, twice in the same week.

"Stella is too important." There was a low growl in Dion's voice.

"I know I screwed up," Oz admitted, his voice a tortured whisper.

I didn't need to hear any more. I knew how this ended.

CHAPTER 42

Oz

"I know I screwed up."

"Is that what you dragged me out here for? An apology?"

As I stood before King Dion, a sense of unease gnawed at me, twisting my gut into knots. In my mind, all I saw was Stella as she'd stepped out of the train and the king had gotten his first look at her. She'd been battered and bruised, all marks that announced my failures over the past few days. I'd been responsible for her condition, for the dirt on her perfect skin and the rags covering her body.

Had I really thought myself worthy of such a prize?

The weight of my failures hung heavy on my shoulders, a burden I couldn't shake no matter how hard I tried. How could I have allowed her to come to harm, to face danger after danger? She deserved so much better than this, so much more than what I had been able to give her.

In that last battle, I'd been outmatched, outnumbered, and on the verge of defeat when Dion had intervened, saving us both from certain death. Without his interference, I would have been nothing more than a casualty of war. I pulled my shoulders back and waited for the killing strike.

I knew he sensed what was between me and Stella. If he hadn't paid heed to the way she'd leaned against me, the way she'd defended me, cupped my cheek and kissed it, I knew he'd heard the warning growl I couldn't hold in when he'd touched her.

He'd seen it. The grin on his face told me he found it amusing. A lowly foot soldier with blood on his hands in love with a goddess, his future queen.

I'd promised Stella that my life was hers. She'd needed to get off this planet, needed to get to the safety of Panthera. If my life was what my king would demand as the price, then I'd pay it. Anything to keep her safe.

There was a thundering blow to my back. Yet somehow I was still standing upright. Dion's massive paw squeezed my shoulder. His grin was wide and predatory, like he was eying a juicy steak.

"Mission accomplished."

I blinked. And blinked again. "Mission?"

"I mean, granted, I didn't think it would take you as long as you did to retrieve her and bring her here. But what an adventure: pirates, a flying horse. Had I seen the flying horse before I sent you, I would've gone with you."

"You saw that?"

"I saw everything... eventually. That portal opening was like an adrenaline shot; it boosted my powers. The things I've seen."

Dion grinned broadly as he looked off into the distance,

his canines glinting in the sunlight. His tongue snuck out and licked at the upper canine like he could taste the blood that I had spilled all in an effort to protect his mate.

"Pirates? How fun was that fight? And a kelpie. I would've loved to take a bite out of her. Do you think she does it in the water?"

And here we were, back to the king's favorite topic: fucking. Only Dion would take a moment to think about sex positions during a fight for his life.

"What? Why are you looking at me like that? Are you pissed because I cut in on your fun with the pirate ship? You're good, my friend, but even you have to admit you were outnumbered there. You would've lost her in that battle."

"Yet you saw all the other times we were in danger, and you didn't decide to intervene then?"

Dion shrugged. "You had it under control. Besides, I had things to attend to."

His gaze trailed off again. This time, instead of looking off into the distance, his obsidian eyes landed on two fairies walking by, swishing their hips and brushing their hair away from their lifted breasts.

"But the kelpie, I wish I'd been there for that. I've always wanted to bang one. Was she slimy to the touch?"

I stared.

"Scaly?"

I gaped.

"Tell me about it later. I have a little more business to attend to first."

Dion gave me his back as though he didn't think I'd already pulled out a dagger and stabbed him with it. He said he saw everything, yet he still trusted me? Hadn't he seen that I'd betrayed him?

Then I realized that he was going in the direction of the fairies. He'd just met the woman he was fated for, and he was off to roll around with some leggy fae. When Stella found out, if she found out, she would be devastated. Dion would be nothing but Ken 2.0.

From the moment I'd laid eyes on her, I saw no one else. Just the thought of touching another female made my stomach turn. Made my panther growl in protest. But there was my king, my best friend, being led by his dick. He would never change.

"You need a healing bath, my friend." Dion had his arms around the fairies, pulling them into his sides as he sniffed at their hair, which likely smelled of flowers and morning dew. Nothing like the warm vanilla scent of my Stella.

My Stella.

"Like I was saying, my business here isn't done yet. The portal opening threw a wrench in the talks. I have to stay a while longer. I need you to take Stella back to Panthera."

"Me?"

"Yes, you. Who else? Take her home. Get her settled. She's not safe here now that people here know who and what she is."

"Dion—"

"I know, I know, with you gone I'll be short-staffed, but I'll focus better with her in the palace. I think you will, too."

He winked at me. I watched his hands fall from the fairies' shoulders and go lower. They both gasped, their hips rocking forward. I was certain their asses were being pinched. With two handfuls of ass, Dion turned his willing bunch toward the back of the house.

"Dion?"

"Yeah?"

"What I wanted to say was... What I wanted to say is thank you for everything that you've ever done for me."

"You're my best friend." He shrugged off my words, not giving them another thought as he gave the fairies a shove forward, still using their asses as handles. Before he disappeared around the corner, he gave me another wink. And then he was off to get off.

I almost cracked a smile at his antics. But I couldn't. Not when I was about to steal his bride away. Because that's what I had to do to protect her heart.

I was going to take Stella to Panthera. But not to the palace. She said she'd live in a shack with me. That's what she would get as I took her into the outlands, where no one would find us.

I would miss my best friend. But I could not live without my mate. And I could not let him break her heart.

CHAPTER 43

Stella

My skin had been scrubbed clean. Not a speck of dirt remained beneath my fingernails, behind my ears, or between my toes. I'd been lathered in sweet smelling lotions until my skin glistened.

Gone was the dirty, man-funk silk shirt I'd donned when I arrived at Blood and Beryl. The Queen had procured me a sundress, a floral affair of pinks. A strappy pair of sandals completed the outfit.

I'd even gotten my hands on a cup of coffee. The dark elixir was the perfect temperature. Hot enough to warm me through, cool enough that I could gulp it down like the caffeine fiend I was.

Somehow, I still felt dirty beneath the layers of soap and sweet lotions. The power of pink that normally made me feel strong and in control when it covered my body left me feeling exposed, vulnerable, and weak. The coffee landed with a thud in my belly, which was too busy tying itself in knots to appreciate it.

"Papers?" the portal guard barked out at me.

I didn't have a stitch of paperwork on me. I'd left my purse back in that clearing where the massacred bodies of vampires had likely turned to dust. I had no way to prove who I was. I wasn't sure about the answer to that question any longer.

"She is a member of the Royal House of Panthera. Her passage is at the bequest of King Dion."

Just hours ago, Oz's voice had brought me comfort. It had been a safe place where I would not have hesitated to fall. Now his words caused a tension headache. I jerked as his hand came to rest at the small of my back as the guards waved us through.

The moment I stepped through the portal, I gave him my weight as a wave of disorientation washed over me. The sensation of traveling through the magical gateway left me feeling unmoored, untethered, like I was floating in a sea of nothingness. Much like how I felt when I was deep into a vision. Except the only thing I saw was Oz speaking with Dion earlier.

Oz's arms wrapped around me now. He was the anchor to my ship. But he was going to cause me to sink. Just like all of the men in my past. I needed to break free of him, but I was still hooked.

Portal travel happened in an instance. That moment stretched into forever. I let it.

I let Oz hold me to him. I let him breathe in my hair. I let his lips sneak behind my ear. I let his exhalation send a shiver down my back.

And then, once I left behind my old world and came

into this new one, I broke free of his hold. The moment I did, the spinning stopped.

Before I opened my eyes to take my first look at Arcadia, I breathed deeply. The air in this new world was crisp and fresh. There was no smell of chemicals or toxins. There was an undercurrent of funk, but it smelled natural, not magical or technical. Here I was going to get a fresh new start. I was going to be a queen.

A queen to a cheating king. But would that be any different from being the unwitting mistress to nothing but cheaters in the past? At least now I'd have a tiara.

The world of Arcadia unfolded before me, a landscape imbued with magic and ancient power. The colors seemed more vivid here, the sky a deeper shade of blue and the grass underfoot a lush, vibrant green. The air carried the scent of burning sandalwood, a smell that had always soothed me. There was an undercurrent of energy pulsing through the very earth. It felt familiar. It felt like home. Not the house kind of home. This felt like a belonging deep in my veins.

Now that I was through the portal, my visions had returned. I didn't even have to close my eyes to see things clearly. The visions no longer felt like a tidal wave pulling me under. They simply rose from the back of my mind like photographs or a video playing out on a screen.

I saw myself standing beside King Dion, regal and commanding. Around us, a sea of people bowed in reverence, their gestures an acknowledgment of my newfound status as their queen. I saw Oz as well. He stood behind us both, decked out in military finery. His gaze was riveted on me, unblinking, filled with desire.

I turned to face him and saw the reality of what I'd seen in my head. How could he think that this would continue?

That I would allow myself to be shared between two men? That I'd let them continue their game like I was a plaything?

I'd decided to be a queen. I would not be a pawn between them.

I'd have a serious talk with my king later. Right now I needed to talk with the man I'd thought I'd loved. The man who pretended to be my mate to get me to come with him.

The man who still held my heart in his paw.

I would be taking that back promptly.

"Can it be?" An elderly woman stepped forward, her hands outstretched towards me. "You are the spitting image of him."

Him? Who?

"We'd thought Cyrus was lost to us forever."

Cyrus? I knew that name. I'd only heard one other person speak it when I was a little girl. "How do you know my father's name?"

Instead of answering, the elderly woman bowed. So did the small crowd gathered behind her. As people milling about the portal station watched the deference, eyes inevitably traveled to me. I saw flickers of surprise, of disbelief, of reverence. Then one by one, they all bowed as well.

Except Oz. He stood at my back, his eyes sweeping over the crowd as though assessing for danger. It was rich, because he was the only one that posed any real danger to me. And he'd already done his worse.

The journey to the palace was quick and silent. Oz opened his mouth a few times, but then seemed to think better of it and remained mute. I had no words to offer. I was still reeling from everything that had happened to me in just the last few hours.

I'd lost a fated mate. Gained a king as a mate. And was

coming to the realization that my father had not been born on Earth. My mother had told me very little about him before she'd died. Only that he'd been killed because of what he was and that I should never let anybody know about the animal hidden inside of me.

So just like then, I stayed quiet.

Entering the palace, I was struck by its opulence. The grandeur was breathtaking, with high ceilings adorned with intricate frescoes. Walls lined with tapestries that told stories of valor and magic. Floors of polished stone that reflected the light from glittering chandeliers.

This was the home I had seen in my visions, when I'd seen myself standing with Oz. I realized that scene was playing out now. Had I been smiling the first time I'd imagined this? Had he?

I was shown to a suite of rooms that was to be mine, each space more luxurious than the last. The bedroom was vast, with a bed draped in silks and velvets, windows that looked out onto lush gardens and a fireplace that crackled with a welcoming warmth.

It felt like a gilded cage. But no key was turned in the lock. The attendant left the doors wide open as she left me alone with Oz.

The tension that had been building between us reached its breaking point. I wanted to scream at him, to behave coolly, as if he didn't matter, to throw myself in his arms and cry, to turn away from him as though I had never cared an iota for him.

"Where do you live?" I asked. Yes, that was my question. I wanted to know where he would be in this maze. To know where I would find him if I needed him. Not that I would ever use the knowledge.

"I have rooms near the king's suites. But I prefer to stay in a small cottage in the forests beyond the gates."

I nodded. Then there was more quiet between us. "Are you going to quit?"

Oz's brows raised, answering my question with his own.

"It's the only decent thing to do after you sampled the king's goods."

He made a strangled sound in the back of his throat. Instead of denying it, his eyes closed. He looked to me like a villain relieved to have finally been caught.

"Was it part of your duties? To sample the queen-to-be, to make sure she was ripe for your king? Or were you two planning to just pass me back and forth?"

"No, he'd never—"

"Yeah, Dion doesn't seem the type. I could sense he was a decent guy the first time he touched me."

Oz looked strained at that pronouncement. He didn't open his mouth to deny my assessment of his king.

"You disgust me." I was so proud that my voice didn't tremble. Inside, I was breaking down, imploding like a building that had been demolished. Or an ancient structure finally giving way to centuries of neglect and ill use.

"Stella, let me explain."

"I reject you."

Inside my belly, the cat growled. I heard Oz's beast doing the same. Why was there still a connection if none of the mating had been real?

"Leave."

He didn't argue. He didn't hesitate. His legs nearly gave way as he made his way out of the room.

His departure was a physical ache, a void that couldn't

be filled. I was left standing in the middle of splendor and luxury, but all I felt was an overwhelming sense of loss.

CHAPTER 44

Oz

In the stillness of the night, I prowled the dense forest of Panthera in my panther form. The darkness was a comforting cloak. Though comfort was a strong word. I was hiding.

Mostly keeping out of Stella's sight. I'd seen the pain in her eyes when she'd realized I wasn't her fated mate. She'd looked at me with the same disgust as my mother had after I'd suckled her dry and my brother had starved.

It wasn't your fault.

In my mind, I heard an amalgamation of both Stella's and Dion's voices. Both had insisted my runt of a brother wouldn't likely have made it. It happened with shifter twins. Even more frequently during the Call of the Wild. But my parent had accused me of gluttony. Just as my friend, my king, would accuse me of the same when the full force of the mating bond took hold of him.

A roar tore through the forest. At first I was certain it was a lion. But no, the sound of a soul tearing in half came from inside me.

No matter how much I tried to tell myself that Stella wasn't mine, that she was rightfully Dion's mate, that she deserved to be a queen and not pledged to a pauper like me, neither my panther nor my heart bought it.

I'd bound myself to her. In my heart, in my soul, in my very being, she was my mate. Her words of rejection were a blow, but it didn't sever the bond that tied me to her. That bond could only be broken by death, and I wasn't ready to let go. Not yet.

Pangs of hunger gnawed at me as I ran. It was a familiar feeling. Surprisingly, it brought comfort. It reminded me where I'd come from, where I would be again once the king returned. Until then, I had one purpose—watching over Stella, ensuring her safety, even as I kept myself hidden from her view.

By day, I moved through the palace, keeping to the shadows as I watched over her. When I knew she was safely inside her rooms at night, I went out into the darkness and hunted.

She'd taken to palace life like it was her due. Because it was. Her father had been royalty of some kind. Born before my time, the man had slipped through the cracks between worlds and fallen to Earth. As his offspring, Stella was treated with reverence, surrounded by those who saw her as a woman soon to be uplifted as their future queen. Not as the mate to a disgraced soldier.

With her rejection, she had the opportunity for a second chance mating to the king. There wouldn't be a second chance for me. Not in love or in duty.

I felt death at my heels. I knew it was close. So I turned and faced it.

As I moved through the forest, silent and swift, a new scent caught my attention—the unmistakable musk of a lion. It was a scent that evoked memories of my youth, of battles fought and strength tested. And this night, it was a challenge I could not ignore.

The lion emerged from the shadows, a massive creature with a mane that glowed like a halo in the moonlight. Unlike when I was a cub and this world had been on the brink, Panthera was now thriving, as were its inhabitants. This lion showed no bones through its full belly. Its mane was full and proud, its claws sharp, its eyes bright as it took me in.

We sized each other up, two apex predators acknowledging each other's power. In one breath we were still statues. In the next, we were an action scene accelerated to four times the speed.

The impact was louder than thunder as our bodies collided. The ground shook at our growls. The trees swayed in the opposite direction of the battle.

At first, I submitted to the lion's onslaught. Each swipe of his massive claws raked across my sleek black fur. The strikes were powerful, the pain sharp and immediate. But it was a pain I welcomed, a physical manifestation of the emotional torment that had been gnawing at me since Stella's rejection.

Each cut, each drop of blood that mingled with the soil beneath us felt like a necessary atonement. I had failed her. I had failed my king. I had failed myself. This pain was a fitting punishment.

The lion's roars of imminent triumph echoed through the trees. His eyes gleamed with a predator's hunger, his massive body a symbol of raw, untamed power. His movements were brutal as he danced toward my death under the silvery glow of the moon.

He lunged at me again. His massive paws aimed at my head. I didn't dodge or duck. That primal instinct within me didn't stir. I wanted the pain; I craved it. It was a relief from the devastation and loss I felt at Stella's rejection.

A sound pierced the night. I should not have heard it, but I did. It was the sound of laughter; hauntingly familiar. The laughter belonged to Stella.

It cut through the fog of my pain. It reminded me of the love and life that still existed, even in her absence. It made me greedy to hear it again, to know what had made her giggle. To know how far her smile stretched.

It was the first time in days that I didn't feel numb. Fueled by this sudden surge of emotion, something within me shifted. It wasn't so much the need to fight back. It was the desire for knowledge, for details. I needed to know the punch line of the joke, or the story that brought her delight. Once I had that, then... maybe?

A blow to the head sent me sideways. My back had a fight with a tree trunk and lost. Leaves fell into my eyes, obscuring my view as the lion charged, preparing to deliver a killing strike. But I was no longer the passive recipient of his fury.

I needed to know what had made Stella laugh. I needed to see if it lit up her eyes. Did her lower lip stretch as wide as her top lip? What would that taste like?

I blocked the lion's next strike with my paw. Then I head-butted him, causing that mane to become mussed. A deadly growl tore from my throat as I sidestepped his incoming attack. My muscles coiled with pent-up energy.

My counterstrike was swift, a blur of motion as I aimed for his flank, my claws extended.

Our attacks grew more ferocious, more desperate. We were creatures of instinct, of raw power. The forest around us grew rank with the scent of sweat and blood.

The pain of my heartache, the anguish of Stella's rejection, transformed into something else – a burning need to prove my worth. Not as a mate, but as a man capable of strength and resilience. Each movement, each strike, became a testament to my will to endure, to overcome.

I launched myself at the lion. The taste of blood filled my mouth, metallic and raw. With a swift, calculated move, I took him down, my jaws clamped around his throat. The lion's body went limp beneath me.

I looked up toward the palace. I couldn't see it, but I knew exactly where she was. Not bothering to wipe the blood from my mouth, I ran to her.

CHAPTER 45

Stella

I'd always thought reverence was my due. When I'd walked through the streets of the Crossroads, I mostly saw fear. They knew what Uziah would do to them if he was displeased. Walking through the grand corridors of the Panthera palace, the people I passed bowed deeply, their voices a chorus of "Your Highness." I might have always thought royalty was my due, but hearing it made my shoulders hunch upwards.

It was a title that felt foreign on my ears, a mantle that didn't quite fit. Their eyes, wide with a mix of awe and curiosity, followed me as I moved through the halls. It was clear they were eager to attend to my every need, yet it only added to the surreal quality of this new life.

"Your Highness, may we fetch you anything?" a young attendant asked, her eyes lowered in a sign of respect.

That was the other thing; no one looked directly at me. As soon as I came in view, their eyes lowered, their voices hushed. I hadn't made a single friend in the two days I'd been here. Hadn't had a substantive conversation with a soul that wasn't trying to see to my every need.

For the first couple of hours, it was great. Probably because I was still fuming from what I'd learned about Oz and Dion. The anger masked the hurt of the betrayal. What I really needed was a girlfriend to talk to. But inter-world communication was still spotty as the new portal settled.

Queen Dani had sent word that Tori and Niamh were safe, though she hinted that Tori had some stories to tell about her adventures after she went through the portal with an Army general from Tartarus. And Niamh she said was fine but didn't have any other details for me, other than she was safe. Unfortunately, Dani hadn't been able to talk much either. The connection, which had been staticky to begin with, cut off just as she was asking after me.

The attendant asking if I needed anything wasn't a gabber. The other day I'd tried to talk about Dion and was met with wide eyes and zipped lips. I hadn't gotten anything out of anyone. The older woman who had recognized my father in me had insisted I wait until the king's return to get any more details about my past.

While I waited, everyone just sat around smiling and asking if I needed anything. The attention, though well-meaning, was overwhelming. I wasn't used to this level of deference, this eagerness to please. It was as if they saw me not as a person but as a symbol of something greater, something I was still struggling to understand.

"I appreciate your kindness." I forced a smile. "But I'd really like some time alone to... to think."

The woman exchanged hesitant glances with others standing in alcoves and shadows, clearly unused to such a request. As they retreated, I took a deep breath, the weight of their expectations still lingering in the air.

The tension between my new role and my own desires was a constant undercurrent, a reminder that I was in a world where I was still finding my footing. I wasn't actually sure what my new role entailed. My partner in this venture still hadn't returned. My escort into this new world had abandoned me.

Okay, not abandoned. I did reject him. But I didn't like to think about that. I didn't like to remember the way his face fell. The way I felt his heart come to an abrupt stop along the mating bond.

That bond wasn't real. Or it was just one-sided. Actually, I don't know what it was. It wasn't like I had anyone to talk to about it.

As I meandered through the ornate halls of the palace, my eyes caught a glimpse of a portrait hanging regally on the wall. It was a painting of Dion, the panther king. My future mate.

I paused, my gaze drawn to the image, studying the brushstrokes that captured his commanding presence. His eyes in the painting held a depth of wisdom and strength. His posture exuded a noble aura. I searched my heart, looking for a spark, a sign of a connection that should be there.

I did feel a sense of safety envelop me. It was the same kind of security his real presence provided in the brief moments that I'd been in his company. But as I scrutinized my feelings, I realized that the heat of desire, the flutter of excitement that should accompany the sight of a fated mate was absent. I told myself it was something that would grow with time, a connection that would deepen as I accepted my role in this new world.

Then my eyes drifted to another portrait beside Dion's, and my breath caught in my throat. It was Oz, standing loyal and steadfast at Dion's side. The painting captured him perfectly, the intensity in his eyes, the slight tilt of his head, a subtle indication of his protective nature.

I did feel heat as I looked at Oz's portrait. I felt desire prick at the sensitive places all over my body. My heart twisted painfully, remembering the connection we'd shared, a connection that felt so right.

But hadn't I felt that way with Ken? With Allan? How had I gotten it wrong again?

I stood there, transfixed, memories of our time together flooding my mind. Each moment spent with Oz, each laugh, each touch, came rushing back with an aching clarity. The portrait brought him to life in my mind, so vivid, so real, that it felt like he was right there with me.

All that was left of the bond was an ache in my chest. Constant pain when I paid it any mind. There was a persistent lump in my throat. Every other second, tears threatened as they burned behind my eyes.

My past breakups never felt this way. The pain had been superficial. This cut was deep.

I wanted it to stop. I needed a break. I needed to run. Then I realized that I could.

I headed down to the garden level, having to ask servants for directions on the way down. They happily guided me, thankful that I'd finally asked them to do something.

When they left me outside, I found an alcove and took my clothes off. The dress was too nice to have it torn to shreds with the change. Then I let the jaguar have me.

I focused on my inner self. That's all it took for the change to begin. It was an intense, consuming sensation, like a fire igniting in my core. My body trembled, caught in the throes of transformation. Muscles contorted, bones realigned, and skin rippled as if waves were coursing beneath it.

My fingers elongated into sleek, powerful paws, tipped with sharp, retractable claws. My senses sharpened exponentially—the rustling of leaves became a symphony, the scents of the garden a kaleidoscope of fragrances, each distinct and vivid.

Fur like the golden sun sprouted across my skin, a luxurious coat that shielded me and connected me to my new identity. My face elongated into a feline muzzle, my teeth transforming into formidable weapons, perfectly designed for a predator.

As the transformation completed, I stood on all fours, my body a perfect embodiment of feline grace and power. Forgetting the old adage of you have to crawl before you can run, I took off at top speed. The world appeared different from this perspective—more vibrant, more alive. I heard the subtle rustling of small creatures in the underbrush, the distant beat of a bird's wings, the soft gurgling of the stream.

In my jaguar form, I felt a freedom I'd never known as a human. It was a liberation from the constraints of society, of expectations, a return to something pure and untamed. My heart beat with a new rhythm, one that echoed the wildness of the forest, the untamed spirit of the animal I'd become.

I prowled through the gardens, each step a testament to the strength and power I possessed. The sensation of the earth beneath my paws, the brush of leaves against my fur, the wind caressing my whiskers—it was an exhilarating experience, a communion with nature.

I wanted to go farther. But when I crossed the boundary outside of the gardens, I heard a low growl. Looking up, I saw a dark panther in my way. There was blood on his side, and his golden gaze was trained on me.

CHAPTER 46

Oz

I corralled Stella's panther into an alcove so she was away from prying eyes. Nudity wasn't a big deal in shifter culture, but I would rip out the eyes of any man who saw her.

She growled at me, and I forgot to be an insanely possessive male for a moment. The sound of her high-pitched warning instead made me grin. She was so precious. How had I stayed away from her all these days?

I hadn't actually stayed away. I'd dogged her every step, but from the shadows. She was safe here in Panthera. Still didn't mean I didn't want to see her every moment of every day.

Before I could turn my back, she shifted back into her human form. The transformation was as mesmerizing as it was intimate. Her sleek panther form gave way to the curves and lines of her human body.

She stood there, in the midst of the garden, completely bare, her skin kissed by the dappled sunlight filtering through the leaves. My mind reeled with the thought of someone seeing her like this, vulnerable and exposed.

I shifted and stepped forward, my own body still aching from the earlier confrontation with the lion. "You need to cover up. Someone might see you."

The rage fell from her face, and she reached for me. "Why are you bleeding?"

Her gaze fixed on the fresh wounds that marred my flesh, remnants of my brutal fight.

I closed off, unwilling to reveal the depth of my turmoil over her rejection. "It's nothing."

Stella's eyes narrowed. "More secrets, Oz? Just like how you used me."

"I didn't use you, Stella. I've never used you."

"I've been trying to figure it out; did Dion know you'd seduced me into your bed? Or are you keeping it secret from him too?"

She had me there. Her eyes flared wider. I felt the golden heat of accusation.

"Good to know me and my real mate have something in common. We both were betrayed by you."

I struggled to find the words, to explain the conflict that tore at me. My loyalty to Dion, my love for her, it was a tangle of obligations and desires that I couldn't fully articulate. "He sent me to find you and bring you back to him. I knew you were his mate. I never thought for a moment that you would be mine as well."

Stella clenched her jaw. At least she wasn't yelling accusations anymore.

"I tried to fight my feelings for you. I didn't think it

could be true that someone like you would even look at someone like me."

Her brow crinkled at that. She opened her mouth. Her throat worked. But whatever she would have said she swallowed down.

"I don't think he knows about us. I don't think he believes I would betray him in such a way."

"Are you going to ask me to keep our secret?"

"No. I would never ask you to lie. Tell him whatever you wish. But I can't watch you with Dion. It'll tear me apart."

"Are you..." She swallowed twice before continuing. "Are you leaving?"

I shook my head sadly. "The bond is still there."

"Our bond? Or the one between you and your king?"

I cocked my head at her, remaining silent. She looked away, but I knew she felt it too. Even though she'd said the words to break it, it took two to officially destroy a mating bond.

"There are only two options left for me," I said, my gaze fixed on her, trying to convey the depth of my struggle. "I can reject you, which I swore I would never do. Or you can fight me to the death, as a rejected mate must do to earn their freedom."

The words hung heavy in the air. Stella's expression shifted from shock to horror at the gravity of my words.

"I hope you choose to fight me. To feel your lips at my throat one more time would be worth it, princess."

"I'm not a princess, Oz." She balled her fist and punched me in the chest. "I'm going to be queen."

She punched me again, and then again.

"I'm going to marry Dion." Another punch. "I'm going to take him to bed." Another punch. "And I'm going to scream his name."

Tears streamed down her eyes as she continued her assault on me. The punches were ineffectual. The tears undid me.

I pulled her to me. She continued to pound me. Then she slumped against me. I pushed her deeper into the darkness of the alcove as I tried to soothe her with nonsensical words.

"I hate you," she sobbed.

"I know, princess. I deserve it."

I pressed my lips to her forehead, to her temples. I lapped up those tears. She wrapped her arms around me and held me like her life depended on it. My beast demanded that I make it better.

My death warrant was already signed by those tears. What would a little treason in the king's gardens hurt?

Tentatively, fully expecting another rejection, I pulled away from Stella's temple. I moved slowly, millimeter by millimeter, until my lips hovered just in front of hers. It was the only move I dared make. The only distance I dared travel. She would have to—

Stella crushed her lips against mine. Her kiss was pure hunger. I answered, giving her everything she asked for and more. My cock ached between us, eager to answer her hunger in its own way.

She moaned into my mouth. Her hands dug into my back as our bodies pressed together. I felt her heart racing against my chest, matched only by the quickening beat of mine. The lust in her eyes was undeniable.

I was about to lose myself in her. Reaching down, I lifted her thighs up and around me. She locked her ankles behind my back, not once breaking the kiss.

She plunged into my mouth as she reached down to guide my aching erection toward her hot entrance. She moaned in approval as she positioned me. I was all set to plunge up, but Stella sank down, claiming me as her own once again.

I felt her muscles pulsate and clench around my head. With a final push, I found my way into her, both of us releasing a deep groan. As I thrusted up, I felt her heat envelop me. The sensation was indescribable. It was as if my entire world had come down to this moment, and there was no turning back.

She was mine, and I was hers. Her moans of pleasure only fueled my desire. I gripped her hips tightly, thrusting deeper and harder with each stroke.

Stella met my every thrust with her own. Her movements matched mine with a fervor that brought me close to tears because of how much I craved her. It terrified me because I didn't know how I'd let her go again.

Her eyes were half-lidded, lost in the passion of the moment. She was close. Which was good, because I was about to burst. The pleasure was building within me, an intense heat that threatened to consume me. I knew I couldn't hold back for much longer.

Stella threw back her head, her muscles clenching down on me enough to steal my breath, to stop my heart, to claim my soul. I let go of everything I had and gave it all to this woman. She had taken my heart; she could have my life.

I held her tightly as she came down from her orgasm. More than anything, I wanted a round two. This time preferably in a bed or some soft place to lay her down so that I could feast between her legs.

All thoughts of carnal play went out of my head when I heard someone approach. Whoever it was had the common sense to stay back a distance. We both heard them clear their throat.

"I beg your pardon, your highness, but King Dion has returned."

CHAPTER 47

Stella

It was a fast walk and hasty mend kinda interlude as I magicked my clothes back into order. I wasn't sure where Oz got clothing from, but he didn't look at all put together. I stopped myself from reaching back and fitting the low slung trousers he'd pulled on. He hadn't even bothered to cover up his chest—which had numerous scratches over his old wounds that if they were DNA traced would lead right back to me.

Try as I might, I couldn't bring up a single hint of shame about what we'd done. What I'd allowed to happen. What I'd insisted should happen.

Oz was mine. I hadn't decided if I was still his. My heart was still trepidatious at his ownership. Regardless of his intentions, he had broken it. I had the cracks and fissures to prove it.

When it came to Dion... well, I wasn't sure what my

future was with him. My visions had been pretty quiet since I'd come to Panthera. Mostly because I'd turned a blind eye to them all day. Surprisingly, I wasn't plagued with nightmares here. Possibly because I had barely slept every night with thoughts of Oz swirling around my head.

Stepping into the grandeur of the throne room, I saw it was crowded with the people of the realm, all eager to welcome home their king. Dion was a beacon at the center of the room. That golden mane of his would draw any woman's eye. Likely a man's, too. The panther king radiated power, commanded respect.

Just like before, I felt pulled to him. Not a pull of desire. That same voice inside my head insisted that he was safe. That I could unburden myself to him and all would be well.

I wasn't so sure about that. I'd been fucking his best friend. I still wasn't sure if Dion was aware of it or not. If he was in on the seduction or had been played for a fool. I wasn't so sure I cared one way or the other.

Oz was right behind me, dogging my every step. If he feared retribution, he didn't show it. Clad only in pants, his chest and feet bare, he caught many a woman's gaze.

That irked me. I might have hissed at one raven-haired woman who licked her lips at him. She gulped at my censure. Oz didn't even glance at her. His gaze stayed on me, occasionally lifting to meet his king's. Meanwhile the king's gaze turned to me.

Dion stopped mid-sentence in conversation and strode forward, his arms open, his grin toothsome. "Stella, there you are."

The man greeted me like I was a long-lost sibling. But I'd learned he had none. His mother had passed when he was young. His father had died in battle during the Call of the Wild. Dion had become a young king, but there was still a youthfulness about him. That was likely why I didn't hesitate to go into his arms when he opened them to me.

That sense of safety and security of rightness engulfed me once I was in his embrace. What I didn't feel was an ounce of desire for this admittedly viral and sexy man.

"Looks like you and Oz have been enjoying the gardens. A roll in the hay, perhaps?" he teased, his eyes twinkling with mirth.

My cheeks flushed with heat. It wasn't shame, maybe embarrassment due to my station. I was meant to be his queen, and I'd been caught with the help. Why wasn't the king upset? Maybe it was his intention to share me after all?

"You and I have a lot of catching up to do." Dion brought his face close to mine until our noses were almost touching.

Out of the corner of my eye, I saw some women press their hands to their hearts at the gesture. Others eyed me with pure jealousy. I felt nothing but a growing affection for the king who had been responsible for plucking me out of my provincial existence and plopping me down into the seat of luxury.

My ears perked at the low growl that came from just over my right shoulder. I didn't need to turn to know it came from the man who had done the actual physical work of plucking me. What would Dion do when he learned that wasn't the only kind of plucking that Oz had done? What would he do when I told him I wanted Oz to pluck me some more?

Was I seriously about to give up a throne? I threw an annoyed glance over my shoulder at Oz. He was glaring at the hand Dion had on my shoulder.

"I need to speak to Stella alone," announced the king. "And then, Oz, I'd like a word with you. Afterwards."

The throne room emptied quickly at that pronouncement. It was only Oz who lingered. No, lingered was the
wrong word. He stayed put.

"That was an order, soldier."

With those words, Oz's glare softened. Only marginally.
His throat worked as he unrooted first one bare foot, then
another from his spot behind me. He dragged his feet all the
way to the exit. The door closed with a soft snick behind
him that reverberated through my whole body.

Dion's chuckle bounced off the walls of the empty hall
when we were alone. "I knew this day was coming, but it
still tickles the funny bone. Did you know cats don't have
funny bones? The humerus doesn't tingle in the same way
that it does in humans. I still find that humorous—get it?"

He chuckled again as he turned and walked to his
throne. The man moved like the big cat he was. He was all
feline grace, as though nothing could knock him down.
Though as he lowered himself, he suddenly straightened
and peered down at the throne as though he wasn't sure if
he belonged there.

"I suppose this is your seat now," he said.

"Mine?"

"Your great uncle, the king, was lost to us during Pan's
Insanity. Your father was the heir to the throne, but he
slipped through the cracks between realms before I was
born. My father took over the crown, but as a direct descendant of your uncle's line, you have a stronger claim to the
throne than I do."

This was not the conversation starter I'd assumed we'd
be having. Dion waved his hand toward the seat of the
throne. I starred at it numbly. I'd wanted the title of queen,
but could I handle the responsibility to lead all these people
I didn't know in a world I'd just arrived in? Doubtful.

"I knew you would say that," Dion said, taking a seat on the throne and crossing one leg over the other.

"I didn't say anything."

Dion tapped at his temple. Because he had the sight, just like me.

"So does that mean... we need to get married?"

A crease formed in his brow. "Now that question I did not foresee. Why would you ask about marriage to me when you're mated to Oz?"

"I rejected Oz."

There had been a jovialness about the panther king. That melted away with each word I spoke. "Why would you reject your fated mate, Stella?"

"I thought... I thought you sent Oz to bring me to you because I was supposed to be your queen. Your fated mate. Not his." The words tumbled out in a rush of honesty.

"Where would you get that idea?"

Yeah? Where did I get that idea? I'd known Oz was mine the moment he brought me into his arms. I hadn't had a single doubt. Not until the conversation I'd overheard between him and Oz.

"You told him to take care of me. That I was important to you."

"You are important to me. You're my cousin. The only blood family I have left in the universe."

"Did you tell him that?"

"No." Dion shrugged. "I knew at first glance he'd figure out that you were his fated mate, and he would protect you with his life. Why else do you think I sent him instead of coming myself? But had I seen all that the two of you would get up to, I would've come, too."

"You saw what we got up to?"

Dion leaned in conspiratorially, as though he was about

to confide a huge secret to me. I'd never used my powers to spy on people's intimate lives. I wouldn't know how. What had he seen? Our time in the pleasure hotel? On the train? Just now in the gardens?

"Tell me," he said, "was the kelpie's skin scaly or slimy?"

CHAPTER 48

Oz

Pacing restlessly, the weight of my decision pressed heavily on me. I was going to have to kill the king. My best friend. My savior. My brother.

There was no way around it. I couldn't live in this world without my fated mate. It was either me or him.

Dion could provide Stella with the life she deserved, but he would never love her in the way I did. I seriously doubted he would be faithful to her. Not when I saw two of his regular playmates lingering in the halls waiting for him to finish talking to the future queen so they could service his cock.

Was he seducing Stella right now? Only to turn around and whet his wick with these two, then more later? It would devastate Stella.

I'd felt her heartbreak when she thought we'd planned to share her between us. I'd known from the moment I got the lay of the land back in Bite Me, from the time when she'd gasped from the simple act of me sweeping her off her feet and into my arms, from that heartfelt request that I not reject her, all this woman wanted was to be loved and cared for.

Dion would break her heart. The man was incapable of fidelity. I was his only monogamous relationship. Even then he tried to share his conquests with me.

I would not share Stella with him. I wouldn't share her with anyone. So that brought the argument back full circle: I had to kill the king.

The silence on the other side of the door was killing me. I could wait no longer, so I burst into the throne room. There were no guards to stop me. I was the highest ranking of all the king's protectors. No one would assume that I meant him any harm.

Dion looked up at the intrusion. He was sitting with his head bent toward Stella. Stella sat beside him on the throne, looking like she belonged there.

My steps halted at the sight of her. She looked regal, happy. Without a care in the world. I wanted to preserve that sight for all time.

She opened her mouth, preparing to aim words at me. My ears perked wanting to hear anything she said.

Dion lifted his hand toward her in a stop motion. "I believe my best friend has come to challenge me for your hand."

I nodded. I swallowed. I said, "I love you." Though those words could have been directed at either of them.

Dion had saved my life. Had been a friend when the world was cruel.

Stella had given me life. Had been a beacon when I thought I was alone.

I didn't want to live without either of them. But when had life ever been kind to me? I would lose today. It might be my friend. It might be my fated mate. It might be my life. There was no way I was walking out of this unscathed.

Dion shrugged out of his shirt and came at me with claws bared. "This should be good."

I threw the first punch. It connected with his jaw. The feel of it was heavy with sorrow. We had once been friends, allies in this chaotic world of shifting loyalties and uncertain futures. But now, driven by fate and the unyielding demands of destiny, our claws were locked in a deadly dance.

"What do I always tell you?" Dion grinned as he licked the blood away. "With power comes pussy."

"Hey!" called Stella.

There was offense in her voice. It momentarily distracted me, allowing Dion to get a hit in. He lunged at me, his claws gleaming in the light of the chandelier. There was no room for sentimentality.

With a roar that echoed through the throne room, I met Dion head-on, our claws clashing in a flurry of violence. Each strike was fueled by the memories of our friendship, by the pain of betrayal and the desperation of love.

I fought with everything I had, every ounce of strength and skill that I possessed. Dion was stronger than me. The man was born from gods. But my heart would not let me back down. I had a purpose, a reason to fight, and nothing would stand in my way.

The room filled as the battle raged on. Guards and courtiers alike lined the walls. More than once, Dion had to tell the guardsmen to stay back and not interfere. He might have spoken too soon.

I felt the tide turning in my favor. I knew my king's

weaknesses. I'd been studying them all these years. I'd never pulled my punches, but I'd never had any intention of taken the man out. Until now.

He managed to get his forearm around my neck. I let him lock my head. I let him feel like he had the upper hand. I let him think that he'd won. And then I delivered a final, decisive blow.

The king fell to the ground, his body crumpling beneath the weight of my attack. I stood over him, victorious but heartbroken. All I felt was a sense of loss.

"Are you two done now?"

I glanced up at Stella. She looked far from impressed. Not happy at all. She looked annoyed.

"Depends," Dion groaned, clutching the family jewels from his place on the ground. "Let's see if he'll strike the killing blow or not."

Dion trained those obsidian eyes on me. It's when I realized I'd made a mistake. He was prone on the floor. When I'd glanced up at Stella, he could've easily reversed our positions. But he hadn't.

He and Stella shared a look that held more words than any verbal conversation. It was a silent understanding that passed between them, a language I wasn't privy to. Had they already bonded? If they had, why could I still feel my connection to her?

It didn't matter. I'd lost any advantage I'd gained as the king climbed to his feet.

"Oz, you'd better keep that attitude if you want my blessing for mating my cousin."

Cousin? The word echoed in my mind, but the revelation of its meaning was slow in coming. Cousin? That meant family. That meant not fated mates.

"I'm trying to decide if I'm pissed that you would've

tried to steal my girl or if I'm happy about how much it would've torn you up to try. Because if she had been my girl, your scrawny ass wouldn't have stood a chance."

The words hit me like a wave. They washed away the dread and the resolve to fight. I didn't have to challenge Dion. I had his blessing. Relief flooded through me, mingling with the pain. I laughed and tasted iron.

The tension in the room lifted, replaced by a celebration. People clapped and cheered. Dion walked away from me and took his seat at the throne. Two women came to him, eager to kiss what I'd hurt.

Stella's hands glowed with healing magic as she reached for me. I went to her. I would always come whenever this woman called. I let her magic wash over me, feeling the wounds begin to close, the pain start to ebb.

"I never lied to you," I said. "I promised to never reject you, to protect you, to worship you, to love you. I just didn't think I had the right to do so."

She didn't say anything. She continued to touch my flesh even though it was now healed and knitted back together.

"I don't presume I have that right now, but I will still keep every one of those promises until my dying day. Except the dying for you part."

She scowled up at me. She looked like an adorable kitten when she did. Just then I saw it: the vision she had when we were back in the swamp. I saw the cubs we would share. The modest house we would grow old in. The friends who would surround us like family... including Dion's fated mate.

"I want to live for you, with you. I'll fight to stay in this world beside you because though I know my best friend is a great warrior—"

"I'm the best warrior," Dion interjected, receiving healing attention of his own from now three women.

"No one will protect you the way I do. No one will love you as fiercely as I do. No one will give you the loyalty that I will give."

"Hush," Stella said, pressing her lips to mine. "I accept."

She accepted me. The brother who hadn't been able to protect his sibling. The son who'd lost his mother's love. The friend who had nearly betrayed his king for fate.

Stella's kiss absolved me of blame. Her lips poured more love into me than I could have ever hoped to possess. Her mouth solidified where my loyalties lied.

Something shifted in me. I was no longer a fractured, broken thing. Stella's love made me whole.

EPILOGUE

Dion

The lingering scent of sweat and desire hung heavy in the air, a tantalizing reminder of the pleasures of the night before. With a languid stretch, I rose from the bed, feeling the warmth of the sheets cling to my skin before reluctantly releasing their hold.

My muscles rippled beneath my skin as I moved. I should be tired after pleasuring two—no. I looked back and remembered there was a third body beneath the sheets. They didn't stir. I'd satisfied them all. Many times over.

Energy coursed through my veins in the sunlight. I didn't feel an ounce of tiredness. I felt ravenous. Like none of the hunger inside me was slaked.

The panther within me stirred eagerly, its instincts sharp and alert, ready to face whatever challenges lay ahead. Except there were no challenges.

There was peace in the realm. There was no one to fight.

But there was danger lurking in the corner, eager to catch up to me in the light of day.

My time was running out. The day that would mark the end was finally on the calendar. A big red circle drawn around it.

I'd tried to delay the inevitable, to stall Oz and Stella's wedding for as long as possible. But now, with the date fast approaching, I could no longer ignore the truth. The day my friend would be happily shackled, the manacles would fall down on me as well.

The day I'd met my best friend was the day I'd had the vision. My fated mate would be in attendance at his mating ceremony.

Luckily, I still had a week before my fate was sealed. And I planned to make use of every moment. Fuck every willing body I hadn't gotten around to, and a few who had given me the highest pleasure. Because I knew there would be no fighting it when I saw her. I would become something I couldn't fathom: a one-woman man.

I gave myself a full body shake. It did nothing to free me from the inevitability of my fate. And so I prepared for the day ahead.

Leaving the comfort of my bedchamber, I stepped into the expansive closet that housed my wardrobe. Each garment was meticulously chosen to accentuate my physique.

I selected a fitted white shirt. White was my best color. It showed off my golden skin tone and hair. The shirt's fabric clung to my strong chest and broad shoulders, emphasizing the contours of my physique. Paired with tailored trousers that skimmed over my narrow hips, the ensemble created a silhouette that would draw women to me.

Not that my title didn't already do that.

As I dressed, I took pleasure in the way the fabric molded to my body, accentuating my finer points and drawing attention to the attributes that had captivated so many before. I knew the effect my appearance had on others, the way women's eyes lingered on my form, drawn to the promise of strength and sensuality that radiated from me.

Making my way down to breakfast, I found Stella and Oz seated closely together. I pressed a kiss to Stella's forehead in greeting. As expected, Oz emitted a low growl in response to the display of affection, his territorial instincts flaring at my actions.

"Stop teasing him," Stella warned, but she was all smiles.

Stella was devoted to Oz, preparing to marry him, yet I couldn't resist riling my best friend, especially when it came to matters of the heart. And Stella was as much mine as she was his. She had quickly become one of my favorite people to engage with, her genuine friendship a rare and cherished bond.

I just hoped she'd remember that bond when she discovered that it was one of her closest friends who was fated to be my mate. For now, I relished in the warmth of our friendship, hoping that it would endure even in the face of such profound revelations.

"I have to head out," she said, dabbing a cloth at the corner of her mouth.

"Where are you off to?" I asked as I piled my plate. "Last minute dress alterations? A bouquet debacle?"

"No, I'm headed to the portal to pick up a friend."

The serving fork clattered to the serving dish. The ticking clock on the wall sounded like bombs going off in my head. The walls in the expansive dining area felt like they were closing off.

"You're picking up a friend?" I managed to ask, though my throat felt constricted. The wedding was still a week off. Guests shouldn't be arriving for days. I was supposed to have days.

"My friend Niamh. You're going to love her."

Get ready for Niamh and Dion's story in "Reveal Me."
Sign up to my Reader Newsletter for updates at
https://ineswrites.com/ReaderGroup.

Thank you for reading FORBID ME!
I hope you enjoyed Stella and Oz's love story. There's more to come in Niamh and Dion's rocky road to love, so stay tuned.

Also by Ines Johnson

Lover of fairytales, folklore, and mythology, Ines Johnson spends her days reimagining the stories of old in a modern world. She writes books where damsels cause the distress, princesses wield swords, and moms save the world.

You can sign up for her mailing list and receive alerts and free reads at https://ineswrites.com/ReaderGroup.

The Last Dragons

The Dragon's Reluctant Sacrifice

The Dragon's Ambivalent Sacrifice

The Dragon's Willing Sacrifice

The Dragon's Rebellious Sacrifice

The Dragon's Compliant Sacrifice

The Dragon's Forbidden Sacrifice

The Nia Rivers Adventures

Dragon Bones

Demeter's Tablet

Templar Scrolls

Serpent Mound

Eden's Garden

The Misadventures of Loren

Spear of Destiny

Ring of Gyges

Hammer of God

The Knights of Caerleon

First Knight

One Knight

Arabian Knight